JO MAY

Operation Vegetable

Copyright © 2020 by Jo May

All rights reserved. No part of this publication may be reproduced, stored or transmitted in any form or by any means, electronic, mechanical, photocopying, recording, scanning, or otherwise without written permission from the publisher. It is illegal to copy this book, post it to a website, or distribute it by any other means without permission.

This novel is entirely a work of fiction. The names, characters and incidents portrayed in it are the work of the author's imagination. Any resemblance to actual persons, living or dead, events or localities is entirely coincidental.

Jo May asserts the moral right to be identified as the author of this work.

Designations used by companies to distinguish their products are often claimed as trademarks. All brand names and product names used in this book and on its cover are trade names, service marks, trademarks and registered trademarks of their respective owners. The publishers and the book are not associated with any product or vendor mentioned in this book. None of the companies referenced within the book have endorsed the book.

This book was previously published as 'The Marina'.

Second edition

*This book was professionally typeset on Reedsy.
Find out more at reedsy.com*

For our great friends
Alan and Julie

Thanks for the wonderful memories
Rest in peace Al

Contents

1	Thunderheads	1
2	Up to the Plate	12
3	Lord of the Manor	23
4	Reaching Out	28
5	Roger Rabbits	32
6	Enemy Within	40
7	It's Who You Know	43
8	Band of Brothers	56
9	Bullied	62
10	New Recruits	66
11	Hi Di	72
12	Sleepers and Beds	81
13	Joy for John	95
14	Gig, Not Concert!	99
15	Abuse of Power	108
16	One Man and His Goat	110
17	Paul	118
18	Investigations	128
19	The Gaffer Erupts	132
20	That Singer Bloke	140
21	Unravelling	156
22	Sneaky Sandy	160
23	Snert 'n' Goolies	167
24	Gig in the Dog	178
25	Arrest	184
26	A Sixteen-incher	188

27	Unmasked	198
28	Just Desserts	205
29	Plans for the Plot	212
30	The Time, The Place	216
More from Jo May		219

1

Thunderheads

A group of ageing citizens is heading to the pub for a meeting. Slowly in most cases. They all live on narrowboats at Watergrove Marina and they are gathering to plan a strategic defence of their vegetable plot. Planning permission is sought by a local landowner to build houses on their treasured allotments. It's a measure that will annihilate years of hard labour. No, hard labour is inaccurate; most of our elderly bunch only bend down three times a day, and two of those are to tie and untie their shoe laces. Years of …. endeavour, that's better - it's less dynamic, more measured. Anyhow, towering storm clouds are gathering over the boaters' existence. Thunderheads are preparing to unleash Armageddon on our waterborne residents.

'Thunderheads just about sums up some of those relics,' muttered one warrior to her friend as they walked slowly between the hedgerows. She was indicating a cluster of three shuffling males up ahead. Her mate giggled. The boaters didn't know it, but the meeting would set in motion a chain of events that would enter folklore - marina folklore anyway. Let's not get carried away here! Operation Vegetable was not so much a predetermined plan as a series of episodes and incidents. It was only at its conclusion, when all the various scenes had been stitched together, that the outcome could almost have been seen as pre-planned.

Yes, a call to arms went up and the jungle drums beat up and down the pontoons. The marina saw more action in an hour that it had seen in the past month. A frantic search for hearing aids and spectacles ensued and our creaking army was mobilised. Let's be frank - if judged solely on their general appearance no foe would be concerned. But beneath the trusses and orthopaedic braces a fiery spirit fermented. They would have to use cunning and artifice in place of brute force and swordplay (but looking at the rambling assortment of specimens, they wouldn't find that easy either.)

The pub was called the Dog and Rabbit, 'The Dog' to the locals. It was a bare half-mile from the marina but the progress of our flotilla was slow, or stately if we are to be charitable; it allows us time to learn a little about our creaking band...

A couple of months ago, four friends embarked on a short canal trip. It was a sunny Sunday afternoon in April. Winter had shrugged off her quilt. Daffodils and snowdrops danced in the gentle breeze. What could be better? Granted, there may be a few things, but it's not a bad way to spend a few hours. The boat belonged to Roger. He'd just had a new engine installed and wanted to give it a test run to iron out any niggles. He was sharing his mini adventure with three mates, Archie, Sal and Pete. But within two hours of setting off, three of them would be bitterly disappointed and the other would be accused of murder.

As the coffin was lowered into the soft earth Roger sniffed. 'We never really got the chance to know you,' he said. 'Dear, oh dear.' He was distraught; they were burying his chicken. It was an honoured fowl. Before they'd buried it, they'd also cremated it. Or, more accurately, Pete had. He'd been in charge of the cooking but had fallen asleep while his three friends were out walking the dog. Now they were back, hungry and disappointed.

'Twenty-four hours ago that was a perfectly presentable bird,' moaned Roger. He glared at Pete. 'Pristine among its mates in the supermarket. Perfect. Full of potential. Now look what you've done. You're a murderer!'

'Hardly. Besides, it was only a bit overdone. It was probably OK in the middle.'

'Oh yeah, sure.'

'Undercooked chicken can be dangerous, you know.'

'Petrified carbon won't do you much good either!'

'Show some respect,' growled glowering Pete, as he hammered a makeshift wooden cross into the ground with an old boot. *'Cluck'* was scrawled on the horizontal – which just about summed it up. Keen to make up for his culinary shortcomings, Pete had taken charge of the burial party, ensuring the carbonized capon had a dignified send-off. The four friends levelled the earth around the shallow grave with their hands, then stood and contemplated their underground dinner. A Jack Russell trotted up, sniffed at the small mound of earth and cocked its leg against the cross. The embarrassed owner dragged the dog off and left with a profound apology.

'The ignominy,' muttered Pete.

'Lump of cheese anyone?' asked Roger mournfully.

They were standing on the towpath of the Llangollen Canal, a few miles east of the Shropshire town of Ellesmere. Roger's narrowboat was moored close by, doors and hatches wide open to disperse the smell of charred flesh. An hour later they were motoring slowly back into Watergrove Marina.

'We've uncovered one niggle anyway,' said Pete. 'Your oven's too fierce.'

Roger grimaced as his empty tummy burbled in chorus with the engine. He piloted the narrowboat slowly into his residential berth. Roger and Pete were standing on the rear deck while Archie and Sal perched in the triangular well deck at the bow with their golden retriever, Betsy.

'Grab a line one of you,' shouted Roger down the length of the boat. Sal stepped off and tied a bow rope to a cleat on the pontoon.

'Look! See that? Some people are blessed with the ability to carry out simple instructions without the need for an internment.'

Pete grinned and stepped off the boat to tie up the stern.

'There!' he proclaimed. Roger looked suspiciously at the jumbled knot.

'I'll check that in due course.'

Though it wouldn't be immediately obvious to an outsider, Pete and Roger were friends. Both lived solo on their boats. Pete had never married, but Roger and his former wife had an unresolvable disagreement over his career choice – in that he *'couldn't be bothered to do anything financially constructive'* as Wendy, his ex, put it - so she left. Roger ended up with the boat while she took up with an accountant in Wiltshire, ironically living in a house overlooking the Kennet and Avon Canal. Roger's boat was blue with cream trim and immaculate, always clean with gleaming brass appendages. And it had a new engine which had been tested, along with his patience, during their short excursion.

When asked why he spent so much time looking after his boat, he would reply that mindless polishing fuelled his creative bent, allowed his mind to be clear of trivia, and left room for the in-flood of literary inspiration. *'And the out-flood of anything comprehensible'* (Sal). Yes, Roger 'likes to write a bit', describing himself as a self-styled wordsmith. *'Blacksmith more like,'* reckoned Pete, uncharitably. *'Hammering the life out of the English language with an assortment of soot-blackened tools around the dying embers of a forge.'* Roger was undeterred and optimistic, waiting for his literary breakthrough. He thought Pete's vitriol to be merely jealous pique. Roger was grey-haired, grey-bearded and sixty-two years old. He was somewhat overweight but not very tall. Pete had recently pointed out to him (rather robustly) that, according to a recent health directive, if you double a person's waist size it should be equal to, or less than, their height.

'No problem,' Roger had replied, 'I'm one-hundred-and-seventy centimetres tall with a thirty-eight-inch waist. Well within target.'

'It's creative thinking like that that has made you so unsuccessful as a writer.'

Archie wandered down the finger pontoon towards the two men at the back of the boat.

'Well, that little adventure has recharged the batteries,' he said, full of bonhomie. 'Time to get back to the daily grind.'

'Daily grind? What daily grind?'

'Pete, my unkempt old mate, some of us have routines in place to ensure we don't end up looking like floating tramps.'

'A man is not a man solely because of a gleaming exterior.'

'No, but at least you can tell who most of us are without scraping layers of muck off.'

'Stop bickering you two and go home,' said Roger, who was plugging in his mains electricity lead. 'I'm going inside to have a cup of tea and a sandwich.'

The daily grind involved mundane tasks such as polishing paintwork, drinking tea during the day, wine during the evening and being rude to one another. A happy bunch were the residents of Watergrove Marina – usually. Pete's boat was moored at the far end of the marina, about three hundred yards from the posh residential area where, according to Roger, his dog can defecate on the residents' car park in contemplative solitude. Pete's boat was untidy. It was in need of a paint job and the roof was full of detritus, including a pile of insect-ridden wood that he burned on his multi-fuel fire. In addition, there were half a dozen empty jerry cans and a sorry-looking canoe that last saw service around the time of the Cockleshell Heroes. The boat had no name. No, that's inaccurate. Every boat has a name; it's just that the sign-written name had long since succumbed to lack of maintenance. In times gone by a skilled sign-writer had lovingly painted 'PUG' on the rear cabin. All that remained now was the outline of the letter 'G'.

Roger reckoned that Pete's boat looked like a relic from World War II, abandoned during a particularly intense bombing raid, but dirtier. Asked why his boat is so scruffy, he explained that he kept it in a state of undress to deter burglars. 'I've never been robbed,' he pointed out. 'In fact, people feel more inclined to leave me something, they feel so sorry for me. I was left a bag of green beans and a couple of pounds of tomatoes once, down near Milton Keynes.'

Anonymity suited Pete; he was a secretive fellow. Excepting the past nine years when he *'bumbled around the marina annoying people,'* (Roger), nobody knew much about him. Rumours abounded but he was unforthcoming, preferring to live in tatty isolation. Actually the boat inside was quite presentable; he called it his ship in wolf's clothing. Rather like Pete himself. He perpetually sported a weathered, once-red bobble hat, usually with a pencil stub poking out from underneath, and moth-eaten clothes. But he was an educated man of some intellect. *'Not much, but some.'* (Roger). He was the keystone of the marina team when they joined the weekly quiz at the Dog and Rabbit down the road.

Roger's three friends had readily accepted his offer of a trip on the boat because the winter, when the boats are basically stuck in the marina for up to six months, can drag on. Many boat-dwellers tend to get entrenched when the weather is foul. It's all too easy to spend long hours watching television or reading. Broken only by the odd sortie to the shops or to lug in bags of coal, it's all too common for these long periods of stultification to morph into a sedentary, winter-long lethargy – a kind of hibernation known as cabin-fever. Though the boats are warm and cosy with all (or most) home comforts, there's nothing like pottering through the countryside at four miles-per-hour. A waterborne ramble where one can enjoy the re-birth of fauna and flora as winter fades. Come early April most boaters are ready for a change of scene, so Roger's little trip came as a welcome relief.

The idea had been to motor for a couple of hours, moor up, then go for a walk. Invigorated, they would enjoy a leisurely lunch of succulent, freshly cooked chicken accompanied by a glass of Merlot. (Pete had agreed to stay behind and demonstrate culinary wizardry. Unfortunately, the 'excitement' of the outbound trip had got the better of him and he'd nodded off.) Following lunch they would then motor serenely back to the marina.

'Well,' said Pete, as he left to return to his own boat, 'at least you have another stultifying sentence to add to your much to be ignored memoires.'

Archie and Sal's boat, called Wet Dreams, was moored against the bank, first in a line of ten boats housed on the residential pontoon. Next door was Roger. Archie and Sal were husband and wife (lady saddled with husband, if you asked Sal) who shared their boat with their retriever Betsy. Both in their mid-sixties, they had been married for thirty years and enjoyed a bickering familiarity. Twelve years ago they sold their pub in Holbeach, Lincolnshire and bought their boat. Spending their retirement years on a narrowboat had been a life-long dream so they offloaded most of their worldly goods via family, car-boot sales and charity shops. Most of the stuff had become so familiar they barely knew they had it; a ridiculous compilation of useless artefacts that had festered in cupboards or hung on walls, barely noticed for years; things they'd walked past every day that had become ingrained into their sub-conscious world; when purchased, items they simply couldn't be without, must-haves. Off-loading it all had been a cathartic exercise and a new generation would be forced to install cupboards and shelves to house newly-acquired treasures. Finally free, they had moved onto their boat one year into the new millennium and, according to Archie, *'haven't looked forward since.'*

Before they had the pub, Archie had been a military policeman but had ducked out aged forty-five. Sal, a midwife, had put her career on hold, excited by a change of direction in running the pub as a joint venture with her husband. In fact, her career was still on hold twenty years later. At six foot three with a ginger-grey moustache and matching full head of hair, Archie had an upright bearing and was still pretty fit thanks to regular walks with the dog, and a military-inspired daily workout routine. Sal was nearly a foot shorter than Archie and was developing arthritis, particularly in her hands and knees, but she was a bright, blonde 'pocket rocket' (according to her husband) who was perennially cheerful. She refused to bow to her ailment and has a cheery word for everyone.

Sal and Archie's boat was fifty-seven feet long and a little over seven feet wide. Fifty-seven is a peculiar length, but not uncommon. Some of the shorter locks on the canal system are around sixty feet in length and a fifty-seven-foot boat allows owners to cruise the whole canal system. Their boat was dark green with yellow coach lines that, according to Roger, looked like a packet of Golden Virginia tobacco. Internal living space was actually considerably shorter than the overall length, at only about forty feet by six. The engine and diesel tanks at the rear and a large water tank at the front accounted for about fifteen feet, so actual cabin space was pretty restricted. Considering their pub had two bars, spacious living accommodation (including seven letting bedrooms), plus a large beer garden, the confinements of a boat took a little getting used to - but they soon did.

Fairly typical of many narrowboats, the accommodation consisted of lounge, kitchen, bathroom and bedroom, so they had everything they need. Heat was provided by a central heating boiler, run on diesel, in addition to a multi-fuel stove on which they burned smokeless fuel and logs. Their kitchen (or galley, as Archie, getting into the nautical spirit, insists on calling it) had all the basics - gas cooker, hob, fridge, microwave, sink and storage. The bathroom had a three-quarter bath with shower over, loo and basin and they slept in a double bed (albeit slightly narrower than the one they had in the pub). People were always surprised at the level of equipment and comfort. Archie and Sal loved the life, particularly when they were away cruising and could explore the canal system.

Watergrove Marina was home to nearly two hundred boats, the majority of which were narrowboats, but there were a few small cruisers. Six boats had permanent inhabitants – or 'liveaboards', as they are known. The marina was created thirty years ago when an old clay pit was flooded. Access by water was via a small branch off the Llangollen Canal, which in turn is an offshoot of the Shropshire Union Canal. Canals were popular again after a decaying slump when trains and roads took over as freight-carrying mediums and the system fell into disrepair. From the late fifties there was a growing resurgence as the waterways were gradually repaired and renovated for the leisure boater. As far as road access is concerned, Watergrove Marina was pretty isolated. Arrival by motor vehicle was via motorway, A-road, B-road, C-road, unclassified road, then a couple more diminishing byways with a strip of grass down the middle, ending at a rusty gate suffocating in an unkempt hedge.

Turn in through the gate, down a 60-metre gravel drive and one arrived at the beating heart of Watergrove, namely the chandlery and office which overlook the four-acre site. There was a ground-floor flat behind the shop and two-bedroom living accommodation on the first floor. Betty, the marina manager, lived upstairs. It was a two-storey brick building constructed in the 1970s. It didn't exactly compliment the rural surroundings, looking more like an unimaginative architect's idea of social housing in East Berlin, but it was functional. The large marina was laid out before the shop. Row upon row of brightly coloured steel boats swayed gently at their moorings in the breeze. It was a slow-motion ballet not unlike an octogenarians' Tai Chi group where ghostly figures move with agonizing precision, shrouded in early morning mist. According to Roger, the shop stocked plenty of stuff you rarely needed and little of what you actually did.

'Who the hell needs bad watercolour paintings?' he pointed out with some justification.

'What we haven't got we'll order for you,' replied Betty, a trim, bespectacled lady who had run the shop for the previous six years.

'Paintings brighten the place up. Who wants to look at lumps of plumbing bits and coils of rope?'

'Well,' replied Roger with some frustration, 'anyone who actually owns a boat I should imagine.'

'We have to cater for visitors.'

'We don't get any bloody visitors. The only people who come here do so by accident – unless they're missionaries. The last ice-cream you sold from that rusty health-hazard of a fridge was probably fifteen years ago.'

Betty was of the opinion that because the boating aspect of the marina was running like clockwork, they needed to develop other revenue streams. Most of the paintings on display had been done by her sister Doreen, leaving Betty exposed to accusations of nepotism.

'Who the hell wants an out-of-perspective view of Harlech Castle for goodness sake?'

'I think it's rather good.'

'You're biased. And misguided. Anyone unfortunate enough to happen upon this place who is then daft enough to buy a painting, at least wants something canal or boat-related. Not a blurred pile of rubble half-hidden behind a blue tree.'

'You are rude.'

'I'm forthright. I am gently trying to point out that you're marketing strategy may have a flaw. And that your sister should consider amending her choice of hobby.'

'OK then, smarty pants. What do you suggest?'

'Well, first of all I suggest you advise your sister that she may sell more paintings of Harlech Castle somewhere near Harlech Castle. In Harlech, for example.'

'She's tried that. There's a lot of competition.'

'Mmm. Has she actually sold any of her work?'

'A few, certainly.'

'Did you buy them?'

'I have the odd one or two, yes.'

'Has she sold any to anyone who is not her sister?'

'Probably. I don't know. I'm too polite to poke my nose in. Anyhow,' she said, pretending to busy herself with a sheaf of papers, 'what did you come in for? Did you come in to buy something or just be rude?'

'I came in for an oil filter.'

'We're a bit low on filters.'

Roger sighed.

'There are one or two down there under the decaf coffee. I usually get them in to order. No point in having dead stock lying about. Bad for cash-flow.'

'You seem to have plenty of decaying paintings lying about.'

'What's the reference number for your filter?' she said, ignoring Roger's jibe. 'They're due to deliver a week on Tuesday.'

'That's ten days away! I could walk to Japan for one in that time. What if I was in a hurry?'

'You're never in a hurry. The only time you hurry is when you dash over here and criticize my shop. Your mate Pete never complains.'

'He doesn't know what an oil filter is, much less where to find it.'

'Do you want one or not? I'm busy and haven't time to stand here and listen to you moaning.'

'I'll take one of those instead,' he said, pointing to a painting. It depicted two objects he presumed were cows standing by a gate.

'Are you serious?'

'No,' he said, and stomped out.

Roger walked back to his boat. Clambering onto the back deck a voice boomed out, 'And what's put you in such a tizz?'

'It's that place over there,' he replied, waving his arm at the shop. 'She never has anything I need. Useless.'

'There, there. Never mind.'

'I'm going in for a brew.'

This brief exchange was with Judy, whose boat *Dream Catcha* was third in line on the pontoon, next to Roger's. Judy was a large lady the wrong side of fifty (*'but only quite recently'*). She has sparkly blue eyes and a mop of curly grey hair (*'that used to be brown'*) and parades about in a variety of multi-coloured kaftans. That day's was purple with bright green flowers. She played the guitar and was an accomplished musician – or used to be, these days preferring to play for fun. *'Hers, nobody else's'* (Pete). *'Anyone within earshot might well end up in the auditory clinic'* (also Pete). He was aware that Judy was blessed with the ability to play most genres of music, but didn't - instead sticking to mournful, folky stuff. *'Tripe to send the most optimistic in search of the Prozac'* (Archie). Divorced five years ago, she once told Pete, "The secret of our happy marriage remained a secret from the church door onwards." But she was cheerful now, surrounded by a motley assortment of fellow boaters.

From time to time Judy's friend Elaine arrived in her old VW camper. Elderly hearts fluttered when she turns up. Pete, Roger and Archie popped down to The Dog from time to time. During one of these senior get-togethers the consensus among the collection of male ruins was that Elaine is 'very nearly still beautiful.' This collective spite was spoken with a courage brought on by half a gallon of ale. She was beautiful, but not in any overly make-upped, designer gear way. She just shone like some lucky people do. The lads were just miffed that someone of a similar age could look so good without making any apparent effort. Anyhow, when Elaine pulled up with that distinctive VW air-cooled chatter, her van decorated with colourful swirls that look like cheerful sperm, the whole ensemble was a throw-back to the 60's when she and Judy offered highly-charged allure during the music festivals of their youth. These days they didn't engender allure so much as wariness but, unconcerned, the two of them sat on the front of Judy's boat and wailed away long into the evening, singing songs about legendary folk of Middle Earth. Roger complained bitterly that spliff smoke made him start seeing things and acting weird. Pete pointed out that Roger didn't need any help with that.

2

Up to the Plate

People who live on boats come from a wide variety of background. In marinas up and down the country bands of brothers and sisters live together in disparate harmony. Company executives to cleaners are bonded together by the bare necessities. When a toilet packs up it doesn't matter if you're the former boss of a multi-national company or the chap who used to mow the lawn, it's all hands to the pump. The person who doesn't need assistance at some time or other is a very rare breed.

There is a lot to go wrong on a boat. After all, it's a mini-house crammed into a narrow metal tube – then you have the added complication of an engine and all the heartache one of those can bring. There is plenty of opportunity for malfunction within the complicated concoction of electrics, heating and plumbing. If all that wasn't enough, there's the fact that the thing is floating on water so the hull needs looking after. The point is that people try to help others – it's folly not to, because tomorrow it could be you in trouble.

Folk get on with their own lives. Despite their physical proximity, people (usually) respect others' need for privacy. They still have everyday problems - health, cash or whatever, but just because you live on a boat doesn't mean you don't get bunions. Outsiders think that living on a narrowboat is the cheap alternative, but that isn't necessarily the case, at least away from cities, especially London. The cost of running a boat is close to that of running a small house when you take into account mooring fees, services, insurance, maintenance etc. What is different (and better according to some) is the lifestyle, on which it is difficult to put a value (except, according to Archie, if you happened to end up living next door to Pete, *'when no amount of fiscal compensation is adequate'*).

Two boats down from Judy lived Alexander (aka Sandy). The boat between them was owned by a South African man called Gilders who rarely visited, preferring the less hostile climate of Cape Town during the winter months. Sandy had cultivated the image of a man of means with a boaty twist – moleskin waistcoat, check shirts, loafers, red-spotted neckerchief and half-moons. A man of dogged determination with an analytical mind. Originally from the Black Country, he'd spent thirty years trying to rid himself of the distinctive accent, largely successfully. It was when he got stressed or someone wound him up that his roots surfaced. Roger goaded him regularly, reminding him that he was from Birmingham. 'Black coontroi, not Beermingham,' he snarled.

Anyone who asked Sandy a technical question had better have an hour or so to waste, because once he got going it was impossible to shut him up. If an engine was running a bit 'lumpy,' or there was a red light on a piece of electrical equipment, Sandy was your man. What he didn't know about boats could be written on the back of a fag packet – *'preferably in Spain'* (Pete). In any genuine emergency he was handy - it's the rhetorical question you had to be careful with. For example: 'I wonder why my batteries don't charge as quickly in warm weather?' - particularly dangerous if you have a sprained ankle and can't run away.

If he didn't know the answer straight off he'd research it and present a paper on the subject. The point is that he'd spout with such authority in a blizzard of technical analysis that people rarely questioned his know-how. This was usually fine. It was on the rare occasion that he was wrong when the difficulties surfaced. Like a couple of years ago, when he advised Roger to use a particular brand of paint while repainting his beloved boat. All was fine for a few days but gradually the whole exterior began to look like it had developed psoriasis. Roger's pride and joy had to visit the boat doctor for a complete outer re-paint. Three thousand pounds and a fortnight later Roger vowed revenge. The mini saga is worth relating ...

Roger's previous paint job had been self-administered by random sanding, rubbing down with pairs of old underpants soaked in white spirit, and the liberal application of Dulux Weathershield – a paint of good repute designed for house exteriors. That paint had lasted for four years - not perhaps the glossy mirror finish achieved by a professional coach painter, but perfectly adequate. Sandy's recommendation (after extensive research) had been to apply eye-wateringly expensive 'quality coach enamel' after sanding down with 240-gauge grit paper and cleaning with a tack cloth. But the new paint had objected to something and parted company with the steel, leaving an oily scum on the water around Roger's boat.

'It obviously didn't like that cheap stuff you put on last time,' reasoned Sandy. 'Preparation is the key.'

'Thanks for the advice,' replied Roger, as he scooped flakes of paint off the water with a child's fishing net.

Sandy was thick-skinned, treating criticism and abuse as a stepping-stone on his quest for perfection – particularly when it was someone else's stones he was stepping on. He described himself as 'the type of bloke who gets on with anybody.' The use of the word 'bloke' was stage-managed because his extensive knowledge and general acumen was on a plane so far above his minions that he had to descend to a lower level to integrate. He was shy by nature but blossomed within the anonymity of an internet canal forum, where he regularly posted, dispensing mind-numbing advice to anyone in difficulty, hiding behind his screen name – 'PPP' (Professor Pat. Pending). He was also gay. Sadly, he had yet to find his soul mate. Not so easy perhaps when, on a number of dating sites, he listed among his interests 'the refurbishment of vintage engines, electrical engineering, ambling and American poetry.' In effect he wanted to be loved but remained single. *'Well, would you?'* (Archie).

Roger was still planning revenge for the paint job, and had just settled down with his cup of tea. Seated before his computer, he flexed his fingers, gearing up to begin the next chapter in his latest literary masterpiece, when a klaxon sounded, then another, and before long it was a cacophony.

'Hell's teeth,' he muttered.

The horn-blowing salvo sounded like a sick, multi-toned air-raid warning - like the welcome afforded one of the great liners approaching port. It was a ritual designed to take the mickey out of Mike and Terri, who had just set off across the marina in their boat to empty their lavatory. There are a number of methods of sewage disposal on boats; Mike and Terri had an on-board tank that must be emptied weekly. This meant a trip to the pumping station about fifty yards away across the marina, where a large vacuum-pump was attached to the tank outlet via means of a long flexible proboscis.

Mike hated being the centre of attention, always had done. He was OK when he could hide away in metallic solitude; it's when he emerged to perform the regular rituals of boating life that he became uncomfortable. It's not easy to be discreet when you're trying to manoeuvre twenty tonnes of red steel between avenues of expensive boats. So, knowing his discomfort, the other boaters mercilessly drew attention to him by sounding their horns. All very amusing for everyone, except Mike and wife Terri. 'Thimply childisth', she said with the aid of a lisp that was prominent when she hadn't put her teeth in.

Mike was forced to retire after a 'mental blockage' and the once successful toy salesman was now insecure and a bit shaky. His retirement was managed by Terri, who nudged and cajoled him in a direction of her choosing with 'an iron fist inside a velvet boxing glove.' Life on a boat was really her idea - a place where Mike could rediscover himself and she could pester him without the inconvenience of a prolonged hunt. When they first bought their boat and moved aboard, about eighteen months ago, Mike was a nervous captain. This was not helped by the fact that his engine smoked. When he fired it up a filthy black cloud was driven before the wind, drawing attention to his tentative dawdling. Worse, he was subjected to a lengthy lecture from Sandy about why diesel engines smoke, and he was so cheesed off at this point that he was tempted to return to work. He was getting the hang of the boat now, but his early insecurity was pounced upon by the other residents. He'd even ditched the tweed cap he used to wear in an effort to appear competent. Consequently, the weekly foray to the toilet block was a thing loved and loathed by different factions for differing reasons.

So, the air was filled with the sound of horns. A nervous chap, without a hat, going fifty yards to empty his toilet isn't quite in the same bracket as the Queen Mary coming up the Solent, but it was a joyous occasion nevertheless - for everyone except Mike and Terri. Terri had odd eyes. One looked straight ahead while the other was off to starboard by a few degrees. Consequently, it wasn't easy to tell if you were the subject of a tongue-lashing or someone standing over your left shoulder. Whichever, it was advisable to pay attention *'because she does go on a bit, like a judge berating a petty criminal from the safety of their dais'* (Archie). (Roger liked that phrase and jotted it down to use in a future story.) Terri, a former P.A., was actually smart and quite proper - *'would make a formidable headmistress'* (Sal). She was less than pleased a couple of weeks ago when Mike, on a rare excursion off his leash, told a couple of rude jokes in the pub. Terri huffed and puffed like an old steam train and everyone agreed that they wouldn't want to be in Mike's shoes when he got home – if he got home.

But right now there loomed a problem that would affect them collectively – a direct threat to their meandering, pottering lifestyle. Someone had applied for planning permission to build on their vegetable patch. The residents each paid ten pounds a year to grow vegetables on a one-acre plot beyond the residents' car park at the far end of the marina. A local farmer (and land-owner, it must be said) had decided he wanted to build three detached houses on it. Mike had learned of this unsettling news from Betty, the marina manager. Archie exploded, and in very unmilitary language declared, 'Not only does the selfish twat own half of Shropshire, he also has enough livestock to fill Wembley Stadium, so what the hell does he want with a few more grand in the bank?'

An air of indignation drifted over the marina as the jungle drums beat. This unsavoury information waddled its way down the information towpath and within minutes the residents had a collective purpose. They decided to form a committee. All eight households (the remaining two of which you'll meet in due course) were hastily invited to a council of war down at the Dog that very evening.

'I need more time to prepare,' said Sandy.

'Mike's not going on his own,' said Terri, 'and it's my hair-wash night.'

However, they both realized the urgency of the situation, so Terri came lank and Sandy came preparedly naked. Everyone forewent regular routines and they gathered together in the pub at six-thirty.

'We need a chairman,' said Sandy when they were all settled in the snug.

'Person!' spluttered Terri, 'chairperson!'

Mike glared at his wife.

There was a pause of indecision.

'Chairwoman,' said Judy with some authority. Then, inflating herself to maximum dimensions, she proclaimed, 'I'll do it. There won't be any objections because none of you wants to go home with a black eye. Right,' she boomed, 'let's get going. Objections? No. Good. Archie, go and get some drinks in. When you get back, we'll decide on how to fund our campaign.'

'Couldn't we discuss a campaign fund before I go?'

'Don't be so tight, we're all in this together. Go on, get on with it. I'll have half a lager ... no, make it a pint. We may be a while.'

'Roger, you are a semi-competent writer. Could you take the minutes? Good, thank you. There's every chance that this lot will have forgotten everything before they get out of the door, never mind next week.'

An hour later Archie was twenty-five quid worse off and Roger was still muttering about the description of semi-competency, but they had set a rudimentary campaign in place. Sal and Roger were put in charge of publicity. Sal, who'd once written to David Bowie suggesting a lyric amendment and thus deemed capable of penning something comprehensible, was to be joint I.C. communications with Roger, who would write a series of articles for distribution to local news and radio outlets.

Archie, already substantially out of pocket, and to his disgust, was elected fund-raiser-in-chief, assisted by Paul, who'd got off to a bad start by coming without his wallet. Sandy was tasked with looking into the legalities – planning issues, rights of access, security of tenure etc.

'That should keep him out of our hair for a day or two,' said Pete, after Sandy had popped off to use the facilities.

'We'll doubtless pay for it later though,' said Judy mournfully, 'after he's prepared a raft of incomprehensible statistics. OK, Pete, you're in charge of environmental issues. You can also keep an eye on physical developments, people surveying or digging holes – that kind of thing. You're in the perfect position living in your squalid box by the car park. Everyone in favour? Right. Good.'

Pete scowled.

'Haaang on...', he began to protest, but was interrupted by Colin.

'My brother's a palaeontologist,' he declared.

There was a period of bemusement and everyone staring at him, including his wife Cassy.

'Oh. Very good,' said the Chair, 'errrm...'

'There may be cause for objection to the development on archaeological grounds,' he continued. 'Has anyone investigated the site? Palaeontology is not just the study of fossils, you know. Well, it is basically, but there may be the remains of rare plants or animals there that will need time-consuming, detailed investigation.'

'It's worth a try,' said Sal. 'Has your sibling got a shovel?'

'Of course he has. He's got some very impressive equipment. I'll have a word with him to see if he'll get involved.'

'Right, good. Positive stuff,' said Judy. 'Archie, pop over and get another round in, there's a love.'

'As chief fund-raiser, I propose we have a kitty.'

'We'll vote on that when you get back. We haven't time for trivia; this is an important matter. Go on! Times pressing.'

Colin and Cassy lived on their tug-style narrowboat boat called XP 49 – a dual reference to Colin's love of aircraft and a (witty?) reminder of his bureaucratic history when he used to be something in local government working for Bristol council. The P49 was not only an American Aeroplane, it was also some sort of booklet relating to employment, though nobody had the slightest interest when Colin tried to explain the fact. He was a tall, slim man with white hair and a pair of horn-rimmed glasses that he constantly shoved back up his nose. Cassy was the grand-daughter of a Scottish Laird who lived on, and managed, an eight-hundred-acre estate north of Fort William on the

Scottish west coast. Her father had sold up, invested in a series of disasters and lost the lot while Cassy was a teenager.

Her mother left in disgust (and lack of money) and emigrated to New Zealand where she now lived with a prosperous sheep farmer. She has spoken to neither Cassy nor her ex-husband for over forty years. Cassy was pulled out of private school and they'd ended up living in a council house in Rotherham before she left, aged seventeen. She went to live in Bristol where she gained a college degree in interior design, funding herself with a series of waitressing jobs. The pair met when Cassy, living in a council flat at the time, visited the council offices to complain about sewage in her back passage. She and Colin struck up an immediate affinity concerning the vagaries of Bristol plumbing and were married eight months later; a romantic tale, if ever there was one.

Paul, the most recent member of the boating community, and second in command of fundraising, was looking for work with some determination. '*Some, but not much*' (Roger). He was the youngest of the liveaboard community by about thirty years and, though you wouldn't know it from his appearance (shoulder-length blond hair, jeans ripped at the knee and ever-present brown boots), he was well educated. He earned a 2nd in electrical engineering at the University of Southampton. Failing to find a suitable post (despite a reported 96% of graduates from that establishment gaining professional employment within 6 months) he said, 'Sod this!' and bought a fibre-glass cruiser on which he now lived. Archie reckons he failed to find work for one of two reasons; either because he had Tourette's Syndrome or because he looked like he's just stuck his finger in an electrical socket; whichever, he had never got past the first interview stage. His boat was actually rather smart, '*amazingly so for a slob*' (Roger). It was his only physical asset, and he lived on the interest from an inheritance received when his godmother died while he was at university.

'As a member of the fund-raising committee I would like to suggest that we run a series of events here at the pub. A quiz or a games night for example,' said Paul, as a way of joining in.

'You can't even remember to bring your blasted wallet with you. God knows why you're my number two,' said Archie, still smarting from two expensive rounds of drinks. 'Besides, we'll need serious money if it comes to a legal battle. Getting pickled with a few locals won't even cover the phone calls. No, what we need is a celebrity on board, someone who can get us on the news and encourage companies to fork out. Anyone know anybody famous?'

Judy leant back in her chair and crossed her arms. Blue training shoes poked out from beneath the red and green kaftan. She caught Pete staring at her feet.

'Yes, Pete? Anything useful to add?'

'I was just admiring your trainers. Very, er, cool.'

'They're for velocity, not aesthetics.'

'Really?' he replied, grinning.

She smiled back.

'Well,' she continued, 'anybody?' There was an ominous silence for a moment before Sal piped up.

'Old Sam who lives in that red brick farm on the way to the marina, perhaps he can help. He used to operate one of the Woodentops on children's television back in the day, remember? Those puppets?'

There was a longer silence as the gathering digested this information.

'I suppose he could pull some strings,' said Judy. Sal tutted.

'Well, maybe not him. But I bet he's still in contact with people from his TV days.'

'We could get 'Weed' to run the tombola,' said Paul. 'That'll bring 'em flocking.'

'I'm only trying to help,' muttered Sal.

'You're doing fine, Sal,' said Judy. 'Don't be put off. You've offered up more than any of these dimwits.' She indicated the assembled with a sweep of a substantial arm. 'It's a good idea. But perhaps we need someone rather more, uh, visible. Someone current.'

'Oh yeah, sure. Let's get Johnny Depp to bring his galleon up the canal. Come on, get real! You're not going to get anyone recognizable to come to a pond in the middle of nowhere.'

'Pipe down, Sandy. Let's try and be positive. Sal, you've written to the great and good before – drop him a line. You never know. Besides, I read that his marriage is in disarray and he could perhaps do with some publicity. As chairwoman I decree that every avenue should be explored,' adding after a pause, 'However unlikely. Pete, apart from insulting my footwear, you've been quiet. What have you got to say?'

He smiled as his eyes slowly scanned the assembled.

'Leave it to me.'

There was yet another pause before Roger reacted.

'Leave it to you? Leave what to you? Christ! If we left it to you, we'd have a block of flats on the veg patch within the week.'

'Could be the Gherkin of the Midlands,' offered Paul. Pete winked and tapped the side of his nose.

'Leave it to me.'

'Well, that's one cul-de-sac,' muttered Roger, now in a state of some agitation. 'Anyone else?'

'Stop bickering. Like it or not, I was elected Chair and it's me who will direct operations. Right, anyone else anything to say before we close?'

'Can we have a kitty?' asked Archie, expecting the answer to be no.

'We can discuss that at the next meeting, which I suggest should be a week from today at seven sharp, same place. Unless of course we feel the need for an extraordinary meeting?'

'This one's been ordinary?' muttered Paul.

'Don't mutter. Right, that's it for now. Until next time we all have jobs to do. Let's just clarify. Sal and Roger, press and publicity. Archie and Paul, fund-raising. Sandy, legals. Pete, you're environmental - you can work with Colin whose brother is coming along with his tackle. Cassy love, can you work with those two? They might need some guidance and it's an important area - and there's a lot to cover. Besides, Pete seems to be in a world of his own — perhaps he will return to our planet with an A-lister. OK, anything else?'

'What about us?' asked Mike. 'What should we do?'

Terri, believing they'd got away with it, gave her husband a filthy look.

'Oh, right. Yes. Sorry Mike. Er … tell you what, why don't you guys get in touch with the waterways authorities, The Canal and River Trust? See if they have any ideas. And have a word with the marina management. Speak to Betty; she's the one who gave us the heads up in the first place. See if she wants to join us at the next meeting. That OK?'

'Yes, we'll do that,' said Mike. 'I need something to get my teeth into, what with being stuck on the boat day in day out.' Terri glared at him, and everybody else silently wished him luck.

'Fine. OK, all clear? Right, adjourned till Saturday at seven. Tally ho!'

'Just a minute,' said Roger. 'What about you? What will you be doing to further our cause?'

Inflating herself to maximum proportions once more, she declared, 'I will coordinate. I will be on hand night and day to offer any advice necessary in any area. I will be ready at a moment's notice to step in and fill any operational void - and knowing you lot there will doubtless be plenty of voids.' She laughed. 'I will do anything to prevent that moron building on our vegetables.'

'Anything?'

'I will move heaven and earth to put a stop to this blight.'

'Can you start by buying a round of drinks?'

'Don't be petty, Archie. We haven't time for socializing; we have work to do.'

Operation Vegetable was a go.

3

Lord of the Manor

A world away, in a seven-bedroom farmhouse, Edward Hordley was about to discuss plans for three detached dwellings with his architect, Simon Mossley. They were facing each other over Edward's large oak desk in his substantial office. Edward was sitting in a dark green leather chair before a sweeping bay window. His wife, Alison, delivered a silver tray on which were a silver percolator, mugs, napkins and biscuits. The bone china mugs and cotton serviettes were each adorned with the Hordley Estate logo. Designed by Edward's father, the logo incorporated the face of three yellow leopards on a royal blue background. Behind the leopards were a set of ornate gates adorned with the letters H.E. – 'Hordley Estates.' The leopards' faces were the traditional emblem of Shropshire and were colloquially referred to as 'loggerheads.' To local people, the gates symbolized the near feudal constriction of the powerful organisation's influence.

'Lovely. Thank you, my dear.'

Alison was a diminutive lady, a little over five feet tall, with neatly coiffured grey hair and large, watery blue eyes that gave her a mournful appearance, not unlike a grieving puppy. Dressed in brown tweed skirt and rust-red cashmere turtle-neck jumper below a neat white pinafore, she smiled nervously and left the two men alone. Alison was rarely seen in public. Excepting larger social occasions, she remained largely confined to the rambling house. Shopping was done by one of the Hordley's two full-time house keepers, chosen by Edward. Alison's hairdresser and beautician each visited by appointment once a week. The large oak door clicked solidly shut behind Alison.

Edward's office was on the first floor and offered a panoramic view of the flat North Shropshire countryside. Oak panelled throughout, a pair of stag's heads looked on threateningly from the right-hand side of a dark marble fireplace. To the left of the fireplace, a second door opened on to a set of stone steps leading to the ground-floor dining room. It was the office of a country squire. Half a dozen ancient oil paintings were dotted around the walls, typical hunting scenes where flashes of red jacket peered out from gloomy backgrounds. A log fire roared to keep out the early spring chill and light from the flames illuminated the gold-embossed leather of Edward's collection of rare textbooks. They were housed on floor-to-ceiling shelves along the wall either side of the main door.

Relaxed in grey corduroy trousers, tweed jacket and carpet slippers, Edward was in a good mood. It was the morning following the North Shropshire Farmers Annual Spring Ball where the great and not-so-great had gathered. Neil Grant, Edward's farm manager, saw the Ball to be an occasion 'to get pickled at somebody else's expense,' a view shared by most of the estate workers. Edward, mindful of his position within the community, had been circumspect and left before midnight in his black Range Rover while Neil had been poured into his six-year-old Subaru three hours later by co-workers under instruction from his wife, Jenny.

Even after his late night, Neil had been patrolling the estate since 6.00 AM in a beaten-up estate Land Rover. Despite having to stop once to vomit into a hedge, he coped pretty well with his daily inspection of the estate's livestock and crops. He knew full well that any dereliction of duty would be reported to Edward. Slacking, even after a heavy night, would not be tolerated. Edward meanwhile had breakfasted at leisure (porridge, kippers and Earl Grey) and was in relaxed form for his nine-thirty meeting.

Fairburn, Mossley and Hind were Shrewsbury-based architects with a high-end clientele and a reputation for getting things done – particularly in rural Shropshire where planning considerations could be sensitive. Simon

Mossley was the son of Paul, one of the firm's founder members. The new housing development, though not a major project, was one that Edward was determined to pursue and he didn't foresee a great deal of objection. After all, he'd completed projects that could potentially have been far more troublesome; for example, the construction of a reservoir two years previously to supply his huge acreage during the drier months. Water for the reservoir was sourced dually, from a small river that crossed the estate and a local spring. To the chagrin of many local people, and those further downstream who also relied on the river for water, the reservoir had been built.

'Bloody hell,' Toby Weatherall, a local plumber, had said at the time, 'I've had more trouble trying to extend my outside lavatory than Lord Edward had building that thing. How on earth did he get away with that?'

His feelings were echoed by others. Someone had put up a hand-painted sign on the dam's bank that stated simply, *'Crooked Git.'* Neil Grant had removed the sign the following day, but not before a photo had been taken and published in the North Shropshire Advertiser. Locals muttered, but as time went by the new lake became part of the landscape and the furore was resignedly accepted. Edward was a big local employer, not just directly but also of tradesmen and women who worked on and around the estate. People had to be careful what they said out loud so as not to upset their meal ticket. In fact, it's fair to say that, with his benevolence to local councillors and charitable causes, his influence reached far and wide.

Edward's country pile may have been a metaphoric world away from the marina, but geographically it was a mile and a half. The huge edifice loomed above the flat landscape like the giant nose of Aires Rock in the Australian outback. The whole estate encompassed more than three thousand acres of North Shropshire, the main crop being potatoes destined for crisp manufacturers. There was also a healthy herd of fifteen-hundred milking cattle producing milk for a large yoghurt producer in nearby Market Drayton.

Edward was tolerated and disliked in equal measure. When you've that much cash you are fawned over and relied on; many of his thirty-strong workforce lived in estate cottages rent-free, but were paid a miserly wage.

They were tied, in effect. They had a lifestyle little above subsistence, but a reasonable place to live (although general maintenance was an issue due to Edward's notorious tightfistedness). Unfortunately (or by design) his staff did not have enough money to break away and start on their own. Many workers had been there so long they knew nothing else. They followed the path of least resistance and lived their basic but mundane lives.

'They will sell for about half a million each I would expect,' said Simon. 'Here are the most recent plans. You see I've extended each property here, here and here,' he explained, pointing at the plans with a gold pen, 'to add a fourth bedroom and extra bathroom to each. One third of an acre per plot provides ample space for landscaping which will include formal gardens, extended patios and plenty of parking in addition to integrated triple garages. As you can see, each property will be wholly independent, isolated from one another by wrought-iron fencing. The exclusive community will be accessed via a gate hung between two four-metre sandstone pillars. The gate itself will be fob-activated and bear the Hordley Estate logo in red and gold. I believe it will develop into a highly desirable address. In addition, I've also commissioned a report on the feasibility of solar and geothermal energy sources. Here,' he said, handing Edward an A4 blue folder.

'Wonderful, Simon. How is the planning going?'

'Outline is approved and detailed plans will be submitted forthwith, subject to your approval of these latest amendments. I don't see any insurmountable objections and expect final approval within a month.'

'Splendid! The plans look fine to me. Presumably we can decide on the solar and geothermal in due course. I'd like to look over the figures.'

'That's fine. I'll prepare to submit the final plans later today when I'm back in the office.'

'Perfect. More coffee?'

'Thanks, I'd love one.'

'How are the family?' he asked as he poured.

'Oh, fine thank you. All happy and healthy. Mary has recently gone back to work part time; she's glad to be getting out of the house again. Tom and Molly are doing well at pre-school. My brother is having a tough time, though.'

'Oh? What's the matter?'

'He works for Meadows, you know, the Land Rover dealership in town. He's in dispute over some missing funds, been accused, at least indirectly, of fiddling commissions in their used car division. It's totally untrue. He's worked there for years and would never cheat on them. He's angry and upset. It's making him ill and his whole family is suffering as a consequence.'

'Oh, that's sad to hear. I'm acquainted with Bill Telfer who owns the place. I'll have a word; see if we can't get it sorted out.'

'That's most kind. Please don't go out of your way. I'm sure it will be resolved before long.'

'It's no trouble, really. I bought my new car from there last month. Bill seems a reasonable fellow. I'll give him a call.'

'Oh goodness, I feel rather embarrassed. I wish I hadn't mentioned it. But thank you all the same; it is much appreciated.'

'Think nothing of it. It's only a phone call.'

As he chatted with Simon, Edward Hordley was a contented man. He was, however, quite unaware of the tsunami of opposition brewing on the horizon. If he been aware of the rumbling, grumbling wall of water, fuelled by the rag-tag bunch on their boats on a pond in a field, he may have been rather less contented.

4

Reaching Out

Roughly a hundred miles away, in Littleborough on the Rochdale Canal, Len Johnson was getting a bit irate. His engine wouldn't start. He'd just given his boat its annual service (oil and filter change, new anti-freeze) and, though it had been running sweet as a nut an hour ago, his Beta Marine 38 motor was getting on his nerves. When he turned the key, the engine turned over but flatly refused to fire up. A wisp of grey-white smoke drifted out of the exhaust. It was being as stubborn as his goat. Yes, goat. He was, as far as he was aware, the only narrowboater to share his boat with a goat. He'd won it in a game of three-card brag in a pub in Skipton the year before while traversing the northern hills on the Leeds Liverpool Canal. One of the players, a farmer called Geoff Proctor, was in town for the weekly market and got himself in a financial muddle while playing cards. He'd gambled to the point where he was so in hock that the only thing of worth with which he could settle the debt was one of three goats he'd bought to market. So Len ended up with 'Proctor,' as he'd subsequently named him.

Proctor was a Golden Guernsey, native to the Channels Isles, but popular in mainland Britain. They are a small breed, known to be affectionate and docile and Proctor had a golden coat with white highlighting. He'd also turned out to be pretty adaptable, taking boating life in his stride without much complaint. Although he was very dubious about the benefits of a goat, Len had become attached to the beast. His boat was a tug-style narrowboat and Proctor spent the majority of time on the long fore deck tethered by a suitable chain while Len travelled. Proctor ate well, availing himself of grass and bits of hedgerow on the canal-side when Len pulled up for the evening, and seemed perfectly happy to hop back on board when bidden.

Len considered the engine malfunction to be fuel-supply related and was bent over checking the pump when his phone rang.

'Bugger,' he muttered, wiping his oily hands on a rag. 'Hello.'

'Len, it's Pete. Pete Crowther.'

'Hi, Pete. Blimey, haven't heard from you for a while. How's things?'

'Fine, thanks. How about you, you doing OK?'

'Just in the middle of an oil change and the old girl won't start - apart from that, great.'

'Oh dear. Well, I just wondered if I could run something by you, pick your brains.'

'I won't state the obvious; but yes, by all means.'

'Me and my boating friends down here in Shropshire have a little problem and I thought of you. Are you still in touch with the rest of the band?'

'Sure, we meet up from time to time for a jam. Nothing big, just in a pub or club. More for old times' sake than anything else. How can I help?'

'How do you fancy doing a gig at our local? We're trying to raise some cash to fight some idiot who wants to build on part of our marina. So far all we've come up with is a quiz night which might raise about twenty quid if we're lucky, and that certainly won't get us very far.'

'You know, I'd love to,' said Len without hesitation. 'Be great to see you again and meet your mates. Let me make some phone calls and I'll be in touch. When are we looking at?'

'Sometime quite soon, I guess. As far as I know they already have outline permission. The guy doing the build is a local big-knob, so I can't see it taking long to get the full go-ahead. In two or three weeks? Is that feasible?'

'I'll have to speak to Doug and Jerry. I need to sub in a keyboard player. John's in South Africa for a couple of months on a solo tour, but leave it with me and I'll do my best. I'm up in the wilds of Lancashire, so it'll take a good week or ten days to get down to you anyway – if I can get this bloody engine started. I'll introduce you to Proctor. You'll like him.'

'Proctor?'

'Friend of mine. I'll call you as soon as I can.'

'Thanks, Len. I appreciate it.'

***

Diane Markham had just returned to her hotel in Exeter. As co-presenter of Gardeners' Choice, a weekly television show on BBC2, she had just completed the first of four days filming in nearby Woodbury and was ready for a soak in the bath swiftly followed by a glass of wine, dinner and an early night. She and her team were in the process of recreating an Italian garden in the grounds of Emmerley Hall, a fine country house set on the hill overlooking Woodbury. The owner, Margaret Cambourne-Smythe, had spent many years and many thousands of pounds renovating the house and gardens. Her only living relative was an estranged sister and it was an open secret that Emmerley Hall would be taken on by The National Trust when the old lady died. Sadly, that moment was fast approaching. She was suffering from lung cancer and not expected to live more than three or four months.

Her oldest friend, Catherine Poole, phoned Gardeners' Choice in the hope that they could help Margaret complete the last project on her beloved garden before she succumbed to her illness. Diane, understanding the urgency, readily agreed to help. The idea was rubber-stamped by her production team and, eight days following the request, work started. It was the first day, and Diane and her co-presenter Simon Goode had worked hard with the other seven members of the team, initially clearing the ground before laying the foundations for the low walls that would define the Italian garden. The original garden had been laid down over a century before but had fallen into ruin. They were now working to a set of original plans found during the renovation of the house itself. After an active life Mrs Cambourne-Smythe is now confined to a wheel-chair, much to her dismay. Frustrated and frightened, she watches the distant works from her bedroom window. Diane had met her before they started work that morning and, seeing the determination and spirit in the old lady, promised to complete the project on time.

Diane had one foot in the bath when her phone rang.

'Damn!' she muttered, putting on her dressing gown and returning to the bedroom.

'Hello. Yes.'

'Diane. It's Pete. Pete Crowther...

5

Roger Rabbits

'Ready?' asked Roger. 'Everyone got a drink?'

'You got any Valium?' Cassy piped up. 'I have the feeling that I may need something to calm down.'

Archie chuckled. From time to time Roger would invite fellow residents to his boat, where he would entertain them with a story. His stock of vintage malt whiskeys took a hit each time, but it was worth it to gain an audience for his writing. He considered it training for when he would read a chapter to a doting public following the release of his latest best-seller. He was serving his apprenticeship for the time when a publisher (or anyone) would realize that his writing was worthy of a wider audience and he would mount the literary ladder; he knew that worldly acclaim was some way down the road (to mix metaphors). To be candid, the traffic lights had only just turned amber - but he reasoned that if he could entertain this lot for a few minutes then anything in the future would be child's play.

'Come on, let's get it over with,' muttered Colin, who was not known for his patience, or benevolence. He was slouched in Roger's best chair, a green leather thing on four splayed wooden legs that both rocked and swivelled. He clutched a crystal tumbler containing an inch of Talisker. In addition to Colin, Cassy, Archie, Sal, Mike and Terri waited with fevered anticipation. The six guests perched in varying degrees of discomfort on an assortment of stools and folding chairs facing the galley from where Roger, standing in splendid isolation, would deliver his reading.

'Could you move back a bit?' asked Archie. 'That spotlight over your head is casting shadows. It makes you look like something from a horror movie.'

Roger moved back half a pace and glared at Archie.

'Right,' he said. 'Ready?'

Sal held up an empty glass. 'Just help yourself,' said Roger, 'but do try and appreciate it. It's for sipping and savouring; it's not Babycham.' Sal examined the tray and settled on a Bowmore Islay single malt. She poured herself a generous inch and returned to her stool. Roger reckoned that the better his tale the more captivated his audience, and the less they drank. He measured the success of an evening in inches. On a good night he would get away with about eight; if his story rambled or got lost in translation it could cost him a foot and a half - and at about £1.50 a shot it began to get expensive. There was inducement to polish a story before a public airing. In the days leading up to a reading, he could be heard muttering and performing various eyebrow arches and hand wafts as he walked round the marina. Everyone knew *An Audience With...* was imminent depending on the ferocity of Roger's scythes and twitches.

'Something a little different this time,' he began. 'As you're aware, I am involved with a literary group. Each month someone comes up with a topic around which we must create a story. It can be anything. Two months ago, it was sun, sea and salmonella. This month's title was 'Who would own a religious medal, Rayban sunglasses and a bicycle pump?' 'So, here we go...' Roger cleared his throat, took a sip of 18-year-old Dalmore, and began.

'So, who would own a religious medal, some Rayban sunglasses and a bicycle pump? Well, initially there were three separate owners. The religious medal was in the possession of a vicar who saved a monastery from demolition, a clueless sailor sported the Ray Ban sunglasses and a bloke called Frank, who's football had gone flat, had a bicycle pump. Quite by chance. however, all three items ended up in the possession of the same person. Allow me to explain. It all started a couple of years ago with the chap with the faulty football. He'd travelled from Bury (Lancashire) to Lourdes (France). There was nothing wrong with Frank actually; he was in reasonable health, but by claiming he had some lingering malady he was able to join a coach load of optimists hoping that a dunk in the holy waters would perk them up. The trip was sponsored by a local coach company who concentrated on the budget end of the market. Due to the festering atmospheres in their buses. they usually had a few passengers fall ill. The Lourdes trip was the coach firm's idea of atonement; not an admission of guilt exactly, more a complimentary jaunt for regulars who, quite by chance, all happened to have been ill – except Frank of course, who'd faked it.

'He actually wanted to get to Monaco to watch the Formula One Grand Prix and, as Lourdes is well down south, reckoned that he could do the remainder of the journey by bicycle. He always travelled with a holdall full of black puddings (created in his home town of Bury), the quality of which had few, if any, equals. He would swap some puddings for a bicycle and barter for accommodation with the rest. The French, despite having their own puddings known as boudin noirs, were partial to the 'real' English version and had historically been quite amenable to an exchange. He'd got this idea after once meeting an Icelandic man in an airport lounge. He had travelled with a small suitcase full of salted cod (an Icelandic delicacy) and bartered that for accommodation in small hotels in Portugal.

'By the time he got to Lourdes, Frank was genuinely ill due to spending fourteen hours cooped up in a stagnant coach. So, before he procured a bike, he partook of the waters to restore some equilibrium. He bartered with a local cycle dealership, mounted up and headed east. He suffered four punctures en route, so was welcome of his bicycle pump and repair kit. Not realizing that it was in excess of 750 kilometres to Monaco, he missed the Grand Prix by a month but, determined to make the most of it when he finally arrived, he lingered by the harbour for a day or two before being encouraged to go and have a wash by an over-sensitive gendarme. Enter our hapless sailor, a man whose cash reserves outweighed his nautical prowess by some margin. Cedric he was called, pronounced Said Reek, a French National who sported a pair of trendy Ray-Ban sunglasses. He also had prodigious chest-hair within which lived a religious medallion.

'He'd won the medal from a vicar in a game of strip poker a couple of months previously in an Abbey perched atop a gorge in the Dordogne. He wore very revealing bathing trunks that emphasised his 'viande et deux legumes' (that's meat and two veg for the non-linguists among you), designed to attract the attention of the Madames of the Mediterranean. Cedric had lashed out on a rather smart yacht - more for the social status than for the joy of the open water. When Frank first encountered our shambolic sailor, it was not so much a social introduction as a rescue mission. Cedric was hanging by his left leg, strung up in the rigging. His ankle had been snared in a loop of rope when a gust of wind had whipped his unsecured sail out over the water, leaving the poor chap dangling upside down over the harbour. Frank, recognising a fellow deity in difficulty, asked the inverted sailor if he could be of assistance.

'No, no, I always spend my holidays like this,' replied Cedric. Then, with a grin, 'Oui, oui, bien sur, vite!' – 'Yes, quickly please!' Frank leapt speedily into action, or as speedily as a man full of black pudding can. He boarded the yacht and hauled Cedric to safety. Red in the face and rather unsteady after his inversion, Cedric was effusive in his thanks and offered Frank a glass of Merlot. Never one to turn down a free glass of anything, Frank readily accepted. They communicated in a sort of Franglais or Fringlish, a language born somewhere out in the English Channel during one of the brief periods when trade, as opposed to cannon balls, was exchanged between their respective countries. Frank bemoaned the blisters on his behind after his long ride and Cedric, hiding his embarrassment behind his Ray-Bans, grumbled about his sore ankle and the shortcomings of modern yachts.

'Three hours later it didn't matter which language they spoke because four bottles of wine had rendered them both incapable of delivering anything coherent. They admitted defeat and fell asleep under the yacht's rear awning, content, pickled and sheltered from the late afternoon sun.'

This alcoholic reference prompted a dash for Roger's malts. The storyteller sighed as a total of seven inches was poured. He continued.

'Frank awoke in the early hours. There was no sign of Cedric, so he lumbered ashore to try and find an all-night chemist and something to ease his vicious hangover. Although not in peak condition, he was aware enough to realize that his bike had been stolen. Despite suffering the type of hangover only usually for sale in Dublin, he was furious and decided on a course of action – he set off on foot in search of his stolen bike. He'd only walked fifteen metres when a police car screeched up alongside and he was arrested. He'd been spotted leaving Cedric's yacht and reported by an interfering native. It all got a bit complicated because Cedric was already in the Gendarmerie with a temporary bandage round his head. He'd been attacked and the Gendarmes, seeking an early conclusion to the matter, took the path of least resistance and arrested Frank. Ten minutes later he was in the room next to Cedric accused of assault, trespass and attempted robbery. Frank was having language difficulties and, no matter how much he shouted and gesticulated, he couldn't persuade the Gendarmes of his innocence. Fortunately, Cedric recognized Frank's voice and eventually everyone came together in the same room in an effort to sort the mess out. Frank was belligerent and immediately went on the attack, stating that if he ever got hold of the bugger who stole his bike he would chuck him in the harbour.

'That was me,' said Cedric, with rather a mournful look. 'I borrowed it to go and get some bread and milk. I'm sorry, but you were asleep.'

'Oh!' said Frank. 'Well, thank goodness for that. At least I haven't lost my bike.'

'Uh, you have actually. I was robbed. Someone bashed me on the head and stole your bike. They also took my money, my sunglasses, medallion. In fact everything except my bathing trunks and T-shirt.'

'Oh!' said Frank again. 'Oh dear. Are you OK?'

'A lump and a headache, that is all.'

There was a silence before Frank, still smarting from being hauled into the police station, went on the attack again.

'So what are you doing?' he asked the senior of the two Gendarmes.

Frank received a Gallic shrug in reply, accompanied by the sound of a horse blowing out through rubbery lips.

'We will do all we can. Till a few moments ago we believed the perpetrator of the crime to be a lurking Englishman.'

'I was not lurking,' said Frank indignantly. 'I was walking the streets of this crime-ridden principality in search of my stolen bicycle.'

'I realize that now. Look, why do you not accompany your friend to the hospital so they can check his injuries, and make sure he is not concussed? In the interim we will make every effort to retrieve your stolen goods. Call back later to see if we have made any progress.'

'So off they went, both sporting spectacular headaches. At the hospital, which in Frank's view was smarter than the majority of hotels in which he'd stayed, Cedric registered with a fearsome-looking receptionist who looked more suited to road-mending than tending the needy. The two new friends waited on orange plastic chairs to be seen by a doctor. To the left of the reception area a corridor led away. Roughly ten cubicles were visible, some open, some with their curtains drawn. Despite the late hour, nurses and white-coated doctors bustled about. Cedric's name was called and he set off down the corridor. He glanced in one of the open cubicles and stopped dead. He stared for a moment then gestured for Frank to join him. Lying on the bed was a man, apparently asleep, with a drip in his arm. On the bedside cupboard beside him were a pair of smart sunglasses, a religious medal and a bicycle pump.

'Well, I'll be damned,' said Frank. Cedric walked towards the prone figure.

'And who have we here, then?'

A doctor approached, not best pleased that the privacy of one of his patients was being invaded.

'Out! Get out of there immediately,' he said.

'I'm sorry,' replied Cedric, 'but this man is my brother. What is the matter with him?'

Frank looked astonished.

'Your brother, eh?' said the doctor, staring at Cedric's head bandage.

'Yes. Is he very ill? Will he be alright?' he asked, not looking at all concerned.

The doctor looked suspicious, but reassured Cedric that his brother had a nasty case of food-poisoning. He'd had his stomach pumped and was sedated. 'He'll be fine in the morning,' he said. The doctor went into the cubicle, opened the bedside cabinet and took out a small canvas bag – he delved inside and held up a black pudding. 'This revolting thing appears to be the cause of his trouble.'

Frank suppressed a snigger. So that's how one man ended up with a religious medal, a pair of Ray-bans and a bicycle pump – at least for a short time. Frank was reacquainted with his bike, the pump was reacquainted with the bike and Cedric, none the worse for his blow on the head, was happy to have his medal and glasses returned.

Brother?' said Frank.

'Never seen him before.'

Frank grinned.

'Watch those ropes,' shouted Frank as he mounted his bike the following morning.

'And you, look after your bottom,' replied Cedric.

Frank laughed as he rode away towards the railway station.

He'd have a tale to tell his mates back in the club.'

There was a moment's silence. Then another.

'Well,' muttered Colin, 'if that story had been a meal I'd be rushing for the lavatory.'

Terri leapt to Roger's defence. 'Don't be mean. I rather enjoyed it. I certainly couldn't come up with anything like that.'

'Nobody could come up with anything like that. In fact, why would anyone?'

'Entertainment, my dear old thing,' said Archie. 'A way to pass a little time in the company of friends while giving audience to a man struggling with his inner demons.' He continued into the static-laden silence. 'Just joking, Roger. Well done! I applaud your endeavours. I look forward to the next one. Particularly if you could source something from North East Scotland where the malts tend to be less peaty, less aggressive. Overall, though, a wonderful way to relax and a pleasant interlude. Thank you.'

'Thanks, Archie. I'm glad you enjoyed it.'

Mike, who had been very relaxed, startled himself awake with a rasping snore. Sal drained her glass.

'It does take a certain courage to expose yourself in public,' she commented. 'Self-promotion is not easy, but at least you're among friends here. We're glass half-full people, so if you do cock it up you'll get sympathy not ridicule.'

'Rubbish,' said Colin. 'It's only by hearing harsh realities that you will be steeled for less appreciative audiences. It's a tough world out there away from the pampered isolation we enjoy. You will have to learn to take criticism and deal with hecklers.'

'Oh, right then,' said Roger. 'If that's the way you feel I won't invite you back. You'd better bugger off.'

Everyone stared at the mild-mannered wordsmith. He'd inched forward again so the light once again distorted his features. He broke into a smile which looked rather menacing.

'Just joking,' he said, staring at Colin, who felt the uncomfortable centre of attention.

The company disbanded a short time later, and Roger was left to reflect on the relative success of the evening – a fourteen-incher.

6

Enemy Within

As Roger's guests headed home, a short distance away a figure was spotted leaving Edward Hordley's farmhouse via the kitchen door. Whoever it was crossed the dimly lit yard and donned a helmet before mounting a motor scooter and riding away – twenty-five pounds wealthier. John Greenway, smoking a quiet cigarette in a shadowed doorway, watched the figure disappear into the Shropshire night. Female, he thought, though he couldn't be certain. 'Dirty bugger,' he muttered to himself, presuming Edward to be having a late-night liaison.

John was a groom, one of three who helped care for Edward's six horses. He was checking up on Victor, a young stallion who had gone lame during his morning run out. The local vet had attended and John was there to make sure the horse was OK before he went home to his cottage in nearby Witherington, a cottage shared with his parents. His Dad, Sam, was a farm worker, and had been for years. Sam drove tractors and combine harvesters - multi-thousand-pound behemoths geared to making Edward richer. His mother, Angie, worked in the farm buttery where cream was processed and packaged to be marketed as 'hand-crafted local produce' by the people of North Shropshire. The fact that cream went in one end of a stainless steel machine and came out the other end wrapped in foil was by the by. The machine was indeed located on a local farm and the buttons were pressed by local people, but 'hand-made' was pushing it. It was an initiative devised by

Edward to humanize the soulless, money-making machine that was Hordley Estates. Nobody was really fooled, but at least his mum was paid a little and they had a place to live.

John was taking evening classes at a local agricultural college as a stockman/shepherd. He had dreams of managing his own animals. Sheep or cattle, he hadn't decided yet, but funding the dream would be a problem – a big one. The point was that he'd sniffed the outside world and was increasingly aware that there were opportunities beyond Edward's net. He was also alarmed that the same net that closed on his parents many years before was now closing around him. His parents were privates in Edward's army with no prospect for promotion – John wanted more. He'd rather be a colonel in his own platoon than a private in a faceless battalion.

'We live a good, honest life,' his father had said when John had shared his thoughts. 'You could do a lot worse. We have a roof over our heads, and it's good to be part of a respected organisation.'

'Everything we have, which isn't much, is down to Mr. Hordley. We're stuck, tethered to this damn estate. When was the last time you and Mum had a meal out or went to the cinema? There's a big world out there. I'm not jealous of Edward, in fact in many ways I see him live a lonely life, driven both by his greed and the need to live up to the expectations of his father who, let's be frank, was the real reason this place is so successful. No, I want something I can call my own. I want the work I do to be for me, for us, not someone else. I must try, Dad.'

John knew that he didn't want to end up like his parents. They were both well into their fifties and owned nothing. What would happen when they retired? A council house? The estate cottage would be needed for future workers. What kind of future was in store for them?

'Look, it might sound like I'm damning you and Mum or criticizing, but I'm not. I'm proud of you. You've both worked hard and I really admire you for that, but I want more. I want us to have our own place and have a proper say in how we live. I have no idea how I'll do it but it's what I want for all of us.'

The noise of the motor scooter was swallowed by the night. Very peculiar, he thought to himself, as he crushed his cigarette underfoot on the cobbles. He turned towards the farm and saw a silhouetted, back-lit figure looking out from the kitchen window. Alison Hordley was watching him. She stood for a moment, raised her chin slightly and moved away. Edward was pensive, bordering on irate. He sat in his office before dark green velvet curtains and stared into the crackling log fire. His source had informed him of the boaters' plans to thwart his development. He'd little time for the residents of the marina, believing them to be either free-loaders or people with little ambition frittering their lives away in the discomfort of their twee, steel boxes; little people whose sole aim was to do as little as possible. There was a part of him that believed the boaters couldn't summon the collective wit to mount a challenge to him; but he was annoyed, nevertheless.

There was money to be made and power to savour. Edward ruled his dominion like a despotic chief, dominating his scattered tribe from his lofty perch of privilege. He was the big cheese and lorded it over people's lives, lazily cruising his empire like a shark in a fish tank. He hid an arrogant ruthlessness behind a ratty smile. He owned his employees, who know that a word here or a signature there could all but destroy their lives. His problem here was that he didn't own the boaters and had no sway. He needed an edge. Fiscal compensation was not an option because he hated to part with cash unnecessarily. He could offer them an alternative site for their damn vegetables – but again that would be giving something away and it went against the grain. It would also be an admission that he was concerned. In fact, any show of benevolence would be a sign of weakness, and in all likelihood make them even more intransigent. No, there had to be a better way.

He stood, parted the curtains and gazed out over his endless acres. Lights from scattered cottages and distant farm buildings twinkled in the darkness - dim beacons of dim humanity in his dark galaxy. One light shone brighter than the others in the distance - the floodlight illuminating the marina car park. It polluted the sky like a rogue star peeping over the horizon. It dominated the landscape and intensified his frustration.

7

It's Who You Know

Three days later the boaters were back in The Dog.

'Right,' boomed Judy, 'welcome to Op-Veg Two, the second meeting of Operation Vegetable. I refer, of course, not to the assembled company, rather to our battle to save our allotments. Right, let's see where we're up to. Roger, could you read the minutes of our previous meeting, please?'

'Can you make them seconds, rather than minutes?' whispered Paul, 'I'm sure someone has a train to catch.' Roger glared at the youngster and cleared his throat.

'Saturday 14th April saw the inaugural meeting of Operation Vegetable, held here in the Dog and Rabbit. Present were Judy, Archie, Sal, Jud...'

'Yes, yes,' said Archie. 'We know who was there. Just remind us what happened.'

Roger sighed impatiently.

'In response to a direct threat to our enjoyment of the allotments by Mr. Edward Hordley, a greedy swine who lives nearby, a residents' committee was formed. The assembled cobbled together the rudiments of a plan to combat this threat. That plan was code-named Operation Vegetable. Judy elected herself chairwoman and procee...'

'Point of order,' she called. 'I was unanimously elected.' Elected herself, indeed. 'If you're going to be committee secretary, at least make the effort to record things accurately. Right, carry on.'

Roger took a gulp of his beer while gathering his thoughts.

'Judy was unanimously elected chairwoman,' he continued. He raised his eyes to the ceiling and continued in dramatic tone. 'A dark, bruised cloud glowered menacingly over our existence until Judy, by means of rapier-like incisiveness and pugilistic menace, managed to whip the assembled into a fighting force. The residents of Watergrove Marina, previously a grumbling, rumbling beast at repose in a field of dreams, was poked in the flank by a purple training shoe, and a battalion was raised.'

'For God's sake,' muttered Archie.

'Ignore him. Carry on, Roger,' said Judy. 'I'm rather enjoying this.'

A few minutes later he was finished, most of the relevant detail having been lost in a morass of metaphors.

'You missed something,' said Paul. 'Apologies for absence. Common sense appears to be missing.'

They all chuckled.

'Thank you, Roger. Very, er, succinct. Right, staying with your team, how are you and Sal getting on with the PR campaign?'

'Mixed,' replied Sal. 'We're doing fine considering nobody appears to give a damn about our difficulties.' Judy sighed. 'Vladimir Putin put a bit of a spanner in the works by moving his tanks up to Ukraine's border. Apparently, he feels threatened - consequently the threat of another world war has taken priority in some quarters. But on a more positive note, the community section in the local rag are thinking about including a piece in their North Shropshire slot. The problem is that nobody wants to upset Edward Hordley, not only because he's a big local employer but he's also a major shareholder in United Press who own the paper. Allegedly, he bought a large chunk of shares after they published the 'greedy git' photo, trying to make sure there was no repeat.'

'I did speak to the local reporter on the phone,' said Roger, 'but when I met her for a coffee in Wem it turns out she's a sixteen-year-old schoolgirl on work experience. But I'm hopeful.'

Colin launched a scathing attack.

'Hopeful? What for? You mean she's over the age of consent?'

'Don't be revolting. She's a very pleasant young girl who is sympathetic to our cause. It transpires she is quite a liberal thinker – and a vegetarian.'

'Oh, marvellous. So we've mobilized the fourth estate via a teenage vegan? That'll have Edward quaking in his boots.'

'Stop bickering, you two. Colin, please go through the chair if you wish to make a point. Denigrating Roger isn't helpful.'

'She's only sitting on a built-in bench because she'd go through a chair if she sat on one,' Colin whispered to Sandy.

'Speak up, Colin. If you've something to say, let's all hear it.'

'Er, I was just saying that we're going to need substantial support if we're not going to end up in an undignified heap on the floor.'

'Quite. That's what we're all trying to achieve - so if you've something to mutter, please either share it or shut up.'

'Actually,' said Sal, 'we've done a bit more than contacting the local press. We thought the local press was a logical place to start, but we've also written to the nationals, letters section and editorial. Most submissions are via their websites these days, so it's hard to know if anything has got through but I'll be following up over the next day or so. We've also designed some posters to spread around the area and voiced our objections to the local planning department. Roger also penned a piece for submission to a waterways magazine called Canal Boat, but it turns out the editor is an idiot – that's Roger's assessment by the way, not mine - so I'm not sure how far we'll get with that. They seem more interested in publishing advertorial features on fancy new boats for the wealthy rather than highlighting local issues or printing anything of any real interest. Just for the record, Roger and I have stumped up for the posters, which isn't really a problem, but we could really do with a campaign fund of some sort.'

'We haven't even got a drinks kitty; how the hell are we supposed to accumulate a campaign fund?'

'Oh Archie, do stop being negative,' said Judy. She rooted about in the nether regions of her voluminous pink kaftan and handed him a crumpled fiver. 'Here, go and get some drinks in.' Before Archie could launch a protest,

Judy went on.

'OK, well done Roger and Sal. That's a good start. Pete, Colin, Cassy, anything to report on the environmental side?'

'Well,' said Cassy, 'we probably have reasonable grounds for objection on a number of fronts, but we reckon that they will only delay the inevitable. For example, we can quote various things from previous planning objections. One we came across said: *"We believe that the proposed development is a direct contravention of Policy 4.19. It does not respect local context and street pattern or, in particular, the scale and proportions of surrounding buildings, and would be entirely out of the character of the area, to the detriment of the local environment."* And another says, *"We consider the proposed development to be a direct contravention of the following objective from the same chapter: 'To protect or enhance the local environment, including wildlife habitats, trees and woodland parks and gardens.'"*

'Sal and Roger used some of this when writing their planning objections. We can use loads of flowery language tailored from one of many historical objections, but our number one problem is Edward and his influence. We can object all we like but if he's porking the head of planning we're up against it. I use that phrase in a metaphorical sense of course, but you get the idea. What we need is an edge. Something we can use against him either personally or professionally.'

'Well, it's all grist to the mill. If nothing else, you could mention this to your journalist, Roger,' said Judy. 'OK, anything else?'

'My brother Andy called in the other day,' said Colin, 'and had a poke around.'

He took out his phone and started scrolling through his photographs.

'Did he perchance unearth a triceratops then, or a Roman villa?' enquired Archie.

'Well, no,' he said, smiling, 'but he did find this. Here, look.'

Archie squinted, then held the phone at arms' length, obviously struggling to make sense of it. 'What is it? It looks like a lump of rotting wood.'

'Well, basically, that's what it is. But an interesting one. It's an old tiller arm.'

'Really?' asked Paul. 'Whose?'

'Very funny. It's the tiller arm from a narrowboat, a very early one. Andy thinks that this is the piece that attaches to the rudder. It's just like our modern-day brass ones, but longer, and this one is made of wood. It may well be from a horse-drawn boat, so it could be a hundred years old or more. The point is that there may be more than just this concealed there.'

'Interesting,' said Judy. 'Time Team, eh?'

'Don't know, but it might be worth a further look. There are probably lots of undiscovered artefacts around the canals.'

'Our marina was only created in the 1970s,' said Sandy, 'but it used to be an old clay pit. Clay was extracted to line and repair the canals. It's quite a historical site really. The canal used to extend past the marina on to a place called Prees. It's derelict now, but you can still see the course of the old canal, particularly a bit further down the line. At one time it would have been pretty busy, I reckon, but what we have now is nothing like what was originally intended. As far as I understand it, the initial plans were approved in the late seventeen-hundreds when they intended to link Chester and Shrewsbury, basically a north-south canal. That didn't happen for various reasons, including financial, but without doubt there has been canal-related activity in this area for more than two hundred years.'

'Indeed,' said Colin. 'Andy did a bit of research. The point is that this tiller arm probably belonged to a very old wooden boat. It could be of real historical value and my brother has come up with a suggestion. Why don't we build a replica boat on-site? He says there are old wooden boats still around; not originals, of course, but replicas. We could use them as a template along with old photographs and any plans that may be in existence. He has come across one boat called Saturn that's around somewhere. It's what's known as a fly boat. Fly boats were the horse-drawn express trains of the canals. They would carry cargo and get preferential passage through locks. There would be fresh horses waiting at various points to keep the boats moving as quickly as possible. Anyway, Andy's idea is that we build an open structure, Dutch barn-style perhaps, and build a boat using tools and techniques employed when these boats were first constructed. He reckons that historical societies, particularly those canal-related, may get behind the idea.'

'I like it,' said Judy. 'Well done, your brother. What do you reckon?' she asked, looking round the table.

'If nothing else it might put another spoke in Edward's wheel if we can generate some publicity,' said Sandy. 'I'll put some feelers out to see if the historical bods are interested.'

Much to Judy's chagrin, Pete was at the bar chatting to Eric, the landlord. 'Going to join us, Pete?' she called over. He didn't look round but raised a finger and called over his shoulder, 'Be with you in a minute.'

'Bloody marvellous!' muttered Judy. 'We're all making an effort while old tatty-features slobs around making the place look a mess.' She shook her head. 'OK, let's move on. Welcome Betty, thanks for joining us. Obviously, Mike and Terri had a word with you – this affects you as much as us. Do you have any thoughts, from a marina point of view perhaps?'

'Unlikely,' said Archie, 'judging by the half-empty art gallery she runs.'

Judy glowered at him.

'Oh, do shut up. Pay no heed, Betty. Did you manage to have a word with anyone?'

'Yes, we invited Charles Conran, the local Canal and River Trust bigwig, to come and see us. I have to say he was basically rather unhelpful. His problem is that the canal branch providing access to the marina is straddled by Hordley Estates land, and they could make life difficult if we cause ructions. He said that all Mr. Hordley needs to do is 'accidentally' nudge some stones off one of the bridges into the canal with one of his tractors and we'd be cut off till we have an expensive clear-up. That's being a bit dramatic, perhaps, but we got the point. Plus, any access road to the new development would need substantial upgrading. The marina uses the same road so in getting it upgraded the Trust would only see that as a benefit to their own infrastructure. Unfortunately, I don't think we'll see any help coming from that quarter. The Trust reckon to be always short of money so they don't want to get into any expensive legal wrangling. Unless the proposals pose a direct threat to the marina they won't get involved.'

'We did point out,' said Mike, 'that although the marina itself is privately owned, waterborne access is managed by the Trust and they had a responsibility to protect the rights of both the marina and it's residents, and any visiting boats. In response, Charles rightly pointed out that Hordley Estates were not actually doing anything illegal, and they have more pressing priorities than protecting a vegetable plot with which they have no direct association. I'm afraid that ultimately we had to concur, much as it rankles.'

'Oh well,' said Judy. 'Thanks for trying.'

Pete wandered back from his chat with Eric and sat on a stool between Paul and Sandy, who shuffled up.

'Ah, the scruffy one's joined us. Glad you've dressed up for your big night out,' muttered Sandy.

'Business beckoned, Sandy my old lad.'

'Mmm. Good of you to join us, Pete.' said Judy. 'OK, fundraising. Anyone?'

Paul piped up. 'We've got a quiz booked here next Saturday night. Sandy and I put flyers in all the shops in Wem and Eric here has agreed to lay on some eats. Actually, there was pretty good support from the shopkeepers; they were sympathetic so it should be a good turn-out. Should be a start to the war chest anyway.'

'Come in, Compo,' said Roger, giving Pete a grin along with a pair of arched eyebrows.

Cassy snorted and everyone chuckled.

'Anything to add, Pete?' asked Judy resignedly.

Pete puffed his chest out.

'Well, I've been keeping a keen eye on the plot and nobody has dug any boreholes or been round with theodolites; except Colin's brother, of course.'

'Very good,' said Judy. 'Hope you didn't over-extend yourself.' Pete smiled at the jibe.

'But, as it happens…'

'As it doesn't happen more like,' muttered Roger.

'My dear man, have a little faith.' He paused. 'I've been in touch with a couple of old friends - pals from my younger days when life was full of hope and wonder and mystery. A time when I hadn't had the dubious pleasure of being forced to associate with the likes of old Roger here. A time when life was full of promise and...'

'OK, OK, we get the point. Do get on with it for goodness' sake, before we develop wrinkles.'

Pete gave Judy a big grin.

'Develop?'

'Get knotted.'

'Anyone watch BBC 2's Gardeners' Choice?' asked Pete cheerily looking round, eyebrows raised. There was an expectant pause.

'Actually, I do from time to time,' said Terri. It transpires that Sandy is a fan too, as is Cassy.

'Right, well, Diane Markham who presents it is a friend of mine from Uni and she's...'

'University! You?' spluttered Judy. Pete grinned again.

'Shouldn't judge a book by its cover, my love.'

'Bloody good job in your case!' Paul laughed.

'You'd be surprised where some of us oldies hail from and what we got up to. It's not just you youngsters who have the license to muck about, you know. I did actually have a life before being stranded in this Shropshire swamp. Anyhow, I told Diane of our problem and asked if she had any ideas. She came back to me yesterday and she's come up trumps. She ran an idea by her bosses who jumped at it. They are going to do an 'allotment special' – right here on our veggie patch. They finish filming any day now down near Exeter and, as she puts it, our cause is just - they start filming here next Wednesday. We, my motley crew, will be the stars of the show.'

There was a stunned silence broken eventually by Judy, who whooped! She heaved herself off her bench, lumbered round to Pete and gave him a big kiss on the forehead.

'Brilliant,' she cried. She waved her arms about and hopped from one foot to the other. 'Yes!' she yelled, pumping her fists. (Archie later recorded the episode in his notebook, stating that he feared the assembled could have been smothered within the fabric of a massive half-deflated balloon, or else trampled underfoot.)

'Archie, get the drinks in,' she said and pulled two twenty-pound notes from her nether regions. 'We need to celebrate. Wow, what publicity; that's exactly what we needed. Well done you lovely, unkempt specimen.' She engulfed Pete in another big hug.

Pete chuckled and everyone started gabbling excitedly.

'Just a moment,' said Sandy. 'Surely the programme won't be aired in time, will it? I mean by the time we get any publicity Edward will be well on his way.'

'You're quite right,' Pete acknowledged. 'But Diane says they're going to film a trailer which will go out as soon as possible. Diane's a smart cookie, she'll see us right.'

'Won't Edward protest about them filming on his land?' asked Cassy.

'They just plan to arrive next Wednesday and crack on. That's on the basis that we are, in effect, the leaseholders and it's us that have granted permission. All we're doing is improving the environment. It's not like WE'RE building houses on the field. If he does protest, they'll get it on film. That footage may accidentally be leaked onto YouTube or wherever. At the very least, it should delay things. Even he wouldn't be brazen enough to just plough ahead with his building; he'd never live it down.'

'I can see him suing us or the BBC, or at the very least chucking us off the field for good. We can't afford any legal stuff, can we?' said Sal.

'Sal, you're taking the wind out of our sails,' Archie responded. 'Relax and have a glass of wine on Judy, an event so rare it could easily be termed vintage. The very fact that we're being bought a drink by our chosen leader should be cause for celebration in itself.'

'The one who chose herself, you mean,' muttered Roger. 'But Sal does have a point.'

'We can cross that bridge when we come to it,' said Judy. 'Right now, we need to plan our attack around Pete's mate. And, just for the record, I was democratically elected as chair.'

'Actually, no one objected through abject fear. It's rather different,' Roger pointed out.

'We needed a strong leader. Don't believe for one moment that I accepted the role without careful consideration. I realized my managerial talents far outweigh the requirements needed to lead you lot – in effect I was WAY over-qualified. It was like asking a self-respecting cowboy to go and lasso a tortoise. BUT, I assessed the opposition and saw a worrying deficiency in viable alternatives so, with modesty and after no little soul-searching, I put myself forward. So there!' she said laughing at Roger. 'Now, have a drink and shut up.'

'Quite right,' said Sal and raised her glass. 'To our leader.'

'To our leader,' they all echoed.

'OK, is there anything else?'

One or two started to gather their belongings.

'Well, actually there is something else.'

Everyone sat down again.

'OK, Pete. Go ahead.'

'I have another friend.' He waited for the inevitable. Colin obliged.

'Really?' he asked sceptically. Pete grinned.

'Yes, really. He's called Len and he has a narrowboat. Before that – thirty odd years ago, in fact - he was in a band that was pretty successful. It was called Rounded.'

They all stared at Pete.

'What? You're joking,' said Sal.

'Nope. They started at Uni under another name I can't remember but they became Rounded after they were taken on by a record label and recorded "Times, Places" which did pretty well.'

'Pretty well? They were massive!' said Judy. 'Elaine and I saw them more than once. I don't believe it!'

'Yes, they did well,' Pete went on, 'They were popular for twenty years or so. To be honest, for a year or two after Uni I didn't know who they were until someone pointed them out to me. I got in touch with Len who invited me to a gig in Colchester, and we've been in contact on and off ever since. He's a good lad is Len, quite unaffected by fame. In fact, the reason he bought his boat was to duck out. They don't play in public these days, save for getting together from time to time at a pub or village hall, for their own amusement really. John the keyboard player still tours with another outfit and is away, but the others are around. Len's had a word and they've agreed to come and play for us.'

There was a stunned silence.

'Bloody hell! I don't believe this. How the hell does a scruffy git like you get involved with stars?' said Judy, wide-eyed. Pete chuckled again.

'I was having a word with Eric just now about it. He's up for it, not surprisingly. Two weeks today we thought, here in the Dog. That should give us time to spread the word.' There were further murmurs and head-shaking.

'Well done indeed, Pete. You've put all our paltry efforts to shame,' said Roger.

'Nah, nonsense. We've all pitched in. What matters is that we make the most of it. Len is quite prepared to be exploited for a night, as are his mates – within reason, of course. We need to make the most of their benevolence and there are ways to do that - but we don't want them photo-bombed with naked bimbos or anything.'

'You listening, Judy?'

'Colin, get lost!'

'How can we make the most of it?' asked Sandy, with more than a degree of scepticism.

'Well,' said Pete after a brief pause, 'for example we could get the gig sponsored. The generation who knew the group thirty years ago are now owning or running companies. The folk with the cash basically. I'd be surprised if one decent-sized business hereabouts wouldn't stump up quite a sum to be headline sponsor, or at least get involved in some way. Way back when I was involved with running the odd sporting event and we built packages to attract sponsors, we were struggling to get people to give us a fiver for a small banner. But with such a well-known act I would hope it would be rather easier. The trick is to offer a potential sponsor as much as possible for as little as possible. In other words, we offer them things that cost us nothing but are valuable to them. For example, they could meet the band, have photos taken with them, put their company name on any advertising or an event programme, plus a VIP table right in front of the stage. Stuff like that; we'll have to get creative. I'd have to run it by the guys, but they may even agree to a photo of them at the business itself. Anyway, you get the idea, that sort of thing.'

'Brilliant,' said Judy. 'You're a genius. Underneath all that mud you really are quite a surprise.' She shook her head. 'OK. Now we really have something positive to focus on, let's get to it. Terri, Sandy, Cassy, you're fans of the gardening show. Why don't you get your heads together? We need to get moving on that one - we haven't much time. Anyone else like to pitch in on this? How about you, Paul?'

'Yeah, I guess so.'

'Don't show too much enthusiasm, for goodness sake. We don't want you having a seizure.'

'No, no, it's fine. I'm up for it. I was just thinking.'

'Steady on...' said Archie. Paul grinned.

'No, I was wondering whether we should try and involve Edward. I mean, wouldn't it be better to try and get him on side? We know he's a narcissist, so if we offered him the spotlight it might just appeal to him.'

'No way,' said Colin. 'He's a complete berk who's only interest is getting his own way.' There was a few moments' silence.

'I tend to agree with Colin,' said Mike. Terri glared at him, but he ignored her and went on. 'Even if he showed an interest, there's nothing to stop him playing along for a week or two and then coming back to trample on us again. What we need to do is put a spanner in his works for good. It's not just about the veg plot, it's about next month and the month after that.' They all looked at Judy.

'This is an important one,' she said. 'What does everyone think?'

'Sod him!' They all stared at Sandy.

'Sorry about the language, but he's had plenty of opportunity to show benevolence and it's patently obvious he chooses profit and power over people; even with those who work for him, if the rumours are to be believed. I say we get on with it without him. We've shown enough resourcefulness, or Pete has anyway, to show we're a match for anyone. Let's just do it.'

'We're making a powerful enemy,' said Sal.

'We've got an enemy anyway. It's time he had a kick in the shins.'

Judy raised her eyebrows and looked around the group.

'OK. The consensus seems to be we go it alone. Let's take a vote. All in favour?'

They all raised their hands.

'Right, good. Roger, Sal, you have some real leverage here for publicity. You good with that?'

They both nodded.

'You can get in touch with your child bride again, Roger,' said Colin.

'Ha ha.'

'OK, the rest of us will put our minds to the gig. Pete, you want to ask Eric if he can join us for a few minutes?'

The two sub-committees adjourned to plan. Operation Vegetable was now, as Paul put it, a two-pronged fork with which to poke Edward in the backside.

8

Band of Brothers

Len was chugging south-west on his narrowboat. He'd managed to get his engine going; it had indeed been a fuel supply problem – in that he'd turned the fuel off before servicing his engine and had forgotten to turn it back on again. He was now on the Bridgewater Canal and moored in Lymm. He munched on fish and chips bought from his favourite chippy (imaginatively called Lymm Fish and Chips) just down the hill from the town moorings. He and Proctor attracted no little interest as Len sat on a director's chair on the long front deck. The goat was confined to barracks in built-up areas so happily munched away on a large bowl of oats while restricted on a shortened tether. The laid-back beast was unconcerned as a Jack Russell went bonkers on the towpath. The little dog yapped and jumped as it strained on its lead, venting fury at an alien invading his territory. Finally the dog was dragged away by its grinning owner and peace returned.

A live version of JJ Cale's *After Midnight* played quietly on speakers concealed in the front bulkhead. A man in a Barbour jacket and tweed flat cap leant on a nearby railing, bobbing his head in time with the up-beat song. The sound of Cale's distinctive voice and smooth guitar drifted over the canal like idle mist on an autumn morning. As Eric Clapton joined in for *Call me the Breeze* the man inclined his head and grinned at Len. Len smiled back and raised a finger to a moment shared. Instances such as this were why Len had taken to boating, and why those who walked by sometimes wished they had.

Len was a wealthy man, very wealthy, but you wouldn't know it judging by his attire and demeanour. He was about five foot eight with short hair and a 'No. 1' grey beard. He wore blue jeans, a red-check lumberjack shirt under a black fleece jacket and Karrimor walking boots. Despite the rock-star life, he'd looked after himself and had a trim figure. He'd never taken drugs and only drank conservatively, usually real ale – he'd seen too many contemporaries end up in a heap. His one rebellious trait was a diamond stud in his left ear, a gift from the only woman he'd wanted to share his life with. They'd parted company while he was touring, away from home for much of the time. Maggie had wanted to develop her career in medicine and went on to become a consultant paediatrician. Difficult though it was for them both, they realized that neither wanted to be tied to the other's lifestyle. She'd met a surgeon to whom she remains happily married.

Len was still friendly with both of them, in fact he is godfather to their first-born, Jack. Recently Len had come across a quote from Zig Ziglar who'd said, *"You can get everything in life you want if you will just help enough other people get what they want."* Nearly forty years ago, both Len and Maggie had different priorities and were not prepared to give quite enough to each other. They'd talked about it subsequently and agreed that they'd had the best of both worlds. Both had realized their ambitions and they had remained friends – the best compromise they could hope for.

During the later years with the band he'd tried to buy contentment, but it didn't work. He'd acquired a country pile in Hampshire and parked sports cars on the drive, but he'd been lonely. Rattling from room to room he'd reminisced about times on tour with the band. It wasn't the adulation or the money, but the camaraderie and sense of belonging that he'd loved; the tension before a gig, the nervy, shared jokes or sitting quietly and sipping a drink with his mates after a successful night. The band split because the time was right, all totally amicable.

Once they'd started repeating things, such as visiting the same cities in increasingly familiar countries, the magic began to wane. It's never the same the second or third time; it's never as good even though each tour coincides with a new album. They'd been going for over twenty years, right from the moment they realized they had something in their friend's farmhouse near Skipton, North Yorkshire, to the final gig in The Nynex Arena in Manchester where they'd said goodbye to twenty thousand delirious fans. There were five of them to start with: Len, Jerry, Doug, John and Ed. Ed had been killed in a car smash ten days after the gathering at the farm, before the band really got going. In his memory they had called the fledgling band Round at Ed's in his memory. They later shortened it to Rounded, but they never forgot their mate.

After the split, Doug bought a struggling yacht brokers in Southampton and turned his second love, sailing, into a successful business. He sold a number of boats to people in the music business, but really turned it round when he began leasing super-yachts to wealthy music fans. The packages he sold enabled clients to see their favourite groups in cities by the sea while staying on board luxury boats in some of the most exclusive and sought-after harbours in the world. Bankers and business-people paid a fortune for the privilege. Doug now lived on a converted Motor Torpedo Boat on the River Adur estuary in Shoreham, East Sussex. He played bass in the band, but was now an accomplished acoustic guitarist. In an on-board studio he 'fiddled around' creating bass lines for up-and-coming local bands and enjoyed what he termed 'acoustic ensembles' with friends.

Jerry, the band's drummer, retired to a vineyard near Bordeaux. It was ironic that after Ed's death, caused when a drunk driver smashed head-on into Ed's Ford Fiesta on a small North Yorkshire road, Jerry vowed to give up the booze. Throughout his time with the band he never touched a drop and from then on limited himself to sampling his own wares. 'It's filthy stuff really,' he once confided to Len, 'but if people are prepared to pay for it the least I can do is taste it and try to understand all the rubbish they come out with.' He now divided his time between his château near Bordeaux and a cliff-top house just outside Whitby. North Yorkshire.

John still played keyboard. He had his own band, Up Close, which toured 'boutique' venues around the world. The five-piece outfit played a mix of jazz, blues and anything else that took their fancy. John learned classical piano at the Northern School of Music and even though they had huge success with Rounded it underplayed his talent. He co-wrote most of the songs with Len, and even though musically he was on another planet he just loved being with and performing with his mates. They all learned from him, and it was often John that took an ordinary song and made it something else. He was, and still was, a big fan of 10cc – the way they innovated and developed, their willingness to take risks by trying something new despite success with one genre. He wasn't over-keen on the use of technology in music, but understood the need to try and develop. Probably his greatest asset was his lack of ego and his willingness to share his skills. Despite now living in trendy Notting Hill, he largely kept himself to himself and was described by Len as one of the good guys.

Len sat back and thought about his old mate Pete and what was in store down in Shropshire. Rounded had been lucky with their manager and record label. Many bands had been fleeced, having being forced into stifling contracts with the promise of fame, but Steve Markovich had looked after them, kept them safe from the jackals and had been handsomely rewarded throughout the years. He was still in the business, heavily involved with a spin-off of a well-known talent show in Australia, but was still pally with the guys.

Len had jotted down a play-list for the pub gig but really had no idea of the make-up of his audience. *'It doesn't really matter,'* he thought to himself. *'The band will enjoy it if no one else does.'* It was Sunday, late afternoon, and Len was a contented man.

* * *

On Monday morning, two days following the Watergrove resident's strategy meeting, Diane Markham met with her BBC colleagues. Six of them gathered in a room to plan the Shropshire show. The producer, a feisty sixty-year-old called Audrey Roberts, had taken some convincing that a bunch of 'privileged' boaters warranted air-time, but she had come round and was excited by the prospect of trying to help keep the countryside green. 'Plus,' she said, 'Shropshire is a beautiful county and will give us some great background footage.' It probably helped that her elderly Aunt still lived in Much Wenlock, a lovely medieval town close to Wenlock Edge, featured in A.E Houseman's poem, *A Shropshire Lad*. 'Yes, I think I'll come along on this one,' she added.

Diane and four colleagues agreed to drive up the following day and do some groundwork. She'd arranged to meet her friend Pete to scope out the lay of the land, followed by supper in The Dog and Rabbit. She had reserved rooms in nearby Whitchurch for the crew while she would stay in the pub.

As Diane planned, Edward Hordley was holding a council of war. He'd learned an hour ago that the boaters were revolting. A phone call from his informant had put him in a rage. Fury fizzed around his office like electricity in a plasma ball. At ten-thirty he'd summoned his farm manager. An hour later Neil felt he'd been battered by a typhoon as he listened to his boss rant and rave. He'd heard the boaters called some very ungentlemanly names. Edward had stood up, sat down, repeatedly thumped the table and gone a very unhealthy colour.

'Make no bones about it,' he finished in a threatening voice,' I will terminate your employment immediately if that television crew even reaches my land on Wednesday morning. You will do everything in your power to prevent these morons interfering with my plans. I will not be made a fool of, and I will not accept failure. Do you understand?'

Neil, who'd never seen anyone so unhinged, merely nodded.

'WELL, DO YOU?' yelled Edward, 'Don't just sit there like a nodding donkey! Tell me you will stop these bastards. I don't care what you do, just stop them. I ask you for the final time, do you understand?'

'Yes,' muttered Neil. 'Yes, I understand.'

'Right, then get out and go and do your job.'

John Greenway was in the courtyard with Charlotte James, a bespectacled sixteen-year-old groom, a pretty, timid girl whose blonde hair peeped out from below her riding hat. She loved her job and was a natural with the horses. Both she and John wore black boots, fawn riding breeches and quilted jackets, and both had heard Edward through the open window. They were transfixed as the lord of the manor had raged and berated his farm manager. Charlotte looked genuinely alarmed, and John was angry.

'Bloody hell!' he said under his breath, then turned to Charlotte. 'If you know what's good for you, don't say a word about this to anyone. It's not our business – well, not yours anyway. Come on, let's make ourselves scarce and give these horses a run out.' They clip-clopped their mounts across the cobbles as Neil jumped into his Land Rover and sped away.

9

Bullied

Elaine had responded to a call to arms from Judy and her ancient, sworl-bedecked camper van was parked on the gravel drive near the marina shop.

'I see the sperm-mobile is back,' said Archie to Sal, who giggled.

They could hear the two ladies sharing a joke on the boat next door and Sal wondered if the manic tittering was the result of something slightly more illicit than your usual beverage. She wasn't bothered; she liked the pair, and in some ways envied their zany friendship. Besides, it was only ten-thirty and they were all due to meet up down the allotment at eleven to have a tidy-up. There was also little doubt that Judy was taking her role as head of Operation Veg seriously, so Sal didn't begrudge her a bit of down time. Roger walked by.

'Hey Rog,' called Archie. 'You arranged to meet your infant journalist yet?'

Roger glared. 'Actually, she's coming by any time, bringing someone with her.'

'Play-school leader?'

'Get lost. Actually, I emailed her last night and we're causing a bit of a stir. She's coming with her boss, and a photographer I think. She asked me to keep shtum till I'd spoken to them.'

'I'm not surprised,' said Sal. 'It's probably a scoop of a lifetime for them. But, let's be honest, we need wider coverage than the local section of a provincial newspaper that most people don't read.'

'I realize that, but I did promise. They said that they would do a big splash – and not just in the community bit either. And don't be so scathing. I'm told they have a circulation of over thirty thousand, plus the on-line readers and syndication.'

'Oooh, hark at him,' said Archie. 'Move over Mr. Murdoch.'

Roger shrugged and moved off down the pontoon towards his boat.

'Don't be cruel, Archie. He's doing his best. Besides, from small acorns…'

'I know, I know. I'm only taking the mick. Anyway, come on. Let's get down the way and see if we can do anything to smarten up our plot.'

'You go. I'll stick around and meet the press guys with Roger. It's my brief after all, and I feel that Roger could do with a bit of support.'

'Marvellous,' muttered Archie as he set off. He joined Sandy, Cassy and Colin and they set off down the walkway that divided the marina in two. Three hundred yards distant, beyond the car park, was a rickety wooden gate leading to the allotments. He could see a commotion as he approached and he heard Paul shout, 'The bastard!'

Archie ran across the car park, went through the gate and stopped dead. A herd of cows was grazing on their allotments. The individual lots were unrecognizable. The cows had stomped and munched their way through the whole area, effectively destroying everyone's hard work and turning the field into a trampled mess.

'I don't believe this,' said Terri, who appeared close to tears. 'All that work. I know they are due to build on here, but this is just vindictive.'

Pete came through the gate. 'For goodness sake, what the…?'

They all just stood, staring. Paul, who didn't actually have a patch himself but helped others out from time to time, said, 'Right, let's go find a truck. We can pack this lot off to the livestock market. There's a bob or two here.'

'I'd like to stuff them all in Hordley's bloody sitting-room. The swine.'

'Calm down, Archie. They might not even be his.'

'Don't be so naive…' he began, but stopped short as they heard a VW clattering onto the car park behind the fence. There was a momentary quiet, broken only by the gentle mastication of the blameless beasts.

'Look out,' said Paul. 'There's about to be an explosion; the gaffer's here.'

After a few tense moments a pink, flowery barrage balloon entered the arena, followed by Elaine who peered round the obstruction. 'Oh no! Who...'

But Judy cut her off and said menacingly. 'Don't ask daft questions. You know damn well who.' She stood for a moment, then said in a loud voice, 'Right, if we weren't before, we are now officially at war! Troops, listen up. How do we sort this out, short of hiring a hit man and killing the bugger? Ideas anyone?'

There was silence as the boaters surveyed the sorry scene.

'Shoo,' said Terri as she walked towards her plot.

'Shoo?' said Paul. 'Shoo? What kind of way is that to talk to a cow? You have to talk bovinely. Like this...HUP, HUP, GWONTHEN, that's what you say, then you beat them on the rump with a stick.'

'Bovinely?' said Archie, laughing his head off. 'Talk to them bovinely? What the hell is that supposed to mean?'

The tension was broken and they all chortled, even Terri who turned and smiled as she wiped the tears from her eyes.

'They are rather engaging things, aren't they?' said Mike. 'Despite their destructive capabilities.'

Terri glared at Mike.

'First job,' said Elaine, 'must be surely to get them out the same way they came in. There's a gate down there in the corner, just by the concrete bridge over the abandoned canal branch. I bet that's where they were let in. Let's have a see.' She walked along the fence line followed by Paul and Mike. 'Yes, here, it's obvious,' she called back, 'the chain's hanging loose and the padlock is open.'

Archie ran out of the gate towards the car park.

'OK, come on everyone,' said Judy, 'Except Archie who seemingly has more pressing matters. Let's get behind them and funnel them down to the gate. Elaine,' she shouted, 'open it up, will you?'

It was ten minutes or so before they got them moving. The cows were reluctant to leave their bonus feast and the boaters were obviously nervous about getting too close, but with a chorus of HUPs and SHOOs, the black and white glacier started to creep towards the gate. Much to its displeasure, Paul beat the rear-most cow with a sprig of laurel plucked from the nearby hedge. It mooed loudly, startling everyone.

Archie loped up with a tin of spray paint as the first beast was approaching the gate. As the first animal passed him he sprayed 'EH' on it's flank in large letters. The following three cows were embellished with, 'IS', 'A', and 'MORO…' Unfortunately, the last letter was missed as the cow put on a burst of speed, but the message was obvious, even when the cows got mixed up when they started grazing again in the adjoining field. Paul tied the gate chain in a messy knot before snapping the padlock over the loose ends. Everyone was in fits of giggles as they walked together back up the field.

'Don't worry,' said Archie, 'it's only line-marker used on grass. It won't do them any damage and it'll wash off in the rain.'

'Here, look,' said Elaine, holding her phone up. She'd got a few photos of the four cows.

'You can give that to Roger and Sal for their press release,' said Paul, almost doubled-up with laughter. They stopped by the car park gate and everyone went quiet as they surveyed the devastation.

Mike vocalised everyone's thoughts. 'Look at the mess! What the hell are we going to do?'

'You know what,' said Pete in an upbeat voice, 'it might be a blessing in disguise. Now we'll have to start over, and who better to help with that than Diane and her team? I'll give you a pound to a penny that they'll get us up and running again. They'll probably even rebuild the borders and restock when we give them the sob story. I'll give her a ring and put her in the picture before she gets here tomorrow – tell her she may need more than a crew with forks and spades. There's a plant hire place in Wem. I'll call them first, see if they have anything suitable to help with the heavy work. A Bobcat perhaps or a small digger of some sort.'

Judy came over and pecked him on the cheek. 'What would we do without you, my unkempt friend?'

Pete had the grace to blush before heading off towards his nearby boat with his phone clamped to his ear.

10

New Recruits

It was six-thirty on Monday evening. Archie, Pete and Roger were in The Dog having a pint. Eric called the three friends the 'Pedigree Chums' because of their liking for Marston's Pedigree bitter, one of the pub's regular beers. The place was fairly busy with the early evening crew who stopped off on their way home after work. The pub wasn't exactly on anyone's direct route, it was nearly a mile off the nearest main road and on a direct route to only a few isolated houses, but Eric's reputation for a decent pint had enticed people in. Since he'd got rid of the plastic plants and arty-farty food, more and more folk had come for a chat and an early evening pint. The odd one stayed for a bite to eat, but usually by about seven-thirty most people had drifted home for dinner, particularly on weekdays.

One of those who stayed that evening was Joy, a petite lady, barely five feet tall, with neat, grey hair cut in a youthful bob. She had recently taken to wearing designer glasses which had replaced, as she described them, her 'state sponsored lawn-mower headlamps.' She was always nicely dressed in an ever-changing rotation of smart outfits, sometimes slacks, sometimes skirts, but always with matching, expensive shoes. Whatever she wore there was an ever-present delicate gold chain around her neck on which hung a tiny gold cross and a letter 'W'.

Joy's husband had died fourteen months previously when the light plane he was in had crashed. Joy had bought William the flight as a present for his sixtieth birthday and not a day had gone by when she didn't regret what she'd done - she had re-lived the horror of it time and time again. For months she had awoken from nightmares as her mind tried to make sense of the loss of her beloved man. The pub and the friends she made there, particularly at this time of day, had been a lifeline for her. All the regulars knew her story and many of them had seen her tears as she struggled. Everyone who knew her admired her. They knew her smart appearance hid her inner turmoil. From nervous beginnings she would now come in and greet her friends with a smile and a wave, exchanging banter while ordering her glass of Pinot Grigio.

Twenty-five years ago, William had had an idea. After much soul-searching and many long talks with Joy, he decided to give up his well-salaried job as an accountant with a local fresh produce supplier and start out on his own. He'd realized that Shropshire was being discovered as a place to move to and live. In those days you could still find roads with a strip of grass down the middle, roads that led to single farmsteads or isolated cottages that housed agricultural workers. Some rural homesteads were time-forgotten. As recently as four years ago, he'd met a fifty-year-old man who had never actually seen a set of traffic lights, so insular were the lives of people untouched by the wider world.

He had realized that countrywide, particularly in cities and their satellite towns, the affordability of property was becoming beyond many. People were also getting fed up with the rat race and looking for an alternative. To any clients looking for the good life or a break from the manic, material world many inhabited, he would often quote a ditty he found apposite: 'If you win the rat race you're still a rat.'

The wealthy were also buying holiday homes. Coastal areas were favourites, but the beauty and peace of rural Shropshire offered an affordable alternative; indeed a quarter of a century ago it was possible to pick up property for a song and William reasoned that prices could only go one way. In effect he had anticipated the region's property boom and set up an estate agent and letting agency. Some friends thought he was potty, but ten years down the line he had been proved right. One house he marketed in the early days went for £25,000 and sold ten years later for a dozen times that. William was in on both ends of the deal and made an increasingly healthy living. Today, the company had five offices dotted around the county. He had also invested in a builders' merchant, buying a fifty percent stake when one of the owners wished to retire. The business thrived within the property boom.

William was nearing retirement when he'd been killed. He and Joy had planned a six-month round-the-world cruise and had bought a villa in Malta where they'd intended to spend time during the cold winter months. He had left Joy well-provided for but bereft. She had recently taken to overseeing the estate agency, not interfering, more showing an interest. She had a good team of people and they respected and admired her fortitude. She basically left them to it but had recently started showing more mature clients round larger properties. She enjoyed it and it gave her a focus. She also met new people, a few of whom had become friends.

Much talk around the pub was of the boaters' woes. There was a poster advertising the quiz the following Saturday, and the conversation focussed excitedly on Wednesday's TV visit. Joy ordered a quiche with salad and listened to the chatter. Sitting on his own at a corner table was John Greenway. Edward's head groom came in two or three times a week for an early evening pint and usually joined in the chat, but today he was uncomfortable. He listened as barbed comments were aimed at him, but not to him directly. He was now one of the bad guys by association. Only once was he directly invited to defend his boss, but he'd replied with a forced grin and a small shake of the head. Most people drifted home, leaving Joy sitting at a table on her own eating her meal while the Pedigree Chums sat facing the bar, chatting quietly.

John approached.

'I am sorry for your trouble,' he said quietly to their backs.

The conversation paused and John turned to walk away.

'Oi!' said Archie.

John turned back as Archie poked him in the chest with a forefinger. 'Not half as sorry as we are, my lad. Now bugger off and leave us in peace.'

Pete put his hand on Archie's forearm. 'Steady on, Archie. It's probably not his fault.' He turned and looked the groom in the eye. 'Is it, John?'

'No,' he replied quietly, 'no, it isn't. If it's any consolation, I think Edward is behaving like an arse. I don't like him. And I'm not the only one.' He looked round quickly to see if he'd been overheard, but Eric was at the far end of the bar polishing a glass and Joy was reading a magazine. He leaned in and looked at the three friends in turn. 'Look, I want to help you.' He looked down and shook his head. 'If he knew I was here talking to you I'd be out on my ear. Please don't say anything. I need my job, at least for now. My parents work there, too, and I can't afford to get them in trouble. I'm serious, though. I really would like to help.'

'How?' asked Archie.

'Can I have your word that you will keep me out of it?'

The three friends looked from one to the other.

'You have it,' said Roger.

John sighed. 'Well to start with, I can tell you that he has an informant, someone who is passing on information about what you're up to. A few days ago, I saw someone visit him late in the evening, about ten it was while I was checking up on a horse. They obviously didn't want to be seen. At the time I thought Edward was having a liaison and whoever it was came out the kitchen door into the courtyard and rode off on a motorbike, or a scooter. I'm not a hundred percent sure, but I think it was a woman. They were wearing a helmet and a thick quilted coat of some sort. Then, yesterday morning I overheard Edward yelling at Neil Grant, the estate manager. Edward said that if Neil didn't prevent the TV crew getting access to your field, he would fire him. He'd really lost it, and the whole thing was cringeworthy. But it's obvious he knows what you're planning. If I know Edward, someone is making a few quid out of it.

The three friends stared at him, so John continued. 'I don't blame you for trying to stand up to him. I wish I had the balls, to be honest. But, as I say, I rely on him.' He looked round again, but Joy was still engrossed in her mag and there was nobody else there. 'Look, I'm taking a big risk telling you this, but the fact is I want out; I want to start on my own. I can't afford it yet, so I need my job. But I'm determined to make a go of something for myself. The sooner the better. The fact is that lots of people rely on Edward. That, and his money, are his strengths.'

An uneasy quiet followed as the boaters digested the information. Pete, who'd been unusually quiet, said, 'It doesn't explain why you're sticking your neck out. What's in it for you?'

John sighed. 'To be honest, I don't really know. I suppose I'm just making a stand, sticking up for the little guy. If anyone has a chance to put a spoke in his wheel, it's somebody from outside. You're not reliant on him, so you don't have much to lose. If those houses do get built, you'll lose your field, but it won't affect you too much. In other words, you can afford to fight him - I can't.'

'The point is, though,' continued Pete, 'that even if we manage to stop him you don't stand to gain. Is there something you're not telling us?'

'No...well, there's plenty I haven't told you. Like, for instance, the whispers about him calling on workers' wives during working hours. There are no accusations of actual impropriety, but they feel threatened. It's creepy. He calls under the pretence of checking up on estate property, but it's his way of reminding his tenants who is boss and that he can basically do what he wants. One young couple left last year because they couldn't stand it. Bernard was lucky; he had an uncle down in Somerset where he could go. He was only twenty-odd so could start again, but people shouldn't be forced out of their homes. All their friends were up here, but they just upped and left. Other workers are older, some nearing retiring age - like my parents, for example - but still utterly tied to the estate. He doesn't give a damn about anyone else really. It's not right.'

'What do you want to do if you get out?' asked Archie.

'I want a place of my own, look after a few animals, sheep, cows, horses. I'm easy. But I know I don't want to end up here in thirty years time, like Mum and Dad.'

'This person on the scooter, motor bike, whatever. What can you tell us about them?'

'I don't know. They were wearing a helmet and coat of some sort. As I say, I thought it may have been a woman but I can't be sure.'

'Tall, thin?'

He shrugged. 'Sort of medium, I guess.'

'You didn't get the registration number?'

'No, sorry. It was all over quite quickly and it wasn't really my business. It makes a bit more sense now I know that you guys are having trouble, but I wasn't taking too much interest at the time.'

They were all quiet for a moment.

'OK,' said Roger. 'Keep this under your hat, will you? Leave it with us. Have you got a phone we can get you on?'

He jotted his number on a beer mat. 'I need to get back. Please, don't let on I've talked to you.'

Archie passed him a business card. 'Keep your eyes open. Ring us if you see anything.'

They shook hands.

As John left Joy looked up from her magazine and smiled at the chums.

11

Hi Di

At eight-forty-five the following morning, a black four-wheel drive vehicle pulled up on the gravel outside the marina shop. It was not due to open till nine, but two men climbed out of the car and approached the shop. The taller of the two, wearing jeans and a black leather jacket, rapped on the door and waited. After a couple of minutes, the door was opened by Betty. The first man walked past her as the second placed his hand on the small of her back, encouraging her inside. He looked round briefly before removing his sunglasses and following her in, closing the door behind him.

A few minutes later, Archie was returning from his morning dog-walk with Betsie as the 4x4 turned left out of the gate and came towards them down the single-track road. The car moved towards them, getting pretty close as it churned dust and gravel up from the roadside. Archie was on the grass verge holding Betsie's collar as the black Toyota Landcruiser sped past. Brake lights flared as the car slowed at the end of the lane before turning right and accelerating away with the growl of a powerful engine.

'I could swear the bugger tried to mow us down,' he told Sal when he returned to the boat. 'Going like the clappers it was. Bloody lunatic.'

Sal instinctively looked out of the window. 'Could you see who it was?'

'No, the windows were blacked out. I only know it was a Toyota. Gave us a right old scare, I can tell you. It came out of the gate. Did you see anything?'

Sal shook her head. 'No, I've just got out of the shower. What are you going to do?'

'I've already called the police from my mobile on the way in. Left a message. Mind you we've been here ten years and I've never even seen a police car.'

'You did the right thing, nevertheless.'

They heard someone walking past on the pontoon. Sal popped her head out to see Sandy walking by on his way to empty his toilet cassette.

'Hi Sandy, did you see a black car in here a few minutes ago?'

'No. Why, what's up?'

'Archie reckons someone tried to run him over on the lane.'

'Christ. Who was it?'

'He doesn't know. Someone driving like an idiot.'

They both turned as Betty's red Ford Focus drove out from behind the shop, along the drive and out through the gate.

'Where the hell is she off to?' said Sandy, frowning. 'She's due to open up any time. I need some milk.' He shook his head and turned back towards his boat, muttering under his breath.

The marina was stirring into life. A plume of smoke drifted from Pete's chimney at the far end of the marina as he stoked his fire. Keeping the fire going is one of the basic necessities for live-aboard boaters – for those who didn't have a central heating boiler, that is. A multi-fuel fire is the prime choice for many boaters because gas or diesel for boilers can be expensive. Smokeless coal is relatively cheap and can be supplemented by logs foraged from the nearby hedgerows and woods. Cast iron or steel stoves not only heat the entire boat, but also help keep condensation under control. They combust using air from the cabin, so fresh air is constantly drawn in through vents - which keeps the cabin dry and fresh. The only difficulty is regularly having to lug coal and wood to the boat, which can be a challenge in icy conditions when the pontoons are slippery. But hauling coal, along with topping up with water and emptying the loo, are just an accepted part of boating life.

Sal was drinking a cup of coffee on her small rear deck. Her hands were wrapped round the mug to ease the ache in her arthritic hands. She was reflecting on the earlier goings on. She smiled as she heard Judy on the boat next door telling Elaine to get moving. 'Come on, you lazy lump! Get up, it's time for breakfast and today's a big day.'

'Every day I wake up after eating your cooking is a big day.'

'Cheeky sod! Come on, get on with it.'

Young Paul poked his head out of his boat, moored on the hammerhead about forty yards away down the far end of the pontoon. He lit a cigarette and waved at Sal, who returned the gesture.

A flock of geese honked noisily as they passed overhead, and a pair of mallards paddled through the mist that swirled and rolled over the water. A tractor rumbled in the distance. One of Edward's minions hard at work on the vast acreage. From Roger's boat a metallic whir as a pump expelled soapy water from his shower. Colin and Cassie had been away for the night, staying with Cassie's friend in Alderley Edge to help her celebrate her birthday. They were due back before lunch.

A mile and a half away Edward was fuming again. He'd just read a brief story on the internet. North Shropshire OnLine had featured Wednesday's proposed visit of Gardeners World. Although there was no mention of him personally, there was a strong suggestion of his disagreement with the marina residents. Under the headline *Boaters Fight to Save Their Allotment* the brief article said that local boaters had enlisted the help of 'national treasure' Diane Markham to help oppose a housing development on land adjacent to Watergrove Marina. Scant on detail, the piece focussed on the potential loss of wildlife habitat and questioned whether such a beautiful area would really benefit from the 'blight' of three new luxury properties when much of the local rural economy was on its knees. The piece was by Lucy Pennington-Martin, Reporter for Rural Affairs, North Shropshire. Presumably her name was on the article because she was expendable if Edward decided to use his influence as a shareholder and demand a 'sacrifice.'

Two things really made Edward seethe. Firstly the article ended, '...the land owner/developer was unavailable for comment but an unnamed source, believed to be closely associated with the project, said, 'People are angry, with some justification. The boaters have the sympathy of quite a few local people.' Secondly the attached photograph of monogrammed cows passing through a gate nearly sent Edward into a tail-spin. He picked up a glass inkwell and hurled it across the room to crash into the panelled oak door.

Pete received a disturbing phone call from Betty just after eleven-thirty. She sounded fraught and tearful.

'I've had a problem, Pete and I've had to go away for a while.'

'What on earth's the matter?'

'It's like a bad dream. I had a visit from a couple of thugs this morning. They showed me photographs of my sister and mother - both taken yesterday. My sister was out shopping and my mother was sitting in the residents' lounge of her care home. They said that if I didn't leave the shop and be at my sister's house by midday today there would be trouble. That's where I am now, in Harlech. They told me to stay away for seven days.'

'Christ almighty!'

He asked whether she had called the police.

'They told me not to. I'm scared, Pete. I've told my sister that I just needed a break, but she's surprised that I've just pitched up here. I'm sorry to let you all down. There's a large car with two men in it just down the road. I think they're watching me.'

'It's OK, love. Don't worry about us. Just stay safe; we'll be fine.'

He sat, looking out of the window as he drank his coffee, then made a phone call.

Diane Markham arrived with a male colleague at two-thirty to be met by Pete and Judy. Diane wore jeans and a red and black check blouse. She was a slim, attractive woman with shoulder-length jet-black hair, and looked every inch a TV celebrity. Her beauty masked a sharp mind and her blue eyes shone. Her colleague was dressed in multi-pocket cargo pants and a red fleece top. A tall, blond guy, he wore a tweed flat cap and sturdy black boots. Diane hugged Pete and shook Judy by the hand. Pete's dog had tagged along, a border terrier called Scamp.

'Hello, little fellow,' said Diane, tickling the dog behind the ears.

'Welcome O Great Protector of our Veg,' said Judy.

Diane laughed. 'You haven't much left by the sound of it.'

She introduced Jake, an associate producer, and said, 'Come on. Let's go and have a look see.'

The four set off down the pontoon towards the car park and allotment. They were followed by Archie and Paul who tagged along behind.

'So, this is where you ended up?' said Diane, smiling at Pete.

'Yep. Nice eh?'

'Well, it's certainly quiet.'

'You'd be surprised. There's a seething undercurrent of action.'

She laughed. 'Looks like it.'

'You have to know where to look.'

A couple of minutes later they were through the gate. Diane exclaimed, 'Oh Lord, what a mess! It looks like a herd of wild boar have been through.'

'Believe it or not, they improved Pete's bit,' chortled Judy.

Diane smiled and took a few photos on her phone. 'We're going to need some help with this. Blimey, we've only got a couple of days; we start filming in Catterick on Saturday. We'll have a few helpers and plenty of hand tools, but we're going to need more bodies.'

'Well,' said Judy, 'there are a few of us, ten at a push. Not all of us are in prime condition, more sprinters than long-distance merchants, but we'll certainly do our best.'

Pete raised his eyebrows and smothered a grin.

'Yes?' questioned Judy, scowling at him.

'I was just, er, thinking that perhaps we could get some school kids involved. I'll ask Roger if we can get his child journalist to enlist some of her mates to help.' He turned and walked away a few paces and took his phone out to call Roger, desperately trying not to burst into a fit of giggles.

Diane smiled at Judy, who rolled her eyes.

'He is rude. Scruffy git...' she said. 'Mind you, we can't call him too much. Without him we wouldn't have you guys here, nor Len and his mates next weekend.'

Diane stared at Judy.' What? Len Johnson? Len's coming?'

'Yes, apparently. They're playing a week on Saturday in the local pub. You know him, I gather?'

'From Uni. Haven't seen him for five years or more when I saw them play -

in Bruges, believe it or not. We got together for lunch the next day. Well, I'll be damned. Good old Len.'

Pete wandered back. 'He's going to ring and ask her.'

'You didn't tell me about Len.'

'Well, it's only sort of verbally confirmed, but as far as we know he's chugging his way down here. You might not know, but he lives on his boat now too. Travels around quite a lot, unlike me who basically stays put. He should arrive early next week with any luck.'

'Brilliant. Right, I'm coming back for that!'

'Star-struck, eh?' asked Judy.

Diane chuckled. 'No, he owes me lunch. I ended up paying last time. Cost me seventy Euros, the cheeky blighter.' She smiled to herself then turned back and surveyed the veg plot. 'Right, let's make some plans here. Machinery, Pete?'

'We've got a Bobcat for a couple of days from the local plant hire. Should be here first thing tomorrow. They said that if you can sneak their name into shot a few times we can have them for nothing.'

'Good, that'll be fine.' She looked across the muddy field. 'OK, we're going to need some hardcore for paths and access to the plots, plus something to define the layout - perhaps some railway sleepers or similar to build up some beds. We'll also need about twenty tons of topsoil. Then we'll need something to plant – providing we get that far. Peas, beans, spuds etc. Is there a decent garden centre or agricultural merchant handy?'

'This is rural Shropshire; supplies like that we are not short of,' said Paul, who had joined the group. 'What we are short of is cash. How do we pay for all this?'

'We have a budget for this kind of thing. It's not like we're re-building a fancy orangery or anything, but our producer Audrey, who you'll meet in the morning, is pretty persuasive when it comes to sweet-talking suppliers. Actually, Simon's pretty good too. Hopefully we won't have a problem with supplies.'

'Simon?'

'Yes, my co-presenter, Simon Goode. He'll be with us late this evening, or first thing tomorrow. He's a good guy.'

'Archie,' said Judy, 'you're pretty clued up locally. Could you root out some suppliers for us?'

'Ah, at last,' he replied. 'A task that won't leave me twenty-five quid out of pocket. Yes, OK. I'll go and make some enquiries.'

Diane raised her eyebrows at Judy, who responded with a vague wave of her arm and a snorting noise. Diane shook her head and continued. 'Jake, could you go with Archie and give Audrey and Simon a heads-up, put them in the picture? We need to get the ball rolling today on this. Ideally we'll need hardcore, sleepers and topsoil late tomorrow morning - or early afternoon at the latest - and the veg first thing Thursday.'

'Sure,' replied Jake, obviously a man of few words. The two walked off towards the marina.

'Doesn't say much, but he's a grafter is our Jake.'

'Unlike Pete,' said Judy, 'who never shuts up and is prone to sustained periods of inactivity.'

'That's the type of guff,' countered Pete, pointing at Judy, 'that we have to put up with from our unelected matriarch. It's only because everyone was scared witless that she's head of the Great Veggy Plot to begin with!'

'Scruffy git,' said Judy as she lumbered away towards the gate.

Pete and Diane shared a grin. As they walked back down the pontoon Pete said to Diane, 'The lass who runs the shop over there,' pointing to the two-storey, red brick building at the far end of the marina, 'was threatened by a couple of bully boys this morning. Told her to leave. They threatened her sister and Mum, indirectly at least. Poor lass left straightaway; she must be scared witless.'

'Crikey! What's that all about?'

'It's Hordley, the big cheese, trying to spook us. I told you he's a nasty piece of work. Must have sent a couple of heavies to scare her. Which they obviously did. They're even watching her, she thinks, down near her sister's place across in Harlech. I've had a word with a bloke I know, ex-forces. He said he'd go and have a word.'

Diane raised her eyebrows. 'You can't prove it's the local big-wig of course.'

'No, but it's pretty obvious.'

He told Diane about meeting John in the pub, about how he'd overheard Edward telling his farm manager to stop the filming at all costs.

'He can't get away with that, surely?'

'There's not much we can do. The police know about the thugs, but we haven't heard anything yet. Don't really expect to if the truth be known. But we're turning into a pretty determined bunch. God help anyone who gets up Judy's nose.'

Diane laughed. 'Imposing, isn't she?'

'I take the mickey, but I like her. Let's face it, there's lots to like. I'd never admit it to her face of course, she's insufferable enough already; but I'd rather be with her than against.'

'You've a soft spot, haven't you?'

He reddened. 'I admire her, for sure. But that's as far as it goes. If I got too close, I'd be engulfed in an acre of pink parachute, might never be seen again. I value my freedom too much, particularly after...well, you know.'

Diane nodded. They walked on in silence. Scamp's claws tick-tacked on the wooden duck-boards as he trotted along in front. Jake was waiting on the drive by the shop, which remained in darkness.

'Jake and I are booked into The Dog. We'll head down there now. I need to do some prep work and speak to the crew; they should be well on the way, if not already at their hotel. They're staying in Whitchurch. Let's meet up at 6.30 or so for a bite to eat, eh?'

'Fine, I'll see you there. Turn right at the end of the road, half a mile or so. You can't miss it. I'll go and see if there have been any developments. See if Team Veg has come up with a master plan.'

'I like the beanie hat, by the way.'

'Part of the image,' he replied. 'It's good to see you again.'

'You too.' She smiled, then leaned over and gave him a hug.

Pete called on Roger, who was polishing his brass tiller handle. 'Did you manage to get hold of the child scribbler?'

Roger frowned. 'She called the secondary school, said they would send a dozen Year Elevens on Thursday. They can help with the planting, but don't want them anywhere near the groundworks. Too risky with the machinery around, they said.'

'What's Year Eleven? Four-year-olds?'

'Don't be an idiot. Fifteen or sixteen, and they are budding horticulturalists.'

'Good, that's fair enough. It'll be a lift, and good for the cameras I would imagine.'

'I'm meeting Diane tonight at six-thirty for a bite in The Dog. Pass the word round, see if anyone wants to join us. Be good to have a team bonding session before tomorrow.'

12

Sleepers and Beds

At five forty-five the following morning Roger, a light sleeper at the best of times, was awoken by a low rumbling noise. At first he thought it was coming from his boat - it sounded a little like his water pump. Situated near the front of his cabin the pump draws water from the main tank under the fore deck and pressurizes the boat's fresh water system. When running it did indeed sound like a low rumble, hidden away in a small sound-insulated cupboard. If the pump runs when no tap or other appliance is turned on, it would likely indicate a leak somewhere. It had happened before when a fitting failed on a basin and water had flooded the bathroom and bilge. He was concerned he had a similar problem. However, having clambered out of bed and stumbling into the lounge he realized that the noise was coming from outside.

He looked out of the window. Because Judy's boat was close to his, all he could see above their roof line was the glow of lights in the trees, fifty yards or so distant. He hurried out of the cabin doors onto his front deck. In the lane behind the marina's boundary fence, he could make out a large digger and a truck working under bright lights. They appeared to be working on the lane, the lane that led down past the marina car park to the allotments – the only access to the allotments.

Initially he assumed that it was the TV crew making an early start. Then he realized something wasn't right. At last night's get-together Diane had said the crew were due to arrive at seven-thirty and it wasn't yet six. She'd also said that, in addition to the two machines organised by Pete, there would be three other vans; one for the crew, one for all the equipment and a chuck wagon that would be based on site for the duration of the shoot to feed the workers.

He dashed back inside and dressed. Re-emerging a few minutes later, he set off down the pontoon. He knocked first on Judy's boat next door, then Sal and Archie's. He roused them shouting, 'Oi, come on! Get up! Something's going on.'

He hurried over to the fence and saw a JCB digging up the lane. It was scooping muck and rubble into the back of the large truck. A deep trench had already been dug across the track. Judy puffed and panted as she joined Roger with Sal, Archie and Elaine close behind. Archie's swear-word was drowned out as the digger dumped a load of stones and earth into the truck with a rumbling clang. The friends stood in the gloom of the breaking dawn and looked from one to the other before Judy walked away, extracting her phone from within the folds of a red-spotted kaftan.

Roger shouted at the man operating the digger and waved his arms, but he was either ignored or unheard above the roar of the engine. Archie picked up a rotting branch and threw it at the digger's glass cabin. The startled driver looked round and the engine died to tick-over as he opened the door and leaned out.

'What the hell do you think you're doing?' shouted Archie.

'What's it look like I'm bloody doing? I'm digging!'

'Well, bugger off. We need access - this is a private road.'

'Sorry, mate. No can do - orders. We're preparing the ground for a new water main.'

The truck driver appeared from behind his vehicle. 'What's up?'

'I'll tell you what's up, my friend,' said Roger. 'We have a team arriving in a little over an hour to begin work down the road, and if they can't get through because you're digging up the road there's going to be trouble.'

'We know nothing anything about any team. We're just doing our job, as instructed.'

'You're not from round here, are you?' asked Sal.

'Church Stretton, Mam,' replied the digger driver.

'Could you turn that off for a minute,' she said, pointing to the digger, 'and let me explain what's going on?'

The driver shrugged, ducked inside his cabin and turned off the engine.

'Better make this quick, I'm due in Market Drayton after dinner. More than my jobs' worth to be late.'

'Yes, OK. Look, we've been having problems with a local big-wig. He's due to build houses down the lane there and it's all got rather confrontational. He's using you guys to try and stop us. They haven't even got planning permission yet and there's no way you'd be allowed to start work without us, as local residents, having some form of notice - which we haven't got.

'I have plans,' replied the driver. 'Look.' He reached into his cabin and retrieved a sheet of paper which he passed over the fence. 'There's a cross on the tree over there,' continued the driver, pointing to a sycamore across the opposite side of the lane. 'That's where we had to start digging. It's quite clear on there,' he said, pointing at the plan.

Sal and Archie looked at the paper.

'I can tell you're just following orders,' said Archie, 'but there is a TV programme coming to film this morning. They'll be arriving any time and there'll be a real ruckus if you prevent them filming. You're just pawns in all this. It's not your fault, but...' he leaned over to read the writing on the side of the digger, 'R&M Ground Works will be getting some pretty bad publicity if you're still at it when they arrive.'

The digger driver looked at his mate. 'I need to make a phone call.'

Archie spoke to the truck driver, 'Look, don't you think it's a bit peculiar that your mate's digging a trench straight across a road in the middle of nowhere? I mean where the hell is it going? It's connected to a hedge at one end and a field at the other – it serves no purpose at all. It's just a hole in the middle of nowhere!'

The man looked round. 'That's as maybe, but we're just following orders. If we don't do what we're told, we don't get paid. It's as simple as that.'

'Arseholes,' said Archie, kicking the wire-link fence.

'Calm down, love. It's not their fault,' said Sal, putting her hand on her husband's arm.

'No answer,' said digger man, returning from behind his machine.

'Well, it's hardly surprising, is it?' said Roger angrily. 'It's six in the morning for goodness' sake! You don't really expect your boss to be sitting by the phone waiting for a call from one of his minions who's wrecking somebody else's bloody road.'

Pete arrived with Judy. He surveyed the scene and said, 'Hang on there a minute, lads. I'd like a word. Stop there, and I'll come round.'

'Oi, no heavy stuff,' said digger man warily.

'No, no. Just want a word, that's all.'

Pete walked parallel to the fence towards the gate while everyone stood by, fidgeting. After a couple of minutes, he appeared on the opposite side of the fence on the lane. 'Here lads, please,' he said, waving them behind the truck.

Dawn was breaking and early birds skipped and chattered in the hedgerow. The friends' breath diffused in the digger's floodlights gave the scene an eerie, ghostly hue. A few minutes later, Pete emerged from behind the truck and walked back up the lane. To everyone else's astonishment the digger driver moved his machine, the truck backed up and tipped all the rubble back in the hole, and the digger man started levelling out the road. Pete came walking back towards the group carrying a sign: *Road Closed. We apologize for any inconvenience caused by essential drainage works.*

'Sorted,' he said.

'What on earth did you say to them?' asked Sal.

'Just asked them how much they were on for the day, then doubled it. Told them they could work for us instead, tomorrow too.'

'Blimey, the lord of the manor's not going to like that!'

'Stuff him,' said Archie.

'How much?' asked Sal.

'Eleven hundred total, including a sweetener for fuel.'

'And, uh...where's that coming from? asked Roger.

'Me, if necessary. Look, they're a two-man band, if that makes sense, Rick and Martin, R&M. They'll take a bonus where they can. They're decent lads and they're doing us a big favour. What we've offered will more than cover today's job anyway.'

'What YOU'VE offered, you mean.'

'Yes, OK Archie, what *I've* offered. The point is that they'll not be interfering with Diane and her crew this morning.'

He walked over to the fence and spoke to the drivers as the digger and truck powered down. 'Why don't you go and park up by the gate down there, lads? The rest will be along in less than an hour. See that boat down there near the car park?' he said, pointing. 'The one with smoke coming out of the chimney? That's me. Wander over and I'll make you a brew. And thanks.'

'You're paying us.'

'Yes, well...' said Pete, and with that walked off towards his boat.

At seven-twenty the boaters had gathered near the shop. Diane and Jake arrived in her BMW, followed by the TV crew in a white mini-bus. Behind them came a burger catering truck pulled by a Land Rover Discovery and, finally, a flat-bed lorry with the Bobcat perched on top rumbled into view. Sandy was chuntering because someone had put a *Road Closed* sign on the pontoon right by his boat. 'Bloody childish,' he muttered as everyone acted innocent. 'I nearly tripped over the damn thing,'

Everyone grinned. Roger stood, all innocent, with eyebrows raised. 'Dear, dear,' he commiserated.

Diane directed operations and the convoy rumbled down the lane. The previous evening there had been quite a gathering in The Dog, including most of the marina crowd plus twenty or so locals. In a corner next to the fire, Diane had done a piece to camera recording a preview of the upcoming programme:

"Hello, and welcome to Gardeners' Choice. This time we are in Shropshire. Some of you will have an allotment, but the fact is that many more would love one. There is a nationwide shortage of plots and many people have been on waiting lists for years, both for council and privately-owned sites. For those without their own land, an allotment is a way to enjoy the benefits of producing their own flowers, fruit and vegetables - not just flora in fact; people keep rabbits, hens and bees, even pigs if they are permitted. The fact remains that thousands of people benefit. It is a wonderful, healthy pastime, in addition to being good for the environment. So when we hear of a site under threat, we listen. That seems to be the case here in Shropshire.

"Regular viewers know that we have worked on projects the length and breadth of the UK, including walled gardens and public roundabouts, private gardens and public parks. This programme features the residents of an inland marina called Watergrove in the Shropshire countryside. Planning permission is sought to build houses on the site and the folk here are about to lose their treasured allotments. To be fair, there is probably nothing illegal about what the developer is doing. We are just sad to see a resource, already in short supply, destroyed. We will neither tie ourselves to trees nor use strong-arm tactics, but we will try and convince those involved that there is sometimes more to life than pure profit.

"When the programme airs in a few weeks you will see that the field has been decimated, some believe maliciously. Not only are we going to help reinstate the allotments, we are also going to create a special area for students. Local youngsters, both from nearby schools and a local sixth-form college, will have the opportunity to develop and nurture their own allotments. In this part of the world, working the land is a way of life and many youngsters will go on to have careers in farming and horticulture. Hopefully, we will give them a chance to gain hands-on experience, develop their interest and give them a start."

By lunchtime the job was well underway, and the site defined into three distinct areas. Firstly, close to the marina car park, within a grid of pathways, the residents' new plots took shape. There were sixteen of them, each twelve by two and a half meters. At the end of each plot would be a two-metre strip that would be hard-cored and designated for the erection of sheds and space for storage of equipment. Secondly, two large plots, each approximately fifty metres by five and divided by a central pathway, were laid out for students. Finally, in a corner of the field closest to the marina, an area roughly forty metres square was roped off. This was where the tiller arm was found. Colin's brother Andy had agreed to come and excavate the plot, helped by students from the college. The idea was then to hard-core the area and cover it with an open-sided structure, funds allowing. It would be here, with luck, where the replica narrowboat was to be built.

There wasn't much the residents could do while the machinery shaped the plots, but after lunch the hardcore arrived. Martin had collected two loads from a local quarry in his truck. He'd dumped them inside the gate and left to collect the final load. Then the timber arrived. There were two hundred railway sleepers and some lengths of two-by-two which would be sawn to length and driven into the ground to hold the sleepers in place. While the digger and Bobcat moved and levelled the hard-core, the residents began moving the timber into position. Judy rightly predicted that progress would be slow as the group of retirees used muscles untroubled by physical work for some time. The lads worked in pairs moving one sleeper at a time.

'There seems to be an element of competition here,' commented Judy, who was leaning on the counter of the chuck wagon, 'as to who can be the most sedentary. Archie and Sandy seem to be the slowest so far.' Sal and Elaine laughed. 'Oh, but hang on, there's been a refusal - Mike's sat down! This could change everything. Go on, Archie lad,' she shouted, 'show 'em how it's done!'

There was a certain amount of muttering from the lads; fortunately most of it was drowned out by the noise of the diggers. Meanwhile, a lone figure stood by the rickety gate into the marina car park.

'Isn't that Joy from the pub?' said Elaine.

'Sure is,' replied Judy. She called over and waved. 'Over here, Joy. Come and join us.'

Joy walked towards the catering van. She was immaculately dressed - almost - in a blue two-piece suit with lemon blouse – and red Wellington boots.

'Coffee? Tea?' asked Elaine.

'Tea, thanks,' she said, as Pete and Colin lumbered by with another sleeper. 'Wow, you're making good progress. It's great to see everyone pulling together.'

'The progress is relentless as you can see,' said Judy, smiling.

The three girls laughed as Pete muttered something with an 'F' in it.

'We girls have been sawing the posts up into lengths; we're just having a breather,' said Elaine. 'We need to put some sort of point on the posts afterwards so we can knock them into the ground. The sleepers will go side on, two deep, creating raised beds which will be filled with top soil. These posts will knock in on the outside to hold it all together.'

Martin had dropped off the third load of hard-core and had now returned for a fourth time with the first load of topsoil. Diane had called and doubled the topsoil requirement. With the sleepers in place, Rick's JCB began ferrying the soil into the individual allotments. The two camera crews were filming constantly, and each had a camera and a sound engineer. There was one male crew and one female. Periodically, the residents were fitted with a microphone. As they were filmed going about their business, Diane asked various questions such as, 'How long have you had an allotment?' and 'What do you like to grow?' Some of the replies were lost among the puffing and panting, but gradually Diane reckoned she had enough coherent answers to stitch something together.

During the lunch break, Jacqui, one of the sound engineers, had a quiet word with Archie. Actually she intended to be quiet, but in reality spoke loud enough for everyone to hear: 'Next time you disappear to have a pee in the hedge, would you mind asking me to turn off your microphone beforehand, particularly if there is a danger of you breaking wind? The mics are pretty sensitive pieces of equipment, and I could do without sound-effects. Besides, we can add our own 'sounds of the wonder of nature' at the editing stage if we deem them necessary.' Archie looked crestfallen as everyone chuckled.

By four-thirty they had done all they could for the day. All sixteen allotments and the two student plots were ready for planting, the hard-standings were levelled and ready for each plot's sheds. A large pile of hardcore was heaped up near the area to be excavated. This would be shovelled into place when the excavation was complete. Everyone was gathered round the chuck wagon. Eric from The Dog had provided a couple of crates of beer and a few of the residents took advantage of the BBC's benevolence and chomped on burgers and slices of home-made pizza. PJ (so called because nobody could pronounce his Lithuanian name which, according to Diane, contained too many consonants) ran the chuck wagon. His food was legendary, always freshly prepared, and there was always a hot brew on the go during film shoots. Diane clapped her hands to call for hush. Audrey Roberts had arrived mid-morning in her red Range Rover. The show's producer spoke up. 'Well done, everybody. What a great effort! You've all worked extremely hard - hats off to you.' She raised her bottle. 'Cheers! Here's to tomorrow.'

Some of the marina crowd slouched on the half-dozen sleepers arranged as make-shift seating, in varying degrees of discomfort. There was cheek-blowing and groans as they tried to ease aching muscles.

'I think you'd better have an ambulance on standby tomorrow, looking at some of that lot,' said Judy.

The two freshest-looking were Martin and Rick, guys accustomed to hard labour. Pete walked over and stood between. He put an arm round each of their shoulders. 'Thanks, you two. We appreciate your help. You made a real difference today.'

There was a chorus of 'Hear, hear.'

'I'll have your cash ready for you by close of play tomorrow, lads.' said Pete quietly.

Audrey had agreed to put them up in the hotel for the night, and the pair accepted the offer of a lift with PJ back to Whitchurch. At nine the next morning, they all gathered back at the allotments. There was a whiff of liniment in the air, and Roger was one of many who admitted that he was a touch stiff. 'Had difficulty getting my socks on.' he said. 'Never realized how far away my feet were.'

A box truck from a local agricultural merchant arrived with seed potatoes, carrots, runner beans, courgettes, onions and other veggies. Then came a van from a nearby nursery with bedding plants and shrubs.

'Right, first job is to get that manure onto the beds,' said Diane, indicating a pile of steaming straw that had been donated and deposited near the gate by a local farmer. Rick clambered up into his digger and set to work. A mini-bus arrived bearing twelve students accompanied by their teacher, Vivienne Reynolds. The six lads and six girls all wore wellies and weathered outdoor clothing looking far more fit for purpose than the majority of yesterday's gang.

'OK, anyone who wants to grab a coffee, please do so,' said Diane, 'then we'll have a team talk and allocate duties.'

A few minutes later everyone gathered in front of the chuck wagon.

'Right,' she said to the students, 'good to see you guys, and welcome.'

Most of them smiled but one or two looked a bit self-conscious as both cameras rolled and the two sound engineers held woolly microphones over the gathering.

'OK, firstly I'd like to introduce you to Simon, my co-presenter.'

Simon Goode was a tall, fit-looking man. With his black, neat hair, blue eyes and designer stubble he looked every inch a TV star and was already the focus of attention of a couple of the female students.

'Sorry I couldn't make it yesterday,' he said. 'I was stuck in London. But I'm delighted to be here now and pleased you've made such great progress. Diane showed me some 'before' photos and you've done sterling work - well done.'

Diane addressed the students. 'I had a chat with Mrs. Reynolds last evening and she suggested you split into two groups. We have prepared two raised beds specifically for the school and college. You can see them over there. We'll basically leave it to you to decide what to do with them. As you can see, we have a good choice of product here so you must chat amongst yourselves and decide what you want to plant. Of course, what we have here is just to get us going; you'll be free to come and go as you please and bring whatever you want with you, perhaps things you've cultivated back at school. A local lady has generously donated a large shed for you where you can store supplies and equipment; that will arrive today or tomorrow. I know the marina residents were keen to welcome some new faces, and Judy here would just like to say a few words.'

Judy stepped forward. Resplendent in a voluminous orange kaftan that billowed in the breeze, she addressed the youngsters, one or two of whom looked rather nervous.

'Right, welcome you lot,' she bellowed. 'You don't know how happy I am to see some eager, fresh faces in our field. Having suffered the suffocating company of this dysfunctional, creaking rabble for years,' indicating the residents with a sweep of her arm, 'you are a joy to behold!' The students smiled as one, all except one lad who stared, wide-eyed, at Judy. 'If you need any help with anything, please feel free to ask. I can't guarantee you'll get a sensible answer, but we'll do our best to make you feel at home. Be wary of asking Pete anything - he's the bloke over there in the knackered hat - because what he knows about horticulture you can write on a pin head and still have room for the Lord's Prayer. Finally, if you grow anything illicit, either for personal use or in the interests of medical research, I request...no, demand, first refusal! Good luck to you and thanks for coming.'

Diane was chuckling as she took over again. 'Thanks, Judy. We may have to work wonders in the editing suite!' She looked directly into one of the cameras. 'At this point I would like to thank everyone who has helped with his project: Windsors Nursery for the flowers and shrubs, Wakely's Agricultural Merchants for the topsoil, seeds and vegetables, Forman and Stoddart for the heavy machinery yesterday, and John Jones Timber Merchants for the all the sleepers and other wood. You've all been very generous, and it is very much appreciated. Thank you to all of you.

'Right, let's get to it. I think we'll pitch in first and give the marina residents a start with planting out their allotments, then after lunch,' she said, looking over at the students, 'you guys can get cracking with your own projects. Jake, Simon and I will divvy up the produce and we'll be on hand if you have any problems. OK, good luck!'

Diane looked on as Pete smiled and shook his head at Judy. She called him over. 'One of these days she'll say something complimentary to you.'

'Never,' he replied. Diane grinned.

'You asked me if we could help out with payment for Rick and Martin. Unfortunately, we can't stump for all of it - but Audrey says we can do fifty percent. It's a bit of an unusual one, what with pulling guys in on the morning of the job, but as the firm in Wem let us have the Bob for free she says we'll pay half. Can you just ask them to invoice us for five hundred and fifty?'

'Sure, that's great. Don't worry about the rest - we'll sort it out. It's not a problem.'

They both looked up, hearing a buzzing noise.

'What the...?' said Pete.

'Blimey,' said Diane, peering up into the grey sky. 'It's a drone. Looks like your nemesis is having a snoop.'

The four-propeller machine hovered about twenty feet in the air, rock steady. Roughly eighteen inches in diameter, its high-pitched buzzing sounded like a giant hornet.

'Hey, look,' shouted Pete, pointing skywards, 'you're on camera.'

Archie looked up and raised two fingers in salute. Before long everyone had spotted it and there were various gestures and cat-calls. Paul broke off, ran towards the drone and threw a stone at it - which missed. The drone immediately rose another twenty feet in the air and continued to stare down at them. It hovered for another few minutes before turning and flying away over the marina.

'They're menacing damn things, aren't they?' said Sal, who'd walked over to join Pete and Diane. 'He's a sneaky sod.'

By late afternoon they'd gone as far as they could, and they'd all gathered round the chuck wagon again. Roger was off to one side with a cup of tea, talking quietly with the shy student, a thin lad with crooked teeth and serious face. He broke off and came to join the rest of the crew who were variously drinking tea, coffee or beer.

'He may be a reserved lad, but boy can he work hard. Knowledgeable too, knows his stuff alright. His mum and dad have a farm over towards Oswestry. He stays with his grandparents outside Whitchurch during the week while he's at school and goes home at weekends. Tells me his dad's struggling with arthritis so his mum does a lot of the work, and Wayne, that's his name, helps out at weekends. He's desperate to do well at school and college so he can take over and take the pressure off his mum.'

'Good for him!' said Sal. 'Let's hope what we're doing here gives him a start.'

Judy wandered over towards the students who were sitting together on the sleepers. 'Thanks, you guys. Great job today. How did you find it?'

A pretty blonde girl spoke up, 'Brilliant!' she said. 'It's good to be out of school for a day. And it was great having the cameras around. They're a friendly bunch.'

'Boy, I hope they don't get to build those houses here,' said a lad wearing an Aston Villa baseball cap.

'We'll do all we can to stop them,' promised Judy. 'Let's hope having the TV here has some sway.' She stood and posed with her hands on her hips pouting. 'Think they'll have me on Emmerdale after all this exposure?'

'Fat chance!' said Colin, who'd crept up behind her.

The kids all laughed.

'Who asked you? Star quality, brother. Don't you recognize it when you see it?'

'Uh, yes actually. And you're not it.'

Judy picked up a clod of mud and threw it at Colin, who ducked and scurried away. 'Cheeky blighter! Off with you.'

'Right,' she said to the youngsters, 'who's for a burger before you get back on the bus?'

There was a chorus of approval as Judy shouted at the chuck wagon, 'Twelve of your best for our gallant grafters, PJ. No, make that thirteen – I'll risk one too.'

'I'm a vegan,' said one of the girls.

'Right! Here, have a chew on this,' said Judy, scooping up a handful of grass. The girl pouted.

'Only joking, love,' said Judy, putting her arm round the lass. 'Come with me and we'll sort you something nice out.'

By four-thirty, most people had drifted away, leaving Roger and Archie sitting on the sleepers supping a beer. Diane, Simon and crew were heading south. Rick and Martin had been paid out by Pete and had trundled noisily down the lane back towards Church Stretton. The youngsters had been bussed back to school, and the remaining residents had dragged their aching bodies home for a cuppa, or something stronger. The new layout looked a treat, as Roger surveyed the transformed field.

'Boy, it's amazing what's been achieved in just two days. Look at that, it's superb!'

'The problem's going to be looking after it all,' countered Archie. 'If you feel anything like me you'll need a couple of months on a beach to re-align. Actually, I might see if any students fancy earning a bit of pocket money.'

'You'll probably find your plot full of wacky baccy when you get back.'

'There's probably a ready market on Judy's boat.'

'She's come up trumps, hasn't she?'

'Sure has. A natural leader. Directing operations from a distance while drinking tea.' They chuckled. 'No, you're right. She's pulled us together and doesn't take any messing.'

When Judy and Elaine arrived back at the boat, they found a woman waiting for them. Dressed in a business-like navy skirt and jacket, she handed Judy a letter. 'For you, I believe,' she said pompously, before clacking away down the pontoon in her court shoes. It was addressed to the Residents' Committee and it gave them one months' notice to quit the site.

She phoned Pete.

'We've just been given official notice,' she told him. 'The Fuhrer has just upped the stakes.'

13

Joy for John

At just after five, Archie received a phone call from John Greenway, who wanted to meet. The two of them met in The Dog at six-thirty in the company of Roger and Pete and sat round a table to the right of the fire-place.

'I've been sacked,' said John. 'I was called in to see Edward first thing this morning and he fired me on the spot. He knew I'd been talking to you.'

There was silence as John stared at the Pedigree Chums in turn.

'How did he find out?' he railed. 'I told you what would happen. What am I supposed to do now? How the hell did he know?'

'The bastard,' muttered Archie. 'I'm really sorry, John, but I assure you it's not down to us. We never let on, I can promise you. Guys?' he said, turning to his two mates. They both shook their heads and said no.

'It's a bit of a coincidence though, don't you think?'

'Bugger.' said Pete. 'I'm sorry, John.'

The evening crowd had largely left. Only a few punters were chatting at the bar, finishing their drinks before heading off for dinner. Joy was chatting with three friends at the bar, two men and a woman. Pete caught her eye and waved her over.

'Hi, Joy,' he said. 'Come and join us for a moment. will you? Here, sit down.'

She looked a bit suspicious but sat on the proffered chair.

'It's OK, don't look so worried! We'd just like a word if you have a minute.'

'OK.' she said nervously, looking round the table.

'You were here Monday evening when we spoke with John. You were having a meal over there.'

'Minding my own business, yes.'

'Yes, I know that. But John here was fired this morning for speaking with us. You don't know anything about that, do you?'

'Such as?' she said indignantly.

'I'm not accusing YOU of anything. I just wonder whether you noticed anything, saw anyone? Someone told Edward, and as a result John lost his job.'

'Steady on, Pete,' said Archie. 'You're out of order. It sounds like you're accusing the wrong person here.'

'Correct,' replied Joy, who looked close to tears. 'I can assure you that I said nothing to anyone. Your business is no business of mine and no, I didn't see anyone else that evening apart from you guys and Eric. There was nobody else here.'

'Sorry, Joy,' said Pete. 'That came out all wrong. I apologise.'

She sighed. 'It's OK. I know you're having a difficult time.' She smiled but had tears in her eyes. 'I'm on your side you know.'

'Of course you are. I'm sorry. I just don't like seeing people trodden on. John was only trying to help us and we got him fired.'

'We also got notice to quit the allotments this afternoon,' said Roger. 'We have a month to get off.'

'Oh dear,' Joy replied. 'He really is the most obnoxious character. It's all above board?'

'We don't know. Until we're advised to the contrary, we have to presume so. Problem is from here on in we're going to need legal advice, and that doesn't come cheap.'

'I've been giving that some thought,' said Joy. 'I know you're looking for a sponsor for the concert a week on Saturday. Well, I'd like to help. I've had a word with the people in our office and they'd like to be involved. In fact, it caused quite a stir when I brought it up. We've agreed that we can offer five thousand pounds towards your war chest - in exchange for a little favourable publicity, of course. Nothing comes for free.' She smiled.

'Wow!' said Roger. 'That is generous in the extreme. Thank you!'

'My pleasure, despite the unfounded allegations.' She grinned at Pete. 'We're all looking forward to it. In fact if I'd vetoed the idea, Brad, he's our MD, would probably have lynched me. He's a big fan.' She laughed. 'Actually I could have saved the company some money because he'd probably have stumped up the money personally so he could meet his idols.'

'Tell you what...' said Pete, in a further attempt to placate Joy, 'don't tell him, but we'll get him to introduce the band. That should give him a buzz.'

'He'd love that. We'll never hear the end of it.'

'And you, young fellow,' continued Joy, looking at John, 'I'm going to put your name forward as a maintenance contractor. We rent out some large properties and we're always on the look-out for reliable people. I'm sure with your skills you can help us out.'

John looked at her wide-eyed. 'Thank you,' he mumbled, obviously a bit taken aback.

'Don't think I'm being charitable,' said Joy. 'You'll earn your keep.'

John looked pensive.

'Come on,' said Archie, 'what's up?'

'It's just that... well, we'll probably be booted out of the cottage. It came with the job.'

'Don't worry about that,' said Joy. 'We have empty rental properties on the books, and I'm sure we can persuade one of the owners to give you a favourable deal, at least to begin with. For your Mum and Dad, too, if it comes to it. In fact, we'll put you on our payroll till you're up and running independently. We'll see you right, don't fret.'

'I can't believe this. I came here to let rip at someone.' He looked at her with tears in his eyes. 'Thank you.'

She patted his hand.

'Stop blubbering, man,' said Roger. 'You're a budding maintenance contractor, not a jilted teenager. Pull yourself together.'

'He's just learnt that not everybody is an arse,' said Archie.

'OK,' said Pete. 'I'm off to give Len a call, see how he's getting on.'

14

Gig, Not Concert!

'Right,' yelled Judy, 'let's get started. Op-Veg 3 is now in session. Apologies for absence? Yes, I know, it's difficult to tell with some of you lot - but let's get cracking. Archie, do the honours, please. I'll have a spritzer, large, with ice, no lemon.'

All eyes turned to their leader.

'Alright, alright, what's with the looks? I'm on a bit of health kick, OK? Realized after all that effort down in the field I could do with bit of bodily realignment. It's more of a maintenance issue really; just need to ensure I'm in peak condition to continue the battle.'

'I can get you a glass of water if you'd prefer?'

'No, Archie. White wine and soda is fine, thank you. I need to dull the senses against the diatribe that will doubtless follow during this meeting. Besides I'm not sure of the provenance of the water out here in the sticks; it's rumoured to have lumps in it. Anyway, now you have a kitty it's only right that we all get a fair crack of the whip.'

'Seven quid. That's the sum total of your mass appeal from last time.'

'Well, it's a start. Go on, off you go.'

'For goodness sake,' muttered Archie.

'Here,' said Pete, 'I'll get these.' He handed over three ten-pound notes. 'Can't do with our chief fund-raiser going bankrupt - we'd be the laughing-stock. I'll have a Pedigree.'

Paul and Archie went over to the bar to get the drinks.

When everyone was settled, Judy continued. 'Roger, the floor is yours.'

'Right. Thank you, Madam Chair.' He stood and hoisted up his sagging trousers. 'Good evening. Minutes of Operation Vegetable two held last Wednesday here at The Dog. Present were Pe…, no, I'll skip that.' He cleared his throat. 'Apologies for absence were received from common sense. The PR sub-committee, that's Sal and I for those who had forgotten, a small but determined duo who probably have the most difficult and onerous task, reported steady, if unspectacular, progress. Although failing to favour much national interest, we managed to make direct contact with a vital member of the local press corps. It's fair to say that, overall, local support was spectacular.'

'Hang on,' said Paul. 'Are we talking about the same meeting?'

'It's called creative accounting,' muttered Mike.

Roger grinned.

'Furthermore, my colleague has written both to the producers of the Woodentops and Johnny Depp in an effort to entice a gullible or mentally deranged celebrity to back our worthy cause. We eagerly await their response, more in hope than expectation. This course of action was undertaken despite misgivings from the time-pressured sub-committee, at the behest of our matriarch who ordered that every avenue be explored in the furtherment of our cause.'

Judy grinned.

'Colin reported that his brother arrived with a van-full of tackle. Following a number of hours hacking and scrubbing around, using practical experience and employing techniques he learned through years of intensive training, he unearthed a lump of rotting wood. Due to some imaginative thinking, this sorry-looking specimen morphed into the tiller handle of an ancient relic. Excitement, here I embellish somewhat, reached fever pitch and speculation mounted. Finally, to the amazement of everyone who thought he had indeed just unearthed a lump of old timber, he exclaimed that it had actually dropped off an old narrowboat two hundred years ago. Contact is to be made with archaeological groups and a local canal historical society to see if anyone has the slightest interest.'

'Despite intensive efforts from our 'local relations' sub-committee tasked with garnering support both from the Canal and River Trust and our marina management, there was absolutely no interest whatsoever.

'Finally, a vagrant came and sat down and offered up a couple of wild suggestions regarding gardening and music. For some reason, and out of all proportion to the actual effort involved, this caused our matriarch to stand up and whoop and dance - a fearsome performance, the like of which has not been witnessed since Custer was surrounded by Indians at the Battle of Little Bighorn. That concludes the minutes.'

Everyone applauded. Roger bowed and resumed his seat.

'Thank you, Roger. Can I have someone to propose the minutes.'

'I'll propose that they were the biggest load of cobblers I've ever had the misfortune to listen to,' said Archie.

'Seconded,' said Pete, laughing.

'Good stuff,' said the Chair, giggling. 'OK, let's move on. I think Wednesday went brilliantly. The allotments look fabulous - well done, all of you. Don't know about you guys, but I remember when recovery time after intense exercise was counted in minutes not days, but thankfully most of us look to have survived the ordeal. Roger, both those minutes you put in were more than helpful, a joy to behold.' She winked at him.

'Cheeky blighter.'

'Seriously, good effort all round. OK, we need to move on to planning the gig, which is one week from today – God willing. Yes, one week. Not long and there's lots to do. Anyone got any comments? Actually, before we start that, for those that don't know, we received notice to quit the allotment site from Hordley. A snotty junior from Whoosit, Whoosit and Clackety Heels ambushed me a couple of days ago, just after we'd finished work. To be honest, I don't think we need to worry too much about it. Joy spoke to one of her legal advisors and we've enjoyed use of the field long enough to raise enough objections, if nothing else, to delay planning approval for a period. Besides, with the TV programme and all the attendant publicity, not even Edward would be idiotic enough to carry through with his threat. We have the kids involved now, plus the historical aspect with the old boat, so I believe we'll be OK; or, more importantly, Joy's legal bod believes we'll be OK.'

'With the greatest respect, Madam Chairperson,' said Roger, 'you appear to take credit for things that have gone well, but when the outcome is less than certain, you sneakily abdicate responsibility – in this case onto one of Joy's employees.'

'It's called the privilege of power. Comes with taking on an onerous role such as this,' she replied, smiling at Roger.

'I wouldn't be so sure we've heard the last of it, if I were you,' said Sal.

'We have a spy in his camp actually,' said Archie. 'Young John, his groom, has come over to our side. Poor lad got fired for his troubles, but he's given us some juicy information on dear old Edward. When the dust settles in a day or two, we can maybe act on it.'

'What sort of stuff?' asked Paul.

'Things of a personal nature, amongst others. Let's just say that he may have had some difficulty keeping his private bits in his breeches. I hope that when other people see John taking a stand they may loosen up a bit and give us some ammunition. Roger, Pete and I are on it. We'll keep you posted.'

Sandy pulled a thick buff folder from his holdall and slammed it on the table with a dull thump. People's eyes widened in horror at what they suspected was a raft of barely comprehensible facts and figures.

'I've been looking into the legalities and have come up with a few thoughts.' He rummaged deep within his file, fished out a sheet covered in yellow highlighter and continued. 'Now, if we begin with rights of easements..."

'Hang on, Sandy,' Judy interrupted, 'could you just hold that thought for a moment? I think we may have the legal angle covered, at least initially.'

Sandy was wide-eyed in horror.

'Should this prove not to be the case, we can rest assured that the stuff you've prepared will be invaluable. Joy's lawyer lady is well versed with disputes such as this. Perhaps we can leave you to liaise with her. I'm sure between the two of you you can put a spoke in Hordley's wheel. Besides, most of us won't understand what you're on about. We really appreciate the detailed work you've doubtless put in, but I think that what we should be doing is moving forward with plans that haven't got a plan, if you follow me - the forthcoming concert, for example.'

With his sail well and truly deflated, Sandy slowly removed his half-moon spectacles. He returned his paper to the file and the file to his hold-all, paused a moment then got up and left without another word.

'Oh dear,' said Mike as the door swung closed behind Sandy, 'Poor lad's upset. I'll go and have a word.' He got up and followed.

Judy had a pained look on her face. 'Now look what I've done, I've alienated the oracle. Damn.'

'He'll be OK. Mike'll sort him out,' said Roger. 'Come on, what's done is done. Let's move on.'

Archie returned with a tray of drinks. 'OK, here we go,' he said, passing them out. He raised his own, 'Cheers, Pete.'

'You're welcome. Yaki da everyone.'

Everyone took a slurp.

'Swedish pop group you know, Yaki-Da,' said Sal. 'Not bad either.'

'Good, yes, right, well,' said Judy, looking a bit bemused. 'Anything else useful you'd like to contribute? Talking of pop groups - Pete, over to you.'

'Well, Len's on his way. Couldn't get hold of him yesterday, probably out in the sticks somewhere with no signal, but last I heard he's en route and should be with us in two or three days. Thought I might drive out and meet him if I can find out where he is. Have a chat and see how we can prepare the ground.'

Paul chuckled. 'May be worth warning him about all the adoring fans that could swamp him when he gets here. You listening, Judy? Don't frighten the lad away before he gets settled.'

'Knickers!' she replied, laughing.

'Don't throw THEM for god's sake,' said Colin. 'He'll do a U-turn and bugger off again.'

'Goodness gracious...what a thought,' muttered Archie.

'I'll have you know, my underwear has pride of place in many rock stars' collections. I flung a pair at The Doobie Brothers at Knebworth in 1974. Great band, but I have to admit they never quite achieved the same heights after that.'

'Well, there's a surprise,' said Paul. 'I heard they stuck some poles in them and lived in the Appalachian mountains during their 'wilderness' years. They were going to call their next album *Livin' in a pair of old undies*, but thankfully changed it to *Livin' on the Fault Line*.'

Terri looked horrified at the belittling of her beloved leader, while everybody else giggled.

'You cheeky young blighter. Right, enough of that. Let's move on.'

Mike returned with Sandy in tow.

'Come on Sandy, love,' said Sal, shuffling up. 'Here, sit next to me and finish your drink.'

He looked mournful. 'I only want to do my bit, feel part of things. Everybody else is doing something useful. I'm sorry.'

Judy went over, placed a hand on each cheek and kissed him on the forehead. 'It's me who should apologise, I was out of order. You are part of us. In fact, you're a bigger part of us than most of this dysfunctional rabble.' She patted his cheeks and winked. 'I'm sorry, love. Forgiven?'

Sandy nodded and grinned sheepishly.

'I'm going up to meet Len if I can find out where he is,' said Pete. 'Why don't you come along and we can do some planning for next Saturday?'

A big breath from Sandy. 'Thanks, Pete. I'd like that.'

There was a collective sigh.

'Good, we're back on track,' said Judy.

'I've had twenty-four VIP invitations printed for the concert,' said Sal.

'Gig,' said Archie, 'rock events are called gigs. Concerts are where sweaty people in evening attire pretend to enjoy a collective racket composed by some Hungarian nobody has heard of.'

Sal smiled. 'Very well then - gig. I thought it might be a good idea to say thanks to the folks who have helped us out, the people who donated things for our allotment. I'd like to send a pair each to the plant-hire people and two each to the produce, soil and timber suppliers. I'm sure we won't have difficulty filling the pub, the opposite if anything, but it would be nice to acknowledge local suppliers.'

'Ideal,' said Roger. 'And listen to this: we've had two further local companies offering sponsorship. Trans Logistics, a big local transport firm, are putting up ten thousand. That's been matched by Morden Clayton, Solicitors. They are from Wolverhampton, so goodness knows how they heard about it - but I've welcomed and thanked them both. As Pete suggested at the last meet- up, I said we would give each sponsor two VIP tickets, signed photos and endorsements on the night. To be honest, they would probably have sponsored us without sweeteners but it's nice to be able to offer them something with which they can remember the occasion. With Joy's donation, that's twenty-five thousand - so we've done OK, I think.'

'We have indeed,' said Judy. 'We've done more than OK. From a standing start ten days ago, we've done a fabulous job. Well done, you two. After we've paid Pete back for the construction guys, plus any other expenses we can't scrounge, we'll have to decide what to do with the balance when the dust has settled.'

'It could go towards a cover for the boat restoration project maybe,' suggested Terri.

'Sure,' replied Judy, 'but we probably haven't finished with his Lordship yet. Let's just see how things pan out, eh?'

Pete returned from a chat with Eric. 'Been quite sneaky has old Eric. He's persuaded a local brewery to give us half a dozen barrels of ale, with profits going to our cause. And he'll put some food on for some chosen guests beforehand.'

'Good man. It all helps. Can you send the brewery a couple of tickets, Sal?'

'Sure.'

Judy gave Eric a thumbs up across the pub, and he replied with a wave and a nod.

'Good stuff,' said Judy. 'The problem we have, if there is one, is getting everyone in. Sal was telling me that there's a lot of local interest; we could be swamped.'

'What about a big screen outside?' asked Paul.

'What if it's pissing down?' replied Archie.

'It won't rain,' said Judy with authority. 'Not on our parade.'

'We could erect your underwear tent,' said Paul.

'I'll ignore that. Sal, what about your Woodentops operator? Any luck there?'

'He died last Christmas.'

'Oh dear, what a shame.'

'Pushing up the weeds,' said Paul.

Sal raised her eyebrows, then frowned. 'Have a heart, for goodness' sake.'

'A marquee might be the answer,' suggested Mike, trying to keep things moving.

'Great idea. Any other suggestions?' asked Judy, looking round the group. 'Anyone not inside seeing the gig live will feel a bit left out, isolated, but I don't really know what we can do about it.'

'Well,' said Pete, we'll see if we can rig that big screen up in the marquee and project a live feed outside. I'll also have a word with Len, see if he'll do an acoustic set out there. Even if he only does a few numbers, I'm sure it will go down a storm. I think he'll probably go for it.'

'Good one. I'll leave that with you, Pete. What we will need to do is form some sort of plan as to who does get inside. The sponsors obviously, and us, but there's only room for what - eighty, a hundred, inside? However many, some people might be disappointed. You're right, locals have got behind us and we really have to make them feel part of things.'

'We've got seven days,' said Archie. It's a bit ironic that we had no idea what to do a week ago, now we've potentially got problems with too many folk.'

'We need to inform punters about what's going on. Roger, could you and Sal draft something up and make it plain that not everyone will squeeze into the pub? Tell them about the marquee idea and the acoustic set? Get a release ready and when we've confirmed things with Len we'll be ready to get it out there.'

'Sure, Judy, we can do that.'

'It's the quiz tonight,' said Paul. 'We can give people a heads-up then.'

'Good idea,' said Judy. 'Oh, and congratulations. That's the first thing you've said that isn't facetious. Could you put that in the minutes, Roger?'

'With all the country piles round here there is bound to be a company supplying tents and marquees for weddings and the like. I'll make some enquiries," said Sal. Actually, I bet Joy knows someone. Leave it with me, I'll have a look around.'

'What about a name for the gig?' asked Archie. 'Something to focus the marketing on.'

'Not sure we really need one,' said Mike. 'The band name says it all really.'

'Actually,' said Pete, 'when I mentioned it to Len he suggested 'Bloke on the Water' when he heard he was performing for a bunch of boaters – quite good, I thought, a Deep Purple parody.'

'How about The Gig in The Dog?' suggested Archie.

'Or Knobworth, in honour of Edward Hordley,' suggested Paul.

Everyone laughed.

'The Gig in The Dog sounds good,' said Judy. 'I like that. What do you reckon, Sal?'

'Sounds good,' she replied.

'Everyone?' asked Judy.

They all muttered and nodded.

'Right, let's go with that then. Pete, best just check it's all OK with Len, but if he's no objections we're off and running. Sal, just a thought...with all the extra folk who'll be around next Saturday, we're going to need some extra loos, those tardis-type things. If you track down a marquee company, can you ask them? Also, extra lighting around the place. Don't want any pickled natives coming to grief on the guy ropes.'

'Sure, no problem.'

'OK, presumably most of you'll be back for the quiz in a couple of hours, so let's head off for a bite to eat or whatever. See you later.'

The meeting broke up with a further one scheduled for Tuesday.

15

Abuse of Power

John Greenway had just received a disturbing phone call from Sue Davis. He'd been in his new role with Joy's Estate and Letting agency for a couple of days but had spent some time contacting former colleagues at Hordley Estates. He'd told them he'd been sacked and asked them, if possible, to report anything untoward, either personally or in connection with work. He told them he was very aware how much people relied on their estate jobs and that anything said would be strictly confidential. He'd told them that he just wanted something with which to bring Edward down a peg or two, and that he was now in a position to be a thorn in his side.

Sue's phone call gave him something. Her husband, Keith, worked on the estate in the milking parlour. Though the term conjurers up the image of a bonneted lass sitting on a three-legged stool, the one on the estate is a state-of-the-art rotary system. Keith oversaw the operation where up to one hundred cows were milked every ten minutes, largely controlled by computer. Cows can be milked two or three times a day so it was a busy operation. But Keith, although well trained and paid better than many other estate workers, was not indispensable. There were two other people trained to oversee the milking, and if all else failed there were contractors who could be called on. Edward was many things, but where the operation of the estate was concerned his finger was on the pulse.

Keith and Sue lived in one of the estate cottages. Sue told John that Edward

Hordley had been harassing her. She sounded tearful and frightened. She said that the previous Tuesday, Edward had come to her home shortly after nine in the morning, knowing that Keith was at work. Although he'd come on the pretence of investigating the viability of installing central heating in their house, she had felt uncomfortable.

She had told Edward to speak with her husband, either after he'd finished work or during the day in the milking parlour. He never did speak with Keith, but instead came back to see Sue two days later. On this occasion he had actually propositioned her. Not directly perhaps, but he'd told her how much more comfortable he could make their lives in exchange for certain considerations. She had been left in no doubt what Edward meant as he stood in her doorway, a ratty smile on his face. He'd told her to keep it strictly between themselves. After all, it would be a tragedy if Keith was to lose his livelihood, particularly if the whispers that she had fallen pregnant with their first child were true. Opportunities for people in Keith's line of work were limited, he'd said, and it would be just awful if they were to lose their home through a silly misunderstanding. She hadn't told Keith, knowing that he'd tackle Edward, and God knows where that confrontation might end up. Sue was really scared for their future.

John's response to Sue's situation was frankly unprintable, but he promised to try and do something about it. He'd heard whispers that Edward had tried it on with people, but this was the first direct allegation. He knew of the young couple who had moved away – perhaps he'd try and find them, see if they would write some sort of statement. He asked Sue to quietly have a word with other workers, see if they had received similar approaches. John knew he had been lucky finding alternative work, but more importantly he knew that the estate no longer held sway over him. However, he was also acutely aware of the perilous state of the estate workers' livelihoods. Edward was a powerful man locally.

16

One Man and His Goat

It was Monday lunchtime and Pete and Sandy had driven out in search of Len.

'There he is,' said Pete, turning to Sandy and grinning. 'Dozy old devil looks asleep. Come on, let's go and ruin his day.'

Sandy looked nervous. Although he didn't know much about Rounded, he'd done a little internet research the previous evening and only now began to appreciate the popularity of the band. He'd never met a celebrity before, and the prospect of meeting such a famous person was giving him the collywobbles. Sandy had dressed to impress and wore his full ensemble - waistcoat, neckerchief, the lot.

They were just outside the village of Wrenbury on the Llangollen Canal and Len was moored about fifty metres east of a large, semi-automated lift bridge. It was still early in the boating season so there were only a handful of leisure boaters about. Come high summer this stretch of the canal would be packed. Not only did Wrenbury have two decent pubs, the Llangollen Canal itself was popular with boaters, both privately owned boat and holiday-makers. There were three or four hire-boat bases along the length of the canal; in fact there was one just before the lift bridge in Wrenbury itself.

It was a rural canal and very pretty, but the primary attraction was the Pontcysyllte Aqueduct about fifty miles to the west, which crossed the River Dee near the town of Trevor. The aqueduct, built by Thomas Telford and

William Jessop more than two hundred years ago, offered stunning views from either boat or on foot, as you crossed the Dee Valley over one hundred and twenty feet up in the air. Talk to any boater and a trip across there is a must.

'What the bloody hell's that?' exclaimed Pete, as they walked towards Fender Bender, Len's grey tugboat.

'If I didn't know better, I'd say it was some sort of goat,' replied Sandy.

They approached warily and Pete shouted, 'Oi, Johnson. Wakey-wakey.'

Len stirred and muttered, 'Get lost. Can't a man have a postprandial nap without interruption?' He smiled, clambered out of his director's chair and stretched before jumping down onto the towpath to greet his friend. 'Hi, mate! Great to see you. Come on board.'

'Hi, Len. Uh, what, if I may be so bold, is that?' he asked, pointing at the goat. The beast had looked at them through blue-grey eyes as they'd inched past, giving it a wide berth.

Laughing, he replied, 'Meet Proctor, Chief Petty Officer, and my erstwhile travelling companion.'

'Oh, of course, how silly of me.' Pete turned to the goat. 'Good afternoon, Proctor, delighted I'm sure. He's your new keyboard player, I take it?'

'Rhythm guitar actually, and backing vocals,' said Len, smiling.

Judging them no threat, and obviously uninterested in the newcomers, Proctor returned to his bowl of oats.

'He's a friendly soul,' said Len. 'Just content to watch the world go by. Happy as Larry as long as he gets his oats.'

They laughed.

'Oh, I see...,' said Pete pointedly, 'Just the two of you living on the boat then is there?'

'Hey, don't start malicious rumours. It's taken years for me to cultivate my squeaky-clean image.'

'Here Len, meet Sandy,' said Pete. 'One of my boaty friends from the marina.'

'Hi, pleased to meet you, Sandy,' said Len, extending his hand.

'Yes, me too. Or rather, you too... oh God!'

'Calm down, Sandy! Relax for goodness' sake. You'll unsettle Proctor,' said Pete.

Len smiled, knowing some people got rather tongue-tied when they met him for the first time. 'Come and sit down, Sandy,' he said. 'Like a beer?'

'Sorry,' said Sandy, looking a bit hang-dog. 'It's just that...well...' He petered out.

'Shut up and sit down,' said Pete. 'Here, have a beer. Chill.'

Pete and Sandy sat on a long, wooden-topped steel box as Len collapsed back into his director's chair. Amy Winehouse played quietly through Len's outdoor speakers.

'So how are you, and how's the trip been?' asked Pete.

'I'm fine and the trip was fine, once I got the engine started. No, more than fine - great. I do love pottering about, the freedom and peace and quiet. And this,' he said with a sweep of the arm, 'is a stunning part of the world, my first time this way. Some decent pubs en route, too. When I started this boating lark I decided that I'd navigate with the maxim, 'the shortest distance between two pints' - a fulsome code by which to live, I think you'll agree. Of course, there's not much scope for lateral movement, but I do tend to put a spurt on near a canal-side pub when I smell hops in the air.'

'Indeed! Sounds like you've got it sorted,' replied Pete. 'I've stopped here from time to time; not a bad pint in the Cotton Arms down there. It's changing a bit though; there's a lot of rural pubs gone to the wall recently. The drink-driving thing scuppered a lot I think, and most of those that are surviving have turned into eateries. Lost some of their character. A decent pint is more difficult to find these days – all gassy lager-type stuff that doesn't need the same looking after.'

'Yes, sadly true. What's your local like?' said Len, passing over a couple of bottles of Old Speckled Hen retrieved from a cool box next to his chair.

'Cheers.' He took a swig and smacked his lips. 'The Dog. A proper pub. Eric who owns it, a former copper, has turned it back to a real pub after the previous owners filled it full of plastic greenery and nouvelle cuisine. Now it's back to good ale and proper food. It's a cracker, actually. You'll like it, I hope.'

'Sounds right up my street. I look forward to meeting your mates and having a real ale or two.'

'How long are you planning on staying around?'

'Haven't thought that far ahead really. I don't tend to plan too far ahead. Spoils it in some ways. I like not knowing what's round the next bend.'

Len turned to Sandy. 'How long have you been boating, Sandy?'

'Oh, coming up ten years now. Decided on a change of pace when I got made redundant. From mechanical engineering to slobbing about. Quite a career path.'

'Sandy is our resident technical wizard,' said Pete. 'A big help when things go wrong, but a pain in the arse when you want some peace and quiet and he has a new theory he wants to unleash on the world!'

'Oh, thanks a bunch.'

They all smiled.

'No, he's a good lad. Part of the scene, for sure. We're all different; that's what makes it so enjoyable really. We're all trying to live a simple life in our own ways. But you'll know all about that,' he said, looking at Len.

'Aye, for sure. My life's changed more than most I guess. Wouldn't change any of it, though. Time for this, time for that.'

Two Lycra-clad cyclists sped by on the towpath.

'A right menace they are,' said Len. 'Always in too much of a rush.'

'There's a song there,' said Sandy.

'Eh?' asked Pete.

'Time for this, Time for that. Good song title.'

They both turned to him with arched eyebrows.

'Ooooh. Hark at him,' said Pete with a smile.

'Well, you know,' replied Sandy sheepishly.

Len smiled. 'You could well be right, but my writing days are over really. I just pick about with my guitar from time to time.'

'*The Time, The Place.* That's what came to mind.'

'You have done some research! To be honest, it still amazes me that songs I scribbled on a piece of paper, or first strummed on a guitar all those years ago, can mean so much to people. I tell you, it's pretty humbling, frankly.'

Len took a swig of his beer.

'So,' he said, 'tell me what to expect at, er... what's the marina called?'

'Watergrove.'

'Yes, Watergrove. What's in store when we turn up?'

'A warm welcome to start with,' said Pete. 'Don't get any pre-conceived ideas about a group of pseudo-intellectuals discussing the economic vagaries of commodity markets.'

Len chuckled. 'Oh, how disappointing,'

'We're just a bunch of regular folk, really. We usually just bumble along, but suddenly we have a cause, a unifying objective. The proletariat has risen en masse to try and stop a plonker wrecking our vegetable patch. It doesn't sound like much.' He paused. 'Let's be frank, it isn't much, hardly Black Monday, but we've unified and repelled all boarders to this point. We want to put a spoke in the Big Cheese's wheel. It's turned into a bit of a local monster. We seem to have plenty of support from the natives, boosted when they heard you guys were coming. And,' he continued, 'we have a secret weapon – our bunker-buster, in the shape of our self-elected oligarch, who is a lass not to be trifled with I can tell you. That right, Sandy?'

'Without question, she's rather fearsome for sure. I'm glad she's not an enforcer for the opposition, or life might be very uncomfortable.'

'Blimey, what are we letting ourselves in for?' said Len.

'She's a great lass is our Judy. You'll like her. I'm taking the mickey from a distance because it's safer than crossing her at close quarters. A lot of people have a lot of respect for her. In fact, she told us herself that we must have respect! We don't tend to argue too much.'

Fender Bender strained at her mooring ropes as a boat motored by. It was a hire boat from the nearby base, out for a test run in preparation for the upcoming tourist season. The three guys watched as it inched into a small port in front of a large building serving as the company workshops and office.

'Oh, by the way,' said Pete. 'Never got the chance to tell you - Diane came with her TV show and did a special on us on our veggie plot. Did us proud, I can tell you.'

'No, really?! Blimey, last time I saw her was in Brussels.'

'Bruges, she said it was,' said Sandy.

'Oh yes, quite right, Bruges. I stitched her up for a lunch.' He laughed. 'About ten years ago, probably. Bet she hasn't forgotten.'

'She hasn't!' said Pete. 'She's coming up for the gig if she can make it. Better look out - she's on the war-path.'

'Oh, heck. Where can I turn round?'

'We joked with her, called her posh totty,' said Len with a chuckle. 'Her university nickname. She's originally from the depths of Yorkshire, little village near Howarth from memory, but she did her best to shed her local twang, started putting consonants at the beginning of words. Made an effort to 'upgrade', as she called it. Silly bugger - totally unnecessary; she was a cracker whatever.' He chuckled at the memory. 'Well I never... Diane Markham. When she got her nickname she dropped a few consonants again. Not just smart, but a lovely looking lass too. No surprise she ended up on TV.'

'The gig's at the pub, of course, half a mile down the road,' said Pete. 'I've reserved rooms for the other lads - hope that's OK? There's a twin and a single, so they'll have to scrap as to who gets what. Real rock star stuff, I can tell you. I told Eric the landlord to book out the whole first floor – hang the expense. There are only two rooms.'

Len laughed. 'Love it. Yes, Doug and Jerry can share, unless one of them wants to bunk down in here with me. Doug lives on a boat anyhow. I've got a lass called Bee to play keyboards. She's played with us before; good lass she is, and a really good keyboard player. She freelances quite a bit, in big demand from overseas artists who need session musicians while recording in the UK. She's twenty years younger than the rest of us, so brings a bit of colour to proceedings. An unsung heroine of the music world really. In fact, one of many, many very talented musicians who are little heard of, but play a huge role in making our music scene the success it is. And yes, you're right, best if she has the single. She's gay actually; not that that has anything to do with anything, but Doug and Jerry are used to bunking up. If you can give me directions, I'll tell them where to come. I told them to be there by lunchtime Saturday, so we can get set up and organised.'

'We raised £57 for the war chest on Saturday at the quiz,' said Pete, 'which is OK, and we had a bit of fun; but just to let you know, three local companies have stumped up twenty-five thousand quid between them to sponsor your gig. I'm not surprised people are interested, but coaxing cash out of anybody these days is not easy. Would you guys be prepared to sign photos for them, have your photos taken, that sort of thing?'

'Wow, it's amazing really. When we were getting going it took us three years and a couple of hit records to make that much at one go. Boy, how things change. Anyhow, well done - that's great. And sure, of course we'll sign stuff, no problem. Actually, I've asked Doug to throw some bits in the truck to auction off, if it's appropriate. Shirts, posters, that sort of thing. We'll sign and dedicate them. Actually I've earmarked a guitar signed by us all to do what you want with. Auction, raffle or whatever, if that helps.'

'Too right it does. That's very generous.'

'Nah, not really. In fact, when I told the guys about your plight they were all for pitching in, really up for it. It's the kind of wacky distraction that appeals after all the begging letters we get, mostly from people who can't be bothered to get off their backsides and help themselves. The more I hear the more I'm looking forward to it.'

'A little thing like this, a gig in a pub, must be run of the mill to you guys, eh?' asked Sandy.

'Well, yes and no,' replied Len reflectively. 'Sure, we know the songs and stuff, but we don't want to make ourselves look idiots by mucking it up. And we have a responsibility to our fans. They at least need to recognize our songs, so we have to get them somewhere near right. We'll get set up, have a quick practice and that should do it. You mentioned some gear for a feed to the marquee Pete; well, we have some tackle that can handle that, including a couple of screens that I can scrounge, so I've asked Doug to load them up too. Got a couple of lads coming along to help as well. They used to tour with us in the UK, roadies if you will, and we're all looking forward to meeting up again. And yes, I like the acoustic idea you mentioned for those that can't get inside; we'll sort something out, I'm sure.'

They chatted away for an hour or so over a couple of beers. Suddenly there was a grunting noise and a hoof stamp.

'Blimey!' said Sandy.

'That's Proctor's way of saying he'd like a little stroll down the towpath. I normally take him off so he can have a forage in the hedge and ...well, you know what else. I get some looks, I can tell you, walking about with him on his tether; but he's very amenable and not aggressive.'

'How on earth did you end up with a goat?' asked Sandy.

'Won him at cards. Well, when I say won him, I didn't go out of my way to win a goat, but the farmer in the group we were playing in had a bad day and couldn't pay his debts. I was all for letting the guy off, but he insisted I take Proctor in payment. Proud Yorkshireman and all that. At that point the goat meant more to him than me, but I'm glad I ended up with him. He's a companion and certainly a talking point. Between you and me, I tracked the guy down through the pub landlord and sent him a couple of hundred quid. It was part of his livelihood for goodness' sake; for me it was just mucking around. Mind you, he'll probably give it straight back if I ever see him again.' He looked up at the two friends. 'You want to come for a potter down the towpath?'

'Sandy, you go with Len,' suggested Pete, 'I'll stop here and guard the fort. Save you locking up.'

Sandy looked at Len.

'Sure, come on. We don't go far anyway.'

Len unhooked Proctor's halter from a ring on the deck, handing the loose end to Sandy. 'Here,' he said, 'you hold him. Make friends.'

'Christ!'

'Go on. You'll be fine.'

As they ambled off down the towpath Pete took a photo with his phone. Proctor was in charge, periodically yanking Sandy towards the hedge when he spotted something tasty. Pete chuckled to himself. 'There's one for the album.'

17

Paul

As they drove back to the marina Pete got a call on his car phone. Suddenly the mood of carefree afternoon they'd shared with Len was shattered. It was Judy, panicky and tearful. Through her sobs she said that Paul was in hospital. Pete and Sandy could barely make out what she was saying.

'Calm down, Judy,' said Pete. 'What the hell's happened?'

She told them that Paul's boat had been destroyed in a fire-ball and he had been badly burned. She wasn't sure how serious his condition was, but he'd been flown to Royal Shrewsbury Hospital in the air ambulance. Pete and Sandy listened in stunned silence. She said that Paul had managed to climb out of his boat, but not before he'd been pretty badly injured. He had lost consciousness on the pontoon close to the boat and had been dragged away from the inferno by Colin and Cassy. That act, according to the Fire Service, probably saved his life because within seconds there had been an explosion. Perhaps fuel or a gas bottle had gone up; they were not sure. The fire crew had given Paul emergency first aid until the air ambulance had arrived.

'Jesus Christ!' said Pete. 'What caused it? Does anyone know?'

'It's terrible Pete, just awful. Poor guy.' Judy broke down again in tears. 'There was some sort of explosion, I think - maybe more than one. I heard a muffled boom and the first thing I saw when I got outside was Colin and Cass pulling Paul away. There were flames and smoke everywhere. It was like a nightmare.'

'Nobody else was hurt?'

'No, I don't think so. Just Paul. Poor lad.'

Pete pulled the car to the side of the road and sat still, breathing heavily. He looked at Sandy who had heard the exchange. Sandy just stared out of the windscreen and appeared stupefied.

No one spoke for a full minute.

'Judy?' said Pete.

'Yes, I'm here.'

'Look, I'm with Sandy in the car. We'll go straight to the hospital. Shrewsbury, you said?'

Yes, Shrewsbury Royal.'

There was a pause before Pete asked, 'Are you guys OK there?'

'Yes, we're fine, at least physically. God, I pray he'll be alright.'

'We all do. Look if there's anything I can do, just call. I'll try and phone when I know something. I'll see you later.'

With that he cut the call, started the car and sped off for Shrewsbury. Pete and Sandy arrived at Accident and Emergency thirty-five minutes later. They couldn't get anything out of the reception desk - but after repeated requests of passing staff, who were obviously harassed, a nurse returned and told them that Paul was alive but sedated. He'd suffered burns, primarily to his legs. He was on oxygen therapy but had not been intubated. That in itself, said the nurse, was a good sign, but at this stage they were unsure as to the full extent of his injuries. He also appears to have suffered a blow to the head. She said it may be a while till more was known.

The two boaters sat, consumed by their own thoughts, oblivious to the hustle and bustle of the busy A&E department going on around them; the usual mixture of complaints, wheelchairs squeaking on polished floors and the sigh of the automatic doors as people came and went, some popping outside for a settling smoke before they got the results of tests. Although Cassy and Judy had given a few basic details to the ambulance crew, a doctor came by half an hour later to ask them more details. He found them waiting on lime-green plastic seats in the reception area. Dr. McDonald, a white-coated thirty-something with bags under his eyes and inevitably wearing a stethoscope, asked them to provide further personal information.

They told him that Paul was thirty-two and lived alone on his boat but no, they didn't know who his next of kin was. Pete told the doctor that Paul had been to university in Southampton and suggested that they may have more information in their records, albeit nearly ten years out of date. No, they'd no idea of his blood group nor whether he was allergic to anything, nor indeed if he was on any current medication. Pete realized just how little they knew about Paul. Why? Sure, he kept himself to himself somewhat, but nevertheless they had displayed an inordinate lack of interest in their friend. He felt uncomfortable, and frankly rather ashamed.

'Has he any family?' asked the doctor.

Pete and Sandy both looked blank and shook their heads before Sandy said, 'I've never seen him with anyone. In fact he rarely leaves the marina, except to go shopping.'

'I can tell you this,' said the doctor. 'He is diabetic. He has a monitoring device on his upper arm which constantly measures his sugar levels. He would need to inject insulin regularly. I'm surprised you never noticed.' He arched his eyebrows. 'However, now we know that we can control his glucose levels, but diabetes can cause complications, particularly with the legs.'

Pete and Sandy shared a look. They'd had no idea.

'Can you tell us how he is?' asked Sandy.

'Comfortable,' said the doctor, with a purse of the lips, 'for now. We don't know how badly burned he is yet; that is the main concern. Naturally we're doing all we can. His breathing is steady, but he may have a slight concussion. There's a good chance he'll be transferred to the burns centre at the Queen Elizabeth Hospital in Birmingham where they are geared to properly treating this type of injury. The risk of infection is another worry, but we'll know more later. A specialist will decide if he should be moved.'

'Can we see him? asked Sandy.

'I doubt it, but I'll go and see. Even then it won't be for long because he's had quite a trauma and is sedated. He's also on some pretty strong drugs for the pain, but if you wait here I'll send someone to get you if it's appropriate.'

'Thank you.'

Dr. McDonald nodded and headed back towards the curtained cubicles. Sandy and Pete sat quietly, both shocked and numb.

'How the hell do we know so little about him?' mumbled Sandy.

Pete merely shook his head. Twenty minutes later a young nurse approached and told them it was not possible to see their friend at the moment. She explained that firstly he was asleep but, more importantly, the risk of infection was too great.

'He's in the best place,' she said, and told them that they would do everything they could for him.

'Does he know we're here?' asked Sandy.

'Dr. McDonald did tell him that two friends had come, but whether it registered I'm not sure. I doubt it to be honest; he was pretty incoherent. He kept mumbling, something about a parcel. He's very confused. '

Sandy stood and faced the nurse, gently clutching her elbow. 'When he wakes up please tell him that Sandy and Pete were here and that everyone on the marina sends their love.'

'Of course.'

Sandy turned away and began to weep, taking a handkerchief from his pocket. Pete put his hand on Sandy's shoulder and looked at the nurse.

'When would be a good time to come back and see him?'

'Leave it till tomorrow at least. It's best to phone first. He's been moved to an isolation ward, but he may be moved to Birmingham - we're not sure yet. As I say, ring after nine tomorrow and we'll probably know more.' With that she smiled and left.

The two friends watched the nurse disappear into the bowels of the emergency suite, helpless in the knowledge that they could do nothing for their pal.

'Come on Sandy, let's get back. There's no point hanging around, there's nothing we can do here.'

It was a sombre drive home and dark by the time they drove into the marina car park near the allotments. They walked the three hundred metres along the pontoons between rows of moored boats towards the shop and residential area, then turned left onto the residential pontoon. Pete knocked gently on the side of Judy's boat. She emerged, followed by Elaine.

She clambered off and hugged her friend.

'Oh, Pete. I can hardly believe what's happened. How is he? Will he be alright?'

He relayed what they had been told. 'We'll call tomorrow morning; maybe they'll have some positive news. It's really hard to take.'

'The police are still here,' said Judy. 'They can't see much of Paul's boat but have been asking everyone questions. They're down with Colin and Cass now. Heroes those two. Probably saved Paul's life, they reckon.'

Pete shook his head.

'Do they know what happened? What caused it?' asked Sandy.

'No, I don't think so. They haven't said anything anyway. They're bringing a crane in to lift the boat out of the water tomorrow. It's mostly under water now, hanging from the pontoon cleats by its mooring lines. They've secured it with extra ropes till the morning.'

The boat was about forty yards away down the wooden pontoon. Only the top of the cabin was visible in the subdued pontoon lights, and it was rolled away from them at an angle. There was an acrid smell in the air.

'It's fortunate that the boat was on the 'T' hammer-head down there, otherwise other boats could have been caught up in it.'

Two police officers walked towards them - one male, one female. The male officer was tall and stick-thin. He was young, early thirties. The woman was older, nearer fifty. Both wore high-vis yellow jackets. The wooden pontoon creaked and rocked as they approached. The woman frowned and it was she who spoke. 'Hello. I'm Detective Sergeant Crane, and this is D.C. Williams. We'd like to ask you two gentlemen a couple of questions.'

'Sure, no problem.'

'Can we start with your names?'

'I'm Pete Crowther. I live here, down the other end of the marina near the main car park. This is Sandy Billings.'

'Can't Mr. Billings speak for himself?' Asked the D.S. pointedly.

Pete said nothing. Although he did think something.

'Mr. Crowther, can you shed any light on what's happened here today?'

'No, we've just come back from the hospital. Sandy and I were away visiting a friend. We left before lunch and only learned about this later this afternoon when Judy phoned.'

'I see. Did you know the victim well?'

'I thought I did. Turns out I don't know him as well as I thought.'

'Please explain.'

'Well, a doctor at the hospital asked us to provide personal information about him. I'm afraid we weren't very helpful. It transpires we actually knew very little about his past, his family, anything really. I've lived in the same place as him for about eight years and can't even tell you who his next of kin is. Pretty bloody poor to be honest.'

'Mmm,' muttered the policewoman. 'Has he had any visitors lately? Have you seen anyone snooping around the marina? Anything unusual?'

'Not as far as I'm aware, no.'

'Perhaps you're not the type of person who notices much?'

Pete remained silent staring at the police officer, and had another thought.

She turned her attention to Sandy and fixed him with a hard gaze. 'What about you, Mr. Billings? Presumably you reside here too. Have you happened to notice anything unusual?'

'Yes, I live here. That's my boat just behind you. The green one, and no, I've not seen anything peculiar, relating to Paul directly anyway. But we have been having a disagreement with a local farmer. Things have been getting a bit heated.'

'Yes, your friends here have explained all about that. It appears you've taken it on yourselves to interfere with his business.'

Sandy looked surprised.

'Well, that's one view I suppose.'

D.S. Crane continued. 'In fact, just yesterday afternoon we received a complaint from a prominent local businessman. We will investigate that in due course.'

Sandy bristled. 'Did you also happen to receive a complaint from one of the residents here who was nearly mowed dow....' He was stopped mid-flow by

Pete, who placed his hand on Sandy's arm.

'Perhaps not the time, Sandy,' he said.

Sandy shook his arm free and muttered, 'Tosser.'

D.S. Crane glared at Sandy. 'I think you would do well to heed your friend, Mr. Billings, before you say something you might regret.' She consulted her notepad, then flipped it shut. 'Well, you've both been very helpful,' she said with heavy sarcasm. She glared at each of the two friends in turn. 'Obviously nobody can add anything useful, so we'll leave it for today. But I'll be back tomorrow morning. We'll doubtless have more questions for you all. In the meantime, I request that nobody goes near the boat. Not only may it be dangerous, but it is a possible crime scene.'

With that she marched off towards her car parked near the shop followed by her mute colleague.

The four friends all looked towards Paul's ruined boat.

'Crime scene?' said Judy.

'Possible crime scene,' replied Pete. 'Probably just covering herself - standard fare.'

Sandy took Pete by the arm and walked him a few paces down the pontoon.

'You remember, Pete? The nurse at the hospital told us that Paul mumbled something about a parcel?'

'Yes, Sandy,' he said. 'I do.'

*　*　*

A mile and a half away Edward Hordley sat behind his desk in his first-floor office. Opposite him stood Neil Greenway.

'You heard about the accident down at the marina, Mr. Hordley?'

'I did indeed. Very unfortunate. Unsettling for everyone, I'm sure. Frankly I'm surprised there are not more such incidents, what with gas, fuel and all sorts of odds and ends on scrappy, ill-maintained boats. Death-traps if you ask me. Yes,' he mused, with a crooked grin, 'most unfortunate.'

Neil stared at his boss.

'They'll blame you, of course. Or me. You realize someone nearly died.

Might still.'

Edward's expression soured.

'Are you suggesting that I had something to do with it?' he said angrily. 'If you are, you'd better disavow yourself of that notion immediately. I will not have my name besmirched by you or anyone else. Do you understand?'

Neil nodded and looked over Edward's shoulder out of the window, wringing his flat cap nervously in his hands.

'Now, what did you want to see me about? And be quick - I'm busy.'

Neil looked uncomfortable. After a moment's hesitation he said, 'I've had a number of phone calls - from estate workers, and others. Don't ask me who because I won't reveal their names, but they are concerned that you're going too far in this dispute. People are talking behind your back. Behind mine too. They know damn well what we've been up to, and they don't like it. I had a note through my door yesterday afternoon asking me where my loyalties lie. You know that I've worked hard for you, never shirked from anything, fifteen years now. But when I get these calls and anonymous letters, I start to wonder if we haven't gone too far. I'm feeling very uncomfortable with it all.'

Edward glared at his estate manager.

'I don't give a flying fig what people think. Never have, never will. You shouldn't either. In fact, you,' he said, wagging his finger at Neil, 'had better decide pretty damn quickly where YOUR loyalties lie. I will not hesitate to terminate the employment, immediately, of anybody who shows disrespect to me. I pay the wages and I provide accommodation and security for many families. I'd go so far as to say that quite a few people round here have a pretty cushy time of it. If they want to leave, let them. See how they manage out in the real world. But what I refuse to accept, in any shape or form, at any time, is people questioning my decisions and actions behind my back. That goes for you too. First, YOU must make your mind up. Despite this insubordination, I will allow you to stay if you so choose. But, and listen very carefully, it will be on my terms and under my jurisdiction, nobody else's. Is that clear?'

Neil was silent. Edward breathed heavily and scowled. The clock on the mantelpiece ticked and ticked.

'Well, I've given you a straight choice. What is it to be? Are you staying or do I find myself a new manager? There are plenty who would jump at the chance.'

Neil sighed. 'I want to stay, really. I enjoy the work, you know I do. But, don't ask me to break the law. I just want to do my job. I don't want to get involved in any dirty work. My wife, just this morning, told me she has had enough. She wants us to leave. You have to understand that I see fellow workers daily and I hate the looks I'm getting. I'm ONE of these people; I grew up with most of them, but they see me as the enemy. I see people in town, in the shops, on the streets and they treat at me as if I'm a pariah. My wife, too, and her health is suffering.'

'Is that a yes or a no? Come on, I haven't got all day.'

By now Neil had wrung the life out of his tweed cap, but he was sensing an inner resolve. He realized he was at a crossroads, physically and metaphorically. Yes, he'd done Edward's bidding, on occasion sailing pretty close to the wind, but, as was the case with many estate workers, he needed the security of the house and salary. However, he knew that a hasty decision now could prove very costly for him and his family. Now was not the time to cut himself adrift.

'I'd like to stay. But please, no more unpleasant stuff. Just my work.'

Edward, too, was pondering. His groom had already jumped ship. No great loss there, but were his farm manager to go it would be potentially more troublesome. Others may follow, despite the financial stranglehold he had over them. Much as it went against his principles, he was going to have to show a little conciliation.

'Very well. You can start by speaking with the young girl groom. See if she's capable of stepping up and taking on more responsibility. Ask her if she's up to the job. If not, tell me and I'll advertise the position.'

'Charlotte, Mr. Hordley, she's called Charlotte,' said Neil, staring pointedly at Edward Hordley, 'Les James, her father, works on the estate. Has done for twelve years. A good man.'

'Yes, right then. Very well, see if Ms. James is up to the task. Now, off you go, I have work to do.'

As Neil walked across the courtyard towards the stables, he put his crumpled cap on his head and sighed.

18

Investigations

At eight-thirty the following morning, a crew arrived to re-float and salvage Paul's boat. Three police officers walked down the pontoon, one carrying flotation bags, another rolling a cylinder of helium on a small bogey and a diver in a dry-suit carrying oxygen, mask and fins. A fire appliance, an ambulance and two further police officers waited between the shop and covered dry dock, twenty-five metres away across a short stretch of water. Few chances, it appeared, were being taken after yesterday's explosions. Close to the emergency vehicles, a large mobile crane waited, engine growling. A knot of watchers had gathered along the shore. D.S. Crane arrived with her sidekick D.C. Williams and spoke quietly to the two uniformed officers.

Over the course of the next hour the flotation devices were placed in the boat by the diver and helium pumped in. Slowly the boat righted itself. Now stabilized, the craft was released from its mooring. A monkey's fist was thrown to shore attached to a thin line, which in turn was attached to a sturdier rope. The boat was pulled towards the shore and the waiting crane. Three fire officers hauled on the rope as the diver swam next to the boat across the short stretch of open water. Two yellow life-jackets and a green plastic storage box floated loose in the boat's wake and a film of fuel shimmered on the water like a kaleidoscope.

Once against the bank the diver slipped two thick straps under the boat, each end of which was attached to a thick chain dangling from the crane. With a change in engine pitch and a belch of black smoke, the crane slowly began to lift the shattered craft out into the shore. Water cascaded from the boat as it began to clear the water. The boat's water-line was clearly visible, white above, dark green below. Below the water-line water poured out though three skin fittings, where the plastic pipes inside had been melted away. The boat was guided onto railway sleepers and chocked from each side to secure it in an upright position. The chains and straps were unhooked, and the crane's arm slowly retracted. Ten minutes later the crane left the scene and all was quiet.

Two of the seven cabin windows had been blown out by the explosion; the remainder were soot-blackened. On the side of the boat, two dark grey streaks could be seen above the water-line where fire and smoke had burned through two further skin fittings and the inferno had burst through the holes. The stainless steel railing near the cabin's side door was bent and the cabin roof bulged out.

'Boy, is that a sad sight,' said Archie, as he stood with the other boaters gazing over the water at Paul's former home. Nobody else spoke.

A double-ladder with a short connecting platform was hauled next to the boat and the forensic fire scene investigator mounted the steps and peered into the boat. D.S. Crane walked down the pontoon towards the boaters.

'Look out,' said Sandy, 'the Gestapo's here again.' He then whispered to Pete, 'Should we mention the parcel?'

'Yes, I think we should. If she finds out and we've said nothing, there could be bother.'

'Good morning, ladies and gentlemen. Any further thoughts on yesterday's accident?'

Sandy glanced at Pete and raised his eyebrows. Pete gave a small nod.

'There is one thing I remember,' he said to the policewoman. 'As we spoke to the nurse at the hospital yesterday, she told us that Paul had mumbled something about a parcel. She said also that he was very groggy, in and out of consciousness and confused. But it may be something.'

'I see,' replied the officer. 'Did you not think to mention this last evening?'

'I forgot, I'm sorry. We were all upset. Not you, of course; we were upset, as you may imagine.'

'Mmm. So what's this parcel was he referring to? Any ideas? If indeed he was talking any sense.'

'I've no idea; it's just something he said to the nurse.'

'Mr. Crowther, anything to add?'

Pete thought for a moment.

'I do have one idea, but ... well, it's only that.' He looked at Sandy, who shrugged.

'Very well, let's have it then - however ludicrous.'

Pete gave her a sour look in response to her sarcasm.

'Well, we all receive the odd parcel from time to time, but we found out yesterday that Paul was diabetic. That means regular medication. That would include insulin and probably other things too. I was wondering whether this came by post. If not regular post, perhaps courier. If it did, it would mean regular packages.' He shrugged. 'I don't know - I'm only theorising.'

'Have you seen him carrying anything like that? Or couriers arriving? Presumably he has a postal address here?'

'We all use the marina as our postal address - and yes, of course, deliveries arrive regularly at the shop. Whether they were for Paul, I don't know. Betty is the person to ask. She manages the place but she's, uh, she's away for a few days.'

'Oh, away is she? Do you know where she is by any chance? How I may get in touch with her?'

'I have her phone number on my boat. I'll go and get it if you wish.'

'That would be helpful. Thank you.'

As Pete turned he said to Sandy, 'A word, Sandy please.' As they walked down the pontoon together, Pete whispered, 'Don't give her Betty's number yet. I want to speak to her first, tell her what's happened here and warn her to expect a call.'

Sandy nodded turned to back towards the policewoman.

'What was that all about, Mr. Billings?'

'Oh, nothing really. He was just reminding me of something we have to do in preparation for Saturday night.'

She stared hard at Sandy who tried to look innocent, then looked down at his feet.

'Come on, out with it. There's something you're not telling me.'

Sandy pursed his lips and shook his head.

'No, seriously, he asked me to remind him to call the caterers in relation to our event on Saturday. He's forgetful. You just have to look at him to see how scatter-brained he is.'

'I warn you. Do not interfere with my investigation or I'll come down on you like a tonne of bricks. Is that clear?'

'Absolutely, Officer Crane. I wouldn't dream of it.'

She continued to stare. Sandy tried to ignore her and watch the goings-on across the water. Finally, she looked away and sighed. She turned and approached the rest of the group, who were standing a little way off near Judy's boat. Colin and Cassy were holding hands, Archie was talking quietly to Roger, and Judy and Elaine stood silently holding cups of tea. There was a shout from across the water asking D.S. Crane if she could spare a moment. She waved and walked round to speak to the forensic fire scene investigator.

Pete returned a few minutes later. 'Where is she?'

'Round there,' said Judy, pointing across to Paul's boat.

'Did you get hold of Betty?' asked Sandy.

'Yes, gave her the heads-up. Between us I asked her not to mention the two guys who'd been keeping an eye on her down there. They had a visit from a couple of mates of mine and I want to keep them out of it. You all OK with that?' he asked, looking round the group.

They all nodded their agreement.

'They may have been a bit heavy-handed, and I don't want trouble for them.'

'Can I take it then that the goons are no longer keeping tabs on Betty?' asked Judy.

'Uh, yes. I think it's safe to say that.'

19

The Gaffer Erupts

That same evening at seven-thirty, the boaters gathered in The Dog. The atmosphere was sombre.

'OK, good evening everyone,' said Judy, tapping her glass on the table in an unusual show of business-like protocol. 'The past twenty-four hours have been harrowing and traumatic for all of us. Watching Paul's boat being hauled out brought back the horrors of yesterday and, if you're like me, you're a bit shaken up. Pete called the hospital this morning. For those who don't know, can you bring us up to date, Pete?'

'Yes, sure. I was told by the ward sister on I.T.U. that Paul is due to be transferred to the specialist burns unit in Birmingham later today. He is really pretty poorly and heavily sedated. His burns, particularly to his legs, are severe - third degree - and I'm told he faces many weeks of treatment, therapy and probable multi-surgeries. He may even lose his right leg.' He looked around the group, most of whom had their heads bowed. 'Frankly, it's horrific. I wish the news was better, but sadly it is what it is. If there is a glimmer of hope, it came through an exchange I had with the ward Sister.'

The group all looked up at Pete.

'During the night, the Sister had spoken to Paul. He was pretty dopey but asked if anybody else had been hurt. He also asked after his boat. When I called this morning, at about nine-thirty, she brought me up to speed with his condition. I then asked her to please pass on everyone's love and best wishes. Answering his questions, I was able to tell her that everybody else was fine. I told her that Colin and Cass had dragged him to safety, probably saving his life, but that his boat was destroyed.

'The nurse apparently relayed all this because she called me back again within half an hour at Paul's request. Apparently, he was pretty insistent that she ring me again. She said that Paul was very grateful for the support and glad nobody else was hurt. She also told me, and here she apologized as she believed that what he said was down to the drugs, that Paul had said, with a smile on his face - and I quote her words exactly - "Colin and Cassy, bloody do-gooders. It was a crap boat anyway."

Cass burst into tears and Colin put his arm round her shoulders. 'OK, love. It's OK.'

Sandy blew his nose and Terri worried a beer mat.

Pete smiled, then went on. 'I don't believe for one minute that what Paul said was drug-induced. I don't think you do either.' He looked around the gathering. 'That to me, sounds exactly like him - the humorous guy we all know. It tells me there is spirit in the lad. It tells me he is up for the fight, which in turn tells me we should do everything possible to help him. Of course, it's very early days, but all we can do at this point is pray that he gets through the next hours, days and weeks. When, and I stress when, we know he is on the mend, then we can start thinking of practicalities. This lad is a friend of mine and yours too, I'm sure. He lives with us, is part of us and I for one intend to honour that friendship.'

'Hear, hear,' said Archie. Everyone murmured their approval.

Judy spoke. 'Well said, Pete. I'm sure you echo all our thoughts. Join me in raising a glass to the lad.' She raised her spritzer. 'To Paul.'

'To Paul,' they all replied in unison.

There was a moment of contemplative silence.

'Roger, I think we'll forego the minutes this time, if that's OK with you. I'm sure you've produced something vaguely relevant, but perhaps now is not the occasion.'

Roger nodded his agreement.

'However,' said Judy, 'one thing I do believe is that Paul would want us to carry on. That includes our scrap with Hordley, and the gig. Is everyone OK with that?'

There were nods all round.

'Good. We owe it to ourselves and to Paul to do the very best we can. I don't know about you, but this has strengthened my resolve to do everything I can to put a dent in Hordley's bonnet. He tried, but failed, to stop our allotment re-build - just as he will ultimately fail to see us booted off the site, however much he throws at us. Let's be in no doubt what he's done, and it is down to him, all of it, however much he hides behind his minions. I remind you, he destroyed our hard work with his bloody cows, engaged a pair of innocents to dig up the lane and scared Betty half to death with a couple of hoodlums. In some ways, this is all pretty half-hearted stuff which we, through our collective efforts, have countered. We've come through smiling, until yesterday. But, for me at least, things have changed. If, and it's a big if, I grant you, Hordley had anything to do with Paul's accident, I will personally drive over to his mansion and tear him apart.' She slammed the table with the flat of her hand, startling everyone.

Mike, in the process of raising his glass to his mouth, flinched and spilled his lager over his crotch. 'Christ,' he said. Everyone else looked at their leader wide-eyed. Everyone was silent as Judy took in a gargantuan breath and inflated herself within her bright red kaftan. She sat upright, bosom to the fore, and stared off into the middle distance for what seemed like an age. Then she slowly breathed out through pursed lips. It took forever as she slowly deflated, finally coming to rest with her eyes focused on the table in front of her, hands meekly crossed in her lap.

They all stared.

She looked up slowly and smiled. 'Right, that's better. Bit of nervous tension, that's all.'

'Bloody hell,' said Roger. 'Whatever you do, never, ever consider changing sides. If you have any notions in that direction, I demand a minimum of three hours' notice so I can pack a few treasured belongings and leave the country.'

Everyone giggled and the storm broke.

'If you weren't fired up enough, Judy,' said Archie, 'I had a phone call from

John Greenway late last night. Hordley has been harassing one of the estate worker's wife. Propositioned her by all accounts, threatened her to keep quiet. John was mighty angry, I can tell you.'

'Jesus, is there no limit to this bastard's depravity?' asked Cass.

'You realize,' said Sandy, 'that he actually put in an official complaint to the police about US? We're interfering with HIS business apparently. Bloody cheek.'

'Deranged, that's what he is, deranged,' said Terri.

'Deranged he may be, Terri,' replied Judy, 'but, and I hope I'm not tempting providence here, I don't think he poses an imminent threat. If Paul's accident was down to him, I don't believe he would try anything else so soon. Let's have a go at him when we have time to do it properly. Right now, I suggest we focus on this gig of ours. If we're not careful we'll have a top band turning up to a half-baked shambles. Pete and Sandy confirmed that Len's happy with our suggestions in principle, but what about practical stuff that we can sort out? Sal, any luck with a marquee, for example?'

'Yep, Joy's helped us out there. Border Marquees, with whom she's worked a number of times, have stepped in. They're going to come and erect one on Thursday afternoon. And they'll provide some stand-alone loos. I've put them in touch with Eric, so he can coordinate where he wants everything. It's looking good. Eric's also setting up a temporary bar at the back of the marquee to keep the natives happy.'

'Midlands Today TV is coming along,' said Archie, 'and Shropshire radio. No doubt we'll get some press turning up too. Word's spread pretty quickly. Sal and I have sent out tickets to the sponsors. There are three main ones and I've sent them three tickets each with an extra couple to Joy's outfit. Also two each to the folk who helped with supplies for the allotments. That's a total of nineteen. I've done a list here.' He handed out a few sheets of paper. 'As you'll see, I've totted up rough numbers and I reckon that we,' indicating the group, 'need eleven now that Paul's absent. That includes Elaine, by the way – a group member by association with our leader.' He winked at Judy, who smiled back and nodded. 'So, that's thirty total. I've put another couple aside just in case. Diane Markham may need one, for example. Eric reckons we'll get a hundred in here, plus room for half a dozen press. That's providing Len and co. don't bring enough tackle to play Knebworth and fill the place.'

'Or Knobworth, as Paul called it,' said Roger, smiling.

'Yes, Knobworth.' Archie chuckled. 'Eric has spoken to his insurers, who've agreed to one hundred, plus staff and band. Anyhow, the upshot of all that is we have seventy spare spaces.'

'Just before we get to that,' said Pete, 'Len and his mates did request no TV or radio, at least recording the actual gig. They're OK with some sort of background piece, but not the gig itself. Something to do with broadcast rights or similar, I'm not sure.'

'I'll let them know,' said Archie.

'What about pub regulars?' asked Sandy.

'Mmm. It's a tricky one,' continued Archie. 'Where do we stop handing tickets out? My view is that the remainder should be first come first served.' He paused. 'We really need to keep things as simple as possible. If we start showing undue favouritism, we could have a riot on our hands. Well, not a riot - but you know what I mean. Plus, whoever we invite there's bound to be someone else who'll have their nose put out of joint.'

'I tend to agree,' said Judy. 'Without doubt there will be those who are disappointed, but I take the view that we are, in effect, having a private do to thank our supporters. Anyone else lucky enough to get in, well, good luck to them.'

'Are we charging to get into the pub?' asked Mike.

'Sure. At least I think so. Thirty quid I thought,' replied Archie. 'Bit of a bargain for a group like that to be honest. But that will put over two grand in the old war chest. It'll be free to get into the marquee. It has to be, really, as we won't be able to police it without setting up some kind of extra external perimeter, and that would be nigh impossible. Being free gratis will ease the pain of being out there. Plus they'll have the live feed and they're going to get an acoustic set, so hopefully won't have anything to grumble about. I thought Len or another group member could perhaps ask for voluntary donations to our cause.'

'Sounds good to me,' said Judy. 'What's anyone else think?'

Pete chimed in. 'We could also do an exclusive raffle out in the marquee for a tenner a ticket. Len's donating a guitar signed by the whole band. It's one that Len actually played when they toured Australia in the early nineties. I think he's going to play a song or two on it on Saturday. I'll ask him if he'll announce a raffle. He's also got plenty of bits of memorabilia for runners-up prizes.'

'Sounds brilliant. You're making it sound more appealing to be in the tent,' said Sal with a giggle. 'I'm not sure we should restrict the raffle to just the marquee though. Let's give everyone a chance. Those that want it anyway.'

'I tend to agree, but overall I love the raffle idea. What do you think?' Judy asked the group.

'Yeah, let's give everyone a go,' said Roger. 'Apart from anything else, it'll raise more cash. We have to make the most of this opportunity.'

'All happy with that?' asked Judy.

Nods all round.

'Good. The problem is, how do we stop too many people getting into the pub?'

'That's covered. Eric has a few old mates who will come along to act as doormen and ad hoc security around the place. They're experienced and won't take any messing. Polite yet firm, Eric says they are. The last thing he needs is any trouble. Not that we really expect any. But when alcohol and lively music are thrown into the mix you never know.'

'Hopefully most folk who come will be of a certain age,' said Mike, 'Rounded are hardly hip-hoppers who'll attract the youngsters. But I suppose you never know. Anyhow, sounds like Eric's got it covered.'

Pete continued, 'Len said that sometimes you can over-plan. Sometimes gigs like this are better with a bit of spontaneity. Of course, we need to organize some basics, which we've done, but he reckons that sometimes nights like this should just take their own course.'

'Right, that sounds great,' said Judy. 'Well done. Anything else? Do we need to meet again, you think, before the gig?'

'Eric was saying that he'd like help kitting out the marquee on Saturday morning,' said Pete. 'He could do with a few bodies to give him a lift setting up the bar, put some chairs around, that sort of thing. Len will already be here, I hope. In fact he should be here tomorrow, but the rest of the guys are coming Saturday lunchtime, so perhaps we can earn our free tickets and give a hand wherever it's needed.'

There were general mutterings of approval.

'Good,' said Judy. 'Anything else?'

It was clear from the head shakes that there was not.

'We'll probably need St. John's Ambulance or something similar, I would think,' said Terri.

'Good point,' said Pete, 'but I think Eric is on it. It's a condition of insurance, I think. I'll check with him.'

Judy held her hand up. 'OK, now listen up everybody. There's just one more thing.'

There was an expectant hush.

'Frankly, I am amazed - pleasantly amazed, but amazed nevertheless, that we, as a bunch of stagnant old dodderers, have achieved so much in such a short time in the face of a crisis. When the call to arms went up you hobbled en masse to man the barricades. It took you a while to climb the ramparts, but you got there. The grunting and groaning when you humped those railway sleepers into place sounded like a herd of arthritic pigs foraging on a frozen field. BUT, with the help of liniment, painkillers and not a little alcoholic fortification, you have battled through and prevailed. I'm proud of you. Proud to be part of you.'

There were various chortles and murmurings.

'BUT, and let's be frank here, you couldn't have done it without the right leadership. The more wayward of you needed the guidance of a determined, intelligent commander-in-chief. Someone to unify the rag-tag bevy of boating bird-brains and mould them into a fighting unit. Someone to stand firm when the stockade began to crumble. Some...'

'OK, OK, we get the picture!' interrupted Archie.

'There's really nothing like being humble and self-effacing,' said Roger. 'How gratifying to finally see your modesty rise to the surface. Like green algae on a foetid pond. And there we were thinking you timid and retiring.'

'I wish she was bloody retiring,' muttered Sandy. 'Give us all a break.'

Judy laughed.

'Thanks for those few kind words. Seriously guys, all of you, well done. Right, onward and upward. Oh, and by the way, I've lost three pounds. So there.'

'Did you take your purse out of your pocket?'

'On your bike, Archie. It helps when Elaine cooks - she's terrible. She tried a vegetarian dish last night and managed to make it look like a half-decayed compost heap. Really appealing that was, I can tell you. Right, I'm off back home for a salad. See you all later.'

20

That Singer Bloke

The following morning, just after nine, Judy was preparing breakfast for herself and Elaine - grapefruit, a glass of orange juice and a small bowl of cereal for herself, poached egg on toast for her friend, and tea for both. There was a knock on the side of her boat. She opened the double doors at the front and saw a stocky man standing on the pontoon. He was dressed in blue suit and shirt and tie, under a long, fawn-coloured rain-coat.

'Good morning. I am Detective Inspector Warner. May I have a moment of your time, please?'

'Yes, sure. Come aboard, I'm just doing breakfast. Coffee, tea?'

'Tea, thank you. Milk, no sugar.'

'Sit down. This is my friend Elaine who is staying over.'

As he sat next to Elaine on a cushioned bench-seat, he leaned his elbows on the small cabin table. He exchanged greetings with Elaine as Judy returned to the galley.

'What can I do for you, Inspector?'

'I'm now heading the investigation into Monday's fire and I have some areas of concern.'

Judy looked over at the inspector, who raised his eyes quizzically and inclined his head towards Elaine.

'It's perfectly alright, we have no secrets. Please speak freely.'

Judy passed over his cup of tea.

'Thank you.' He took a sip and paused. 'Very well. Have you any reason to believe that someone may wish to harm Mr. Longfield?'

Judy stared at the policeman.

'No. Why do you ask?'

'Nobody here at the marina, nor anyone you may know from his past, bears him a grudge?'

'Not here, I'm sure of that. He was well liked, a friend to all of us. There's no way anyone would hurt him deliberately.'

'He wasn't in any financial difficulty?'

'Not as far as I know.'

'How well do you know him?'

Judy pursed her lips. 'Reasonably well, I suppose. As well as anyone here I would think. I know he's a decent guy and, as I say, I'm convinced that he has no enemies here.'

'How long has he lived here? What do you know of his history?'

'Well, he's lived here about eight or nine years, I would say. He came here pretty much straight from university. Southampton, I believe. But as to former friends and family, I'm afraid I know very little.' She frowned. 'What's with these questions about Paul?'

'Do you not consider it strange that a man who has lived among you for nine years is such an enigma? Surely if someone lives so closely to you, you'd want to find out a bit about him.'

'No, not really. You find out about people by living with them. People choose to live on a boat for all sorts of reasons. Some of us are private and it's not my job to question other's reasons or motivations. Most of us want a quiet life, and as a result respect other's privacy. We're not snoopers. Prying into fellow residents is no way to exist in such an insular community. Having said that, I have no reason whatsoever to believe that Paul is anything but the friendly, pleasant soul he appears to be.'

'What about you Ms...?'

'Elaine, please!'

'OK, what about you, Elaine? Did you come into close contact with Mr. Longfield?'

'No, I only know him vaguely. We had occasional social contact and passed the time of day when we met. But know him well? No, not really. Not at all in fact. I come to visit my friend here, Judy. I'm not usually around for more than a day or two at a time. I've stayed longer this time because of the trouble the residents have been having.'

'Yes,' mused Inspector Warner, 'I've been hearing about that.'

'Inspector, can you tell us what this is all about?'

'Please bear with me. I need to question the other residents first. I hope all will become clearer in due course. Now, excuse me, I must get on. Can you tell me where to find the other residents?'

He took a drink of tea.

'They are all up and down this pontoon, except Pete - he lives down near the residents' car park at the far end of the marina. Pete Crowther. You'll know which boats are lived on - you'll see lights, or smoke coming from their chimneys. Apart from me there are five other liveaboard boats.'

'Yes, I saw smoky chimneys on the way in. I came to you first because I was told you are head of the residents' committee?'

'I suppose I am, yes - unofficially at least. We're all the same really. Perhaps I just shout loudest. I need to speak up due to my diminutive stature.'

The inspector smiled. 'Quite. Thank you for the tea.'

With that he left and headed off down the pontoon towards Colin and Cassy's boat.

An hour later the boaters had gathered together, at the inspector's request, on the quay near Paul's boat. The senior policeman had been joined by D.S. Crane.

Inspector Warner addressed the gathering.

'Thank you for your time and patience,' he began. 'It appears that the fire was no accident. There was indeed an initial explosion. The forensic fire investigation officer briefed me early this morning and told me there is evidence of explosive material in the boat's cabin. When the resulting fire took hold, it ignited a plastic can of fuel causing a secondary explosion. Mr. Longfield was fortunate to escape. If he hadn't managed to get out before the petrol ignited, we may well have been investigating a charge of manslaughter.'

The boaters, suddenly more alert, stared at the inspector.

'My colleague, D.S. Crane, visited the victim yesterday afternoon in hospital after his move to Birmingham. Mr. Longfield confirmed that a package, purportedly containing medication, caught fire. He wasn't holding it at the time; it was resting in his lap while he was speaking on the telephone. He was fortunate that he had a duvet across his legs; it may well have protected him from the very worst of the initial heat. Had he been holding the device, he may well have lost his hands. It appears to have been some sort of homemade incendiary device. By nature, they are designed to burn quickly and fiercely rather than actually explode. The forensic fire office found traces of pyrophoric material, including magnesium. He is in little doubt that this was a deliberate act and we are investigating it as such.'

The inspector would not normally make as many details public, but the reason was clear. D.S. Crane watched the boaters' faces intently, looking for any reaction to the news.

'Now,' continued the inspector, 'in light of this information, may I ask you all once again if any of you have any reason to suspect why Mr. Longfield may have been a target of this attack?'

There was a stunned silence from the boaters. To a person they looked nonplussed and shook their heads.

'Christ almighty,' muttered Archie. 'This is unbelievable.'

'Hordley,' said Sandy. 'That bastard Hordley is responsible. Mark my words.'

'Let's not jump to conclusions,' said the inspector. 'Digging up a road is one thing, sending a package with the deliberate intent of causing harm, death even, is something else altogether. There may be any number of reasons for this attack. Don't do anything foolish and try and take matters into your own hands. We, the police, will investigate this matter and we'll take a very dim view of anyone interfering with our investigation.'

He looked from one to another.

'Am I making myself quite clear?' The mild-mannered man suddenly looked more threatening.

There were mutterings and nods of assent from the boaters.

'Good. Now, D.S. Crane will leave her contact number for you. If you hear, or think, of anything that may help our enquiries, please get in touch immediately. Finally, I wish to warn you all to be vigilant. We have had one very unpleasant incident, and it's possible that somebody else may also be targeted. Please be careful and report anything suspicious to D.S. Crane. Henceforth she will be your point of contact and I have asked her to keep you appraised of developments, if appropriate. Good morning.'

'D.S. Crane, a moment please,' he said, taking her by the elbow. The two officers walked a short distance towards the shop's parking area. The inspector whispered to his junior who nodded, then briefly replied. Then he climbed into his car and drove out of the gate.

'Just one more thing,' said D.S Crane, walking back towards the group of boaters. She handed out business cards to the group. 'The boat and mooring on the pontoon over there are to be considered crime scenes. They are taped off. Please do not clamber over them or touch anything. In particularly do not try and board the boat, however much you want to play detective. We do not need your sticky fingers contaminating evidence. Am I clear?'

More nods.

'There will be a patrol officer by the boat and another posted at the gate, at least for the remainder of today. P.C. Barton is the one to speak to if you can't get hold of me on that number,' she continued, indicating the cards they were holding. 'She will know how to get a message to me.'

With that she strode off, her raincoat tails flapping in her wake. The mood was sombre as the boaters drifted away.

At two forty-five Len motored slowly into the marina. He'd phoned Pete who now stood on the resident's pontoon and waved him into an empty berth two boats down from Colin and Cassy. Proctor stood out front, his golden coat shining like a Mediterranean sunset.

'What the...?' asked Judy, who'd followed Pete to greet her hero. Fender Bender eased slowly between two boats and came to rest with its nose resting on the pontoon.

'That's Proctor, Len's travelling companion,' chuckled Pete. He tied Len's front line to a cleat. 'He's quite a sight, isn't he?'

'You're not kidding. He sure is a handsome beast.'

Pete walked down the finger pontoon and greeted his friend with a hug and handshake. 'Welcome!' he said.

'Thanks, mate. Good to be here at last. Hey, it's a sizeable place, isn't it?' he said, looking around.

'Couple of hundred boats maybe. Not many folk about yet though; a bit early in the season for casuals. You'll just have the permanent residents to cope with.'

'And that,' he said pointing down the pontoon with his chin, 'must be Judy, your erstwhile leader.'

'Sure is.' He waved and called out. 'Hey, Judy! Come and say hello.'

Judy looked resplendent in a purple kaftan with gold trim as she walked towards them.

'Wow, love the attire,' said Len. 'Hi, Judy, pleased to meet you.'

Judy beamed. 'Likewise. A real pleasure for sure. I'm a bit of a fan. Love the goat by the way.'

'Proctor? Yes, he's quite a character.'

'Bit of a fan?' said Pete with a grin. 'She nearly had a seizure when she knew you were coming.'

'OK then, a lot of a fan. It's not every day we get a rock god landing in our midst. We do get rocks though, like your friend Pete here. When you take the deity out of 'rock god' you're left with a knackered old fossil.'

Len laughed and Judy chuckled and nudged Pete's arm. 'Anyhow, I'm really glad you could come. And thanks for helping us out.'

'It's my pleasure. I'm really looking forward to it actually. It'll be nice to hole up for a few days. Any news on your friend?'

'No, not since I spoke to you earlier. Except that what I didn't get chance to tell you is that apparently it was no accident. Some sick bugger sent him an incendiary device of some sort. Went off in his lap; that's why his legs took the brunt of it. Horrible.' He shook his head and grimaced. 'Look there, behind you - that's his boat.' Len turned.

'Jesus, what a mess. Boy, that must have been some fire.'

'He was really, really lucky to get out at all,' said Judy. 'We've had the police here most of the morning. It's put a serious damper on things, I can tell you. But we've agreed, between us all, that we're going to try and carry on as normal. No disrespect, I'm sure you realize, but, awful as it is, we can't let whoever's done this mess it up for everyone. Paul wouldn't want that.'

'I'm sure he knows that you don't think any less of him.'

'Yes, in effect that's what we think. The upshot is the gig is green for go. And our scrap with our farmer friend goes on.'

'You'll need a crash helmet,' said Pete. 'She's been out and bought some new underwear to chuck at you. No laughing matter that, I can tell you.'

'As if you would know!'

They all giggled.

'Why don't you get organised, Len, and come down to my boat for a brew? Down there near the main car park,' said Pete, pointing.

'OK, that's good. Give me half an hour. The lad needs to stretch his legs anyway. Is it OK to bring him down?'

'Sure, he can meet Scamp. Might be easier if you walk him down the lane rather than down the rickety pontoons. Far side of that hedge over there. It's private, no cars and quite safe. Just go out the gate and follow it down to the car park. I'll look out for you.'

'OK, fine. See you, Judy. Nice to meet you.'

As she and Pete walked back along the pontoon he said, 'I'm going to give the hospital a call before Len comes down. Later, if he's up for it, why don't we meet down the pub, about six say? Pass the word round - he'd like to meet everyone.'

'Sure. See you later.'

The marina usually breathed a sigh around mid-afternoon. Morning chores done, dogs walked and lunch over, the residents often took to their boats to chill out. Roger would write for a couple of hours, working diligently on his latest tome. Sal, if she wasn't at her Tuesday Pilates class in Ellesmere market hall, would read. Today, Wednesday, she continued to work through her P.D. James collection, alternately reading and snoozing on the bed. Judy would often have a nap; though not today as she'd just been to greet Len, and was still buzzing. Elaine, if she was staying over, would watch the previous day's soaps on catch-up TV - things she was dissuaded from watching in the evening due to Judy's hatred of the things. "Awful damn stuff," according to Judy, "and an utter waste of air-time." She would rather chat or play her guitar, with a glass of something – or the occasional spliff if the mood took her, partaken purely for 'musical awareness.' Today, Elaine was prevented from watching television because of Judy's stream of excitement.

Mike, if Terri hadn't found some task for him, would tinker in his engine room. Despite his ministrations, the engine smoked as fervently as ever - but he kept trying. Terri would knuckle down to her cross-stitch. Their cabin walls were bedecked with small, colourful canal scenes. Mike reckoned it made the boat look like a second-hand craft shop, but wisely refrained from saying so.

Sandy often used the post-lunch period to do research. Currently he was looking into the construction of a Dutch Barn with the expectation that the knowledge would be invaluable (should funds ever be in place) to build the replica narrowboat down in the field. Via the internet, he'd just discovered that there is a Wooden Canal Boat Society, and sent them an email to ask for guidance on their potential project. He also used the afternoon hours to disperse invaluable advice on the boating forums he frequented and seemed to take delight in blinding unknown and unseen victims with science.

Archie was having his usual mid-afternoon siesta when his phone rang. Unhappy at being disturbed, he answered tersely. 'Yes?'

'Archie, it's John. John Greenway.'

'Oh hello, John. Sorry, just having a doze. What can I do for you?'

'Sorry to wake you but, well, just a bit of local info. There's a whisper going round that Hordley's wife has done a runner. Left first thing this morning by all accounts. Packed a couple of cases into her Volvo and left about six. She was spotted creeping around the yard by one of the dairy workers who texted me.'

'Right! Well, thanks for letting me know. I'm not sure how it really helps us, but thanks anyway.'

'Well, she'd be a good person to get on side. If we could find out the reason she left it might give us a bit of ammunition.'

'Yes, I see your point. Mind you, there could be any number of reasons judging by the whispers we've been hearing recently.' He paused. 'Nobody knows where she's gone, I suppose? Does she have family? Siblings?'

'Don't know. No one saw much of her, to be honest. I only spoke to her a couple of times in all my time working there, and that was just good morning or whatever. But something's got to her for sure. I'll put some feelers out, see if anyone knows anything.'

'Right, thanks John. Let me know if you come up with something.'

'I'd better get going. I've a gate to re-hang before a viewing near Ellesmere tomorrow, and I'll lose the light if I'm not careful.'

'OK, bye for now. Speak soon.'

Edward Hordley parked his black Range Rover on the gravel drive and climbed the four stone steps up to the front entrance. He slammed the ancient oak door behind him, crossed the tiled hallway and mounted the wide staircase to his first-floor office. He was alternately seething and bemused. News of his wife's departure had spread. His daily inspection of the estate had been a muted, embarrassing experience. Workers, normally keen to talk, avoided eye contact and offered nothing unless directly spoken to. He imagined them sneering behind his back. He was not accustomed to anything except complete control, and it made him feel very uncomfortable and angry.

He sat behind his desk. It was late afternoon and the sun was beginning to set behind him. It was a cool evening and wisps of mist rose from the vast acreage; beauty unnoticed because mocking him on the desk in front of him was Alison's note. He'd discovered it on his dressing room table just after eight that morning, left while he slept. It had shaken him to his roots. It was brief and explained nothing, just bare facts.

"Edward. I am leaving you. I have had enough, it's over. Please leave me alone. A."

He had marched into her suite to find her bed unmade, her dressing table empty and the bedside lamp switched on. A numb reality settled in. Shock, then anger. Anger was his go-to emotion, where he inwardly returned when he needed control, to exert authority. It was the pulpit from which he could flay and preach to his minions. He had dressed and rushed downstairs, through the kitchen and out into the courtyard. It wasn't a dream; her car was gone. There was an eerie silence about the place as if the house held its breath. He stood on the cobbles, staring into the empty garage, double doors swung back, latched open. He turned and stared through the gate and down the rear driveway, silent and empty. Bordered by post and rail fencing, the private gravel road ran for three hundred yards before joining the public highway - left north, right south. 'You bitch,' he'd cursed under his breath. 'You selfish, bloody bitch!' His breath had leached away into the misty air of the cool morning. There had been no feelings of love or sorrow, just revenge and damage limitation. A horse whinnied across the yard shook him out of his reverie. His day had begun anew.

The fire to his left was burning low, so he threw on another couple of logs. Sparks danced up the chimney and he returned to his desk. He read the note again and swore under his breath. He balled the single sheet of paper and threw it into the fire. He sat for nearly an hour as the sun set behind him, deep in thought. He spun his chair and looked out of the window as darkness cloaked the estate. Individual lights emerged out of the gloom as cottagers returned home and began to settle in for the evening. Families. He turned on his desk lamp and rose to draw the curtains. There was a knock on the door.

'Yes?'

The door opened and Neil Grant peered in, cap in hand.

'Yes, Neil. What can I do for you?'

'Just checking in, Mr. Hordley, before I knock off.'

'Yes, of course. Come in. Anything urgent? I'm rather busy.'

'Not really, no. Nothing that can't keep till the morning.'

'Right, good night then.'

Neil stood and fidgeted and screwed up his cap.

'Well?'

'It's just that, uh, rumours have been going round about your wife, Mr. Hordley. It's none of my business, of course, but people are whispering, talking behind your back.' His cap was now a mangled wreck. 'Well, what I mean is, is there anything you want me to tell people?'

Edward stood abruptly and Neil flinched.

'You're right. It is nobody else's business except mine,' he growled. Then after a pause, he said, 'To lay to rest any rumours, any unfounded rumours, you can tell them, Neil, that my wife is taking a holiday. She will return in due course. You can also tell them that I abhor insubordination and will not stand for it. Anyone speaking out of turn, behind my back, will suffer the consequences.'

Neil looked down at the carpet.

'Is that clear?'

'Yes, Mr. Hordley. Perfectly clear.'

'Good. Then if there is nothing else, I have things to do. I'll see you tomorrow.'

Neil looked his boss in the eye momentarily. 'Very well then. Good evening, Mr. Hordley.'

Neil turned and left.

Edward sat down heavily and thumped the desk. He reached for the phone and dialled.

'It's me,' he said. 'You've heard?' A pause. 'Find the bitch.' He slammed the phone down.

Archie, Sal and Roger had just arrived at The Dog and settled themselves on stools at the bar when Archie felt a tap on his back.

'Hello, guys.'

Archie turned.

'Hi, John. You OK? You look a bit worried.'

'No, I'm fine. Just a bit worn out. Busy day.'

'Have a pint - that'll help.'

'Thanks! I'll have a Guinness, please.'

'This a social visit? asked Roger.

'No, actually. Well, partly. I've got some news. I had an anonymous call from a woman about an hour ago. She told me that Hordley's wife has a brother living in Holland. She says the two have been in regular contact by phone and email.'

'Really. Well, I never. But we don't know she's actually heading there, do we?' said Sal.

'Actually, we do. The lady saw an exchange of emails between Alison and her brother. He's called Simon, by the way; works for a window company in a place called Zwolle. Anyhow, turns out that she'd told her brother that she'd booked a ferry and was heading over. She'll be arriving early to mid-morning tomorrow.'

'Looks like your local network is working,' said Roger.

'It does, doesn't it? But someone's put a lot on the line to tell us this. God knows what'll happen if Edward finds out he's been ratted on.'

'There's no reason for him to find out, is there? You won't tell him, will you? And we certainly won't. It must be someone close, though, with access to Alison's computer.'

'Has to be one of the housekeepers, surely?'

'Or a cleaner? Or her hairdresser?'

'Yes. Well, whoever it is has done us a big favour. And quite the opposite to Edward.'

'Do we know where this brother lives?'

'A place called Staphorst, about 12 miles north of Zwolle. I looked on the internet; it's a small place, little more than a village, pretty rural. I don't have an actual address, though.'

'You don't know Alison's phone number, by any chance?'

'Yes, the woman gave it to me. I've got it here.' He took out his wallet and fished out a piece of paper. 'Here.'

'Right,' said Archie, 'let's...' But he was interrupted, as Pete and a man they'd never seen before came up behind them. They swiveled on their stools.

'Hey, guys! Meet Len.'

Archie jumped off his stool with hand outstretched. 'Hi Len, I'm Archie.'

'Archie, good to meet you. And you must be Roger?'

'Yep, that's me. Welcome to our second home, Len. Pleased to meet you.'

'You too.' He looked round. 'Nice place - I approve. A proper pub.' He delved into his pocket. 'Right, my round, what are you all having?'

'No chance,' said Roger. 'You're the guest here. I'll get these.' Then, after a pause, he added, 'You can get the rest!'

'Sounds like a good deal,' said Len, chuckling. He looked at the line of pumps. 'I'll have a Black Sheep, thanks.'

Eric had sidled up.

'Eric, meet Len. He'll be the one blowing your roof off on Saturday.'

They shook hands. 'Good luck to you mucking in with this lot. A right bunch of old rogues. Black Sheep coming up.'

'And who's this?' asked Len.

John held out his hand. 'Hello.'

'So, you're one of this rabble are you?'

John looked sheepish.

'Actually no, I'm not a boater. I was the enemy till I jumped ship. I'm John. You'll be the singer bloke I've been hearing about?'

'Yep, that's me, the singer bloke.' Len laughed. 'So, tell me John, what kind of bloke are you?'

Pete said, 'He's the bloke who worked for the estate, but we got him fired.'

'Oh, how considerate of you,' said Len.

Pete smiled. 'Blessing in disguise in the end, eh John?'

'Yes, it was really. Man's an arse.'

'Let's get this straight,' boomed Judy, who had crept up behind. 'We rescued him, in a roundabout sort of way. Spritzer please, Eric, when you have a minute. Large one if Roger's getting them. Not a normal rescue, I grant you; more a subtle plan to extract one of the chickens from the hen house before he was smeared by that bloody fox up there.'

'And he's started laying eggs. Listen to this,' said Archie. He explained about Alison's plans.

'Good lad, John. Well done,' said Judy.

'Hang on a mo,' said Pete, 'Len doesn't want to hear about our woes. Let's just relax and have a drink.'

'No, it's OK. I'm interested, really. In fact, if I can poke my oar in, I'm guessing the reason she'll get to central Holland by mid-morning is that she's travelling on the Hull Europort ferry. It leaves Hull about eight in the evening and gets into Europort at six or seven in the morning. It's a good couple of hours drive from Rotterdam to Zwolle. I've done that trip a few times, as I have some friends up that way.'

'There,' said Judy to Pete. 'Told you your mate wasn't just a stuffed shirt. I knew he'd come in useful.'

Everyone laughed.

'Mine of useless information, that's me.'

'Well, what do we do with it?' asked Sal.

'Act on it. Act on it in a decisive, devastating manner,' said Judy.

'How?' asked Sal again.

'No idea,' said Judy. 'But you were right in what you said earlier, Archie. If there's anything untoward concerning Edward, his wife will be the one to know. And let's face it, there must be a reason she's upped and gone now.'

The door swung open and Sandy walked in, followed by Terri and Mike.

Len looked over and waved. 'Sandy, my old chap! Come and join us.'

Sandy bloomed with embarrassment and pride that Len had singled him out. In fact, by the time he'd approached and shaken Len by the hand, he looked close to tears. 'Hi, Len. Good to see you again. This is Terri and Mike, a couple of fellow boaters.' Introductions were made and hellos exchanged.

'Now, no arguments, I'm getting a round in. Roger, you're in prime spot - could you shout them up for me?'

'OK, we're on TV in five minutes. Eric,' Judy called, 'can you turn it up?'

A wide-screen TV in the corner to the left of the fire sprang to life. A game show of some kind was reaching its denouement; blue flashing lights and silly noises signalled that someone was about to win a major cash prize – possibly.

Judy boomed out, 'Right, Vegetable Operatives and honoured guests, settle down.'

They all took chairs in a loose arc before the TV as Gardeners' Choice's familiar theme tune filled the pub.

Diane and Simon stood shoulder to shoulder and introduced the show. Then over a panoramic shot of the marina and ruined allotment, they explained why they were in Shropshire and explained the boater's struggle.

Simon echoed Dian's comments in the programme trailer about open space being lost to development. He said that they'd finished the programme in double-quick time because of the urgency of the boaters' situation; they all thought this was a cause worth going the extra mile for.

The show moved on to show the re-building of the allotments and interviews with the residents, who were shown huffing and puffing during unfamiliar exertions. Catcalls aplenty came from the audience in the pub. Other customers had gathered to watch, too, and everyone was in high spirits. Brief interviews with Pete, Cassie and Roger were greeted with more catcalls, before Diane concluded, 'Gardeners' Choice didn't hesitate to come and help restore order in this delightful corner of the country. It was an unusual assignment for us, but immensely pleasurable. We've made friends here, given them their treasured allotments back and laid the foundations for local youngsters to learn about and enjoy the outdoors.'

Simon Goode took over. 'I have with me Judy, one of the boaters involved in the fight.' The camera focused on Judy. She wore a red and yellow outfit, and was beaming. There were a couple of whistles from the pub and everyone laughed.

'Judy,' said Simon, 'how do you feel about the support you've received?'

'Well, to be honest we're quite overwhelmed. One of our number is an old university friend of Diane's. She responded to our plea without hesitation, and your whole team have been magnificent. You've worked so hard for us and everyone here, including the teachers and pupils from local colleges and schools, wish to say a huge thank you to all. We were pretty low when, just a few days ago the whole place looked like a battlefield, but you've done a terrific job. You've made a lot of people very happy and proved that our cause is just. On behalf of everyone, may I also say thank you to local suppliers who have been so generous.' She broke off and looked around. 'Look at it - it's unrecognizable! How you coordinated everything in such a short space of time is beyond me, but it's a wonderful result - so thank you.' She waved at Diane and blew her a kiss.

Pete patted Judy on the shoulder. 'You're a natural. What a decision it was to elect yourself leader. Well done, lass.' She reached back and patted his hand as she chuckled.

So, what turned out to be a pretty long evening left the station. Len enthralled them with stories of life with the band, because he was asked to do so. He told the tale of when they'd played in Madison Square Garden. It was just as they'd hit the big time and their first trip to the States. He'd flown his mum over first class to come and watch the show and put her up in the Ritz Carlton. They'd played for over two hours to twenty thousand wild fans and performed two encores.

'My mum was watching from the wings,' he concluded. 'I thought she'd be safer there than being among the throng down below. I'm not sure what I expected when we came off. Praise of some sort, I guess. Something like, "Well son, I never thought I'd live to see the day when you were the star of the show in New York." Instead, the first thing she said was, "Go and change that sweaty old shirt this minute. You look revolting!" She never let me get too big for my boots, that's for sure.'

But Len also proved to be self-effacing and a good listener, asking questions of the boaters and listening to their stories. John's verdict was shared by everyone – 'Decent bloke.'

21

Unravelling

Edward Hordley had slept badly. He'd watched the television programme. Although he wasn't mentioned by name, the inference was obvious. He was the villain. He was used to getting his own way, but he could see no way through this situation. How could a rag-tag band of scruffs get the better of him? He swore out loud. Now they had this damn concert getting them publicity too. He had the feeling of being driven into a corner. And he didn't like that. He needed to take his ire out on somebody, or something.

He had been pacing round his vast house since before six. Reminders of his treacherous wife were everywhere. Every vase or bowl, each photograph, wound him tighter and tighter. She had become the focus of his angst. At eight forty-five he made a phone call.

'Well, have you found her?'

'No. But we have found her car. It's parked at Knutsford service station on the M6. No sign of her, no sign of any luggage. Looks very much like she was either meeting someone or swapped vehicles.'

'Where the hell is she, then?'

'The short answer is, I don't know. I checked the airports and there was an A. Hordley booked on the Vienna flight from Manchester at seven-thirty yesterday evening. I sent someone along, but no one of that name showed up. I've also got people checking the ferry ports. We don't have a car registration to go off, but we're checking names. Nothing so far. I've got to be honest, I think she's planned this pretty carefully. We're getting to the point where we'll be lucky to catch up with her. It may help if you could tell me her maiden name. Women do use them, sometimes have bank accounts or other things in their former name.'

'It's Simms, double 'M'. So, you're telling me she's just vanished? You've no clue where she is now or where she might be going?'

'Frankly, she could be anywhere; with a friend, in a hotel, a B&B. She could have driven or been driven. She could have taken the train or bus anywhere in the UK. At this point, I've no idea where she is. But we'll keep looking.'

'Well, get a bloody idea, and quickly. I pay you enough, for goodness' sake.'

With that he slammed the phone down. Thursday was one of the two mornings his secretary came in. Jane Featherstone had been with the family for over twenty years. Fifty-four years old, she was a little over five feet tall. She wore steel-rimmed spectacles, had light grey hair and was very efficient. She buzzed Edward on the phone.

'Mr. Hordley, I have Simon Mossley on the line for you.'

'Right, Jane. Put him through.'

After a moment. 'Simon. You have good news for me, I trust.'

'Good morning, Edward. I'm sorry to report there has been a minor delay. The planners have received a number of objections to our proposals which will have to be resolved before they return to committee for approval. This should take between two and three weeks but, ultimately, I'll be frank, it could cause a real problem.'

'Two or three weeks is not acceptable. We should have had the go-ahead at yesterday's meeting - that's what you told me. I have contractors lined up ready to start. Any delay will cost me a small fortune. What sort of bloody objections anyway? Presumably they came from...no, don't tell me...'

'Times have changed, Edward. Things are not as they were. People have far more access to information these days; they're more savvy. For example, a quick search on the internet can root you out reams of information regarding the viability or otherwise of a proposed development. There are companies and individual consultants who can advise on every aspect of an application.

They can make things pretty difficult. To be perfectly honest, some of the objections regarding our development have gravitas. Historically, local planning issues stayed local and frankly, as we have done in the past, it was possible to influence planners. We have to be far more careful because these days transparency is a major issue. Decisions are open to the closest scrutiny.'

'What objections are we talking about?'

'Well, the primary one focuses on the fact that the proposal is within the green belt or open countryside, where development is usually discouraged. Although tricky, that in isolation is not insurmountable, but tied with other objections it may cause more serious problems. You may be aware that nowadays council authorities have a Local Plan. This used to be called the Local Development Framework. In effect, it sets out each area's planning policies and decides what will be developed, and where. It affects both commercial and residential development. Nothing has been designated in the area we have chosen for our development. Then we add in effect on the character of a neighbourhood, possible loss of privacy, disturbance and the impact of any new development on the landscape. Someone has done their research, Edward. There's no doubt they have raised genuine concerns and we may have real problems with our application.'

'Have you spoken directly to the planning department?' asked Edward, with obvious frustration.

'They're not returning my calls. I've tried to contact Geoff Mason a number of times.'

'I know Mason. I'll ring him myself.'

'Before you do, there's something else you should be aware of. I received a letter. It was addressed to me personally but anonymous. It was hand-delivered to my office but arrived among our regular mail. There's no way to trace its origin and my name alone was written on the envelope. The note stated, and I quote, "Your client, Mr. Edward Hordley, is engaged in nefarious activities in relation to projects with which he is involved. We strongly advise that your continued association with this man may be damaging to both your business and personal well-being."'

There was silence for a moment.

'That, Simon, is libellous,' fumed Edward. 'And, as such, a police matter. Those allegations are wholly unfounded. They are of a criminal nature and written with the scurrilous intention of besmirching me and damaging my reputation. In addition, it poses a threat your livelihood. With that in mind, I advise you to take the strongest possible action. I want you to contact the police and demand that they find the perpetrator of this outrage.'

Simon Mossley was silent.

'Well,' raged Edward, 'are you going to do something about it? Let me be clear – if you won't, I will.'

'I feel very uncomfortable about this, Edward. I hear you and understand your frustration, but I have a wife and young family. To be truthful, I am concerned. My family must come first. With that in mind I have already decided not to take the matter further. You have the protection of wealth and influence. I do not.'

'You're spineless, man! For God's sake fight. Don't let some anonymous coward get the better of you. Your father would turn in his grave if he could hear your whimpering. Now stand up for what is yours and do something.'

'I'm sorry, Edward. My mind is made up.'

'Right, if that's the way you want it, I'll show you how to treat this slanderous insult. Bring me the letter and I'll take it to the authorities myself.'

'I'm afraid that won't be possible. I destroyed it.'

'You did what?! You idiot! I have never encountered such a feeble toad. I need people in my corner who are winners. I need people who have the courage and determination to get a job done. You have let me down and shamed your father's memory.'

There was an ominous silence broken only by Edward's heavy breathing.

Then, he added maliciously, 'Our association is at an end. You're fired.' And for the second time in twenty minutes, he slammed the phone down.

22

Sneaky Sandy

It was ten-thirty and Sandy wandered down the far end of the marina. He knocked on the side of Pete's boat. The double doors swung outwards with a squeak.

'Hello, Sandy. Come in. You want a cuppa?'

'I'll have a coffee, thanks. Decaf if you have it.'

'Decaf? What's that?' he said with a smile.

'Fine, regular then.'

'This a social call? What can I do for you?'

'Actually, I've just come to tell you I'm off to Holland. Booked on this evening's ferry from Hull.'

'You what?'

'Yes, I'm going to find Alison to try and get her to help us.'

'You've no idea where she is. You can't just pitch up in...where was it...Staphorn, and hope to bump into her in the butchers or the bakers.'

'Staphorst, it's called. I've been looking it up. It's only a small place. There can't be many English men living there who work for a window company. I'll ask around.' He continued defiantly. 'I'm going to find her.'

'It's a heck of a long way to go on a whim. Here's your coffee.'

'Thanks.' He took a sip. 'It's not a whim. I need to do something. The more I think about what's going on, especially Paul, the angrier I get and the more I want to do something constructive. I can't just sit around.'

'Well, I understand how you feel, we all do - and I admire your determination, but there's plenty you can do here. And you'll miss Saturday's shindig.'

'I won't actually. It's like Len said, I've checked. The ferry leaves at eight, gets in tomorrow at seven and there's a two-and-a-half-hour drive to Staphorst. Len says it's an easy drive, motorway almost all the way. I'll get the ferry back at eight tomorrow night and be back here around lunchtime Saturday. I'll have a good six hours in Staphorst to find them. Sounds a bit loopy, I know, but I've made my mind up. I'm going.'

'Well, it sounds like you won't be deterred. What can I say except good for you. Good luck.'

Sandy took a sip of his coffee and looked out of the window. Still gazing off into the middle distance he said innocently, 'Actually, I er ... I was wondering if you wanted to come along? I could do with the company and two sets of eyes and ears are better than one.'

Pete stared at his friend and gently shook his head.

'I can't just up and leave. What about all the arrangements here? There's loads to be done. Then there's Len to consider; I invited him after all. I can't just tickle off for a couple of days - that's not on.'

'I've spoken to him. He thinks it's a great idea.'

'What?'

'He's all for it. Says it's time you had a change of scene. And I've spoken to Judy, and she says they'll manage fine without you. In fact, she said she's quite happy to have you in another country for a couple of days.'

'Well, that sounds about right,' he said, laughing.

'Besides,' continued Sandy, 'most things are in place. And we'll be back in time to help on Saturday anyway.'

'What about Scamp?'

'Roger says he'll have him. No problem.'

'I don't know, Sandy. It's all a bit, well, last minute.'

'I want to do something, and I would like your help. And your company - it's a long trip.'

Pete raised his eyebrows in bemusement and shook his head.

'You've got it all covered, haven't you?'

'Yep.'

'OK then. I must be potty but, OK, I'll come along.'

'Great. Because I've already bought your ticket. I won't have to have change the name.' He smiled. 'We'll leave here at one.'

Pete laughed. 'You bugger.'

'Thanks for the brew,' he said jauntily.

With that he left and walked back down the pontoon, whistling.

On Thursday, at just after one, Sandy and Pete walked down to the car park in the company of Archie and Sal.

'Give us a call if there's anything we can do at this end,' said Archie.

'You could have another try at finding Alison's brother's surname and the address where he works. I looked on the internet but couldn't find anything. My Dutch is a bit scratchy, to say the least.'

'Yes, we'll have a go. I'll see if I can root out that window company. Drive safely and see you Saturday.'

Sandy fired up the car and they pulled out of the gate to start their four-hour trip to Hull. Judy watched as Sandy's car passed the main marina gate and she silently wished the pair well. As she looked on, three students cycled down the lane towards the allotments; two girls chatting away, followed by a young lad. It appeared to be the quiet boy to whom Archie had spoken during the works. She decided to walk down and see how they were all getting on.

Donning a pair of Wellington boots she set off down the pontoon. Near the residents' car park she passed close to Pete's boat. She knew him, of course, but not well. She wondered what made him tick. She was curious why an obviously intelligent, resourceful man had ended up looking like a vagrant, living on a messy old boat in the middle of nowhere. Since Paul's incident she'd thought quite a bit about everyone with whom she shared the marina; she was a bit nonplussed that she knew so little about any of them. She knew a little of course. Archie and Sal had run a pub. Mike had been a salesman, but of Terri she knew almost nothing. Sandy was a complicated puzzle, but she knew little more than he was gay and a techno-whizz. She knew something of Colin and Cassy's history, but nothing in depth. She didn't like to pry into anyone's business but their scant knowledge about Paul, when asked by the medical staff, had unnerved her. Maybe some things were better left unknown.

But it was Pete who piqued her curiosity most. Being honest with herself, she had a bit of a soft spot for him and he intrigued her. He was obviously a decent man. She found herself wondering what he thought of her. She had a wistful feeling walking past his boat, knowing he wasn't there. She even felt the compunction to go and tidy his boat up; get rid of the rotting wood on top and give it a clean. But he wouldn't want that. She doubted he'd want to be tamed. He'd probably refer to it as grooming! Smiling at the thought of her scruffy friend, she walked across the car park and through the gate into the allotments.

Roger was there, digging away at his patch away off to the right. She called and waved. He waved back before returning to work. The students had donned boots and were sorting some plants or vegetables ready for planting. The door to their new shed was open. A gift from Joy, it was about twelve feet square and had plenty of room for the storage of mucky clothes, boots and tools. She joined them.

'Hi guys,' she boomed.

'Hi,' said the girls in unison.

'How are you getting on then?'

'Great, thanks! Just getting some veggies in. Potatoes today,' said a blonde girl. 'We're trying four different varieties. We'll treat one batch with different fertilizers, the other with this organic stuff here,' she explained, indicating a small pile of manure. 'We're trying to find the ones that do best without chemicals.'

'Good for you,' said Judy.

'Jen and I want to work together when we qualify and get into organic crops,' said the second girl. A dark-haired lass with piercing blue eyes and dark, defined eyebrows. She reminded Judy of Brooke Shields from the film Blue Lagoon.

The blonde girl talked about yields, growth rate, density and such like. Unwilling to admit she was being blinded by science, Judy nodded and muttered her approval.

'Lovely,' was all she could come up with. 'Good luck.'

The two girls returned to work and Judy turned her attention to the lad who was coming out of the shed with a spade and fork.

'Hi,' she said.

He smiled shyly and nodded a greeting before clambering up onto one of the raised beds.

'If I remember right you live over in Wales?'

'Aye, that's right.'

'With your Mum and Dad.'

'Aye,' he replied again.

She watched him turn over some soil with the fork for a few moments.

'I gather you want to take over your parents farm at some stage.'

'Aye, suppose so,' he said. 'They're strugglin' a bit. Need a lift wi' it. 'E's arthritic and Ma's not really up to the heavy stuff.' He stopped for a moment and looked off into the distance. 'It's 'ard for 'em.'

'You help them out at weekends, I believe?'

'Aye, but it's not enough. Things are getting behind.'

'It must be very difficult.'

'Aye, 'tis really. I've two years at college yet. Don't know what's goin' to 'appen to be honest.'

Judy watched as he returned to work.

'What if I could find you some help?' asked Judy.

He carried on digging. 'What do you mean?'

'Well, perhaps I can find you someone to lend a hand a couple of days a week.'

He stopped and looked warily at Judy.

'Can't afford it,' he said finally. 'They've no spare cash. Besides,' he continued, 'Da wouldn't like it. Don't trust strangers.'

Judy smiled. 'Yes, I can understand that.'

The lad cocked his head as if deciding whether to say something.

'There's a local bloke,' he said eventually, 'wants to buy Da out. But he's not for sellin'. Reckons it's the only thing we have. He's worked 'ard for it and won't let go. Don't blame him neither. It's 'ard mind, watchin' him struggle. Not much money in small farmin' nowadays.'

'I see.'

The lad returned to work.

'Well, best of luck to you.' said Judy as she turned to leave. 'I'll see you again soon, I hope.'

'Aye. See ya.'

As she walked back towards her boat she pondered. Strange how people from so many different backgrounds are thrown together. Through a set of freak circumstances there was now some young blood around the place, at least intermittently. She wished for a moment that she was young again. She could have made more of herself, perhaps. Definitely not married that dick-head, that's for certain. It had all started off in a pleasure blitz, but once the bonking and boozing became a habit it had started to wither. He'd taken her for a small fortune in a failed second-hand car dealership. She'd offered him most of her savings to get him up and running. It had been her inheritance from her Mum, and it rankled to this day how she could have been so short-sighted. He basically drank the money away and let the business crumble beneath him. The eight-year marriage had drained her. She'd lost her spark and her weight had ballooned. She'd never been slim, she'd always been up and down, but at least she'd had some joy and spirit to hide behind. That had all but disappeared when the marriage hit the buffers.

She'd bought the boat as a way to start again. That at least, she acknowledged, had been a good decision. Her mojo had begun to return of late, largely due to her marina friends. And of course they'd all pulled together with the recent hassle. Distant spirits had reawakened as each resident brought their own abilities to the table. It was the spirit of youth, mostly long forgotten, when people in years gone by had channelled energies into fledgling careers or businesses. Purpose, she mused, that was the word. She realized that you needed to have a reason to get out of bed, a goal to focus on. She had thought long and hard about how to resolve their difficulties and wondered what these musings had replaced. What did she focus on before? Nothing basically, and it dawned on her how easy it is to get stuck in a rut. There was a new energy about the place and, even though things were uncertain, everyone had fronted up. But over the years, whether things had been fraught, such as when her marriage crumbled, or sedentary, she and Elaine had remained best buddies. They continued to thrive like college buddies, but thirty years on.

Just the other night Elaine had reminded her of when they'd gone for a drunken dip in the canal and ended up wrapped in prickly, grey blankets in Cheltenham police station. Spotted by a patrol-man while sloshing though a shopping precinct, the bedraggled duo had been 'invited to the station' to dry off and explain themselves. Elaine had invented a dog! That was the reason they'd jumped in the water – to save the poor beast. The dog, Patch they'd called it, had escaped of its own accord so a patrol car had been dispatched into the depths of a Cheltenham night to try and find a non-existent brown and white terrier. As they'd slowly dried out, they'd had an amusing couple of hours joking with two constables, who were happy to pass the time on a quiet night shift in less pressured times. She giggled to herself, realizing that the only experience she'd had of canals before she bought the boat was jumping in while pickled.

'What are you grinning at?' asked Sal as Judy passed.

'Just memories.'

'You're lucky to have something vaguely amusing to look back on.' Indicating her boat, she said, 'You should try being married to this knuckle-head for twenty years.'

'I heard that,' said a voice from within.

The two girls laughed.

'Yes, it wasn't so bad,' thought Judy.

23

Snert 'n' Goolies

Pete and Sandy were having breakfast in the restaurant aboard the *Pride of Hull*. An honour guard of wind turbines off to the left protected the coast of Holland. Topped by red-winking lights, they spun lazily in the wind. With a little over an hour run till they docked in Rotterdam, they were fuelling up on a cholesterol-laden breakfast for the drive through Holland. They'd shared a bunk-bed cabin, fortified by a decent meal and a couple of drinks in the on-board bar listening to a musical duo 'de-constructing' Abba songs, as Sandy had put it.

They'd also got tangled up with a group of twelve fifty-odd-year-old ladies on a hen do to Amsterdam. They all wore T-shirts bearing the words, 'Goolies on the Rampage.' Cautious questioning had revealed that the lasses were from Goole, an east Yorkshire town not far from Hull. The ladies had spent a raucous night on the boat, giggling and getting noisily sozzled. In groups of two or three they'd spent half the evening popping out onto the outdoor smoking deck for a nicotine fix. Dressed totally unsuitably, they'd stand outside puffing away in the freezing wind before staggering back inside to thaw out. While another group nipped off for a puff, the first would down another couple of brandy and cokes to warm up before dashing out again.

'At least they're keeping fit with all that rushing about.' Pete had commented.

When the girls arrived in Holland they would take a shuttle bus into

Amsterdam, lurch from bar to bar for a few hours, no doubt causing mayhem, before returning to Hull on the ferry that same evening, with Pete and Sandy. Both the guys had gone on deck to see the ferry arrive in Europort. They'd enjoyed seeing the massive port waking up in the early morning. Grimy commercial ships, many rust-streaked, waited to load or offload, often with a hosepipe discharging over the side, while pilot boats buzzed around busily. A forest of skeletal cranes stretched into the distance. A huge container ship was being nudged alongside by two powerful tugs. They found it fascinating to see one of the world's largest commercial hubs come to life. A far cry indeed from sleepy Watergrove.

Pete and Sandy left Rotterdam just after nine in the morning. Sandy had primed his Sat Nav for Staphorst - 199 kilometres, just under two hours. Motoring up the A12 they'd passed Gouda and Utrecht. They were making good time and had just joined the A28 when Sandy's phone pinged.

'Get that will you, Pete. It'll be from Archie. Hopefully he's got some info for us.'

Pete fiddled with the phone and opened up the message.

'Er, no. Actually, it's from someone called Tim. Says he wants to meet up.'

'Oh bugger, sorry. That's for me,' said Sandy, rolling his eyes.

'Well, it's your phone. It's likely to be for you, isn't it?'

'Well, yes. What I mean is it's nothing to do with you. Or Archie. Or...'

Sandy sighed as Pete looked over.

'It's from a dating site,' he said sheepishly. 'I got a response to an ad I posted. This guy wants to meet up. Have a drink.'

'Well, that's great, isn't it?'

'Yes, yes, of course it is. I'm just not over keen on getting you involved with my private life. Not that I mind, it's just not what you do, is it?'

'I'm not bothered. Should I give him a ring?'

'No, you won't give him a bloody ring. I'll deal with it later.'

'I could tell him you're in a car with a close friend, cruising through Holland.'

'Knowing my luck, he'd end up taking you out instead.'

'Actually, he wouldn't,' said Pete, chuckling.

'No, well, you know what I mean.'

They settled into a thoughtful silence.

As expected, the landscape was flat and featureless, but they passed over rivers and canals, seeing the odd cargo vessel lumbering along beneath them. Sandy noted how nice it was to see the waterways being used for freight. He'd read somewhere that each laden boat, on average, held the equivalent cargo of forty trucks so it certainly helped keep heavy traffic off the roads. They passed Amersfoort and Zwolle and arrived on the outskirts of Staphorst at eleven-fifteen. They'd had a good run and noted how good the motorways were - excellent condition and not too busy. They pulled in for petrol at a very clean service area.

'Right,' said Sandy, 'let's give Archie a ring - see if he's got anywhere.'

Archie's voice came over the phone's speaker. He asked how they were getting on. Sandy told him they'd made good time and, apart from Pete interfering with his private life, everything was fine.

'Never mind,' he said, when questioned. 'Did you find anything out?'

'Yes. It took a while and a few false starts to get through to someone, but there is a Simon Miller who works at that window company. It's called Schipper Kozijnen.' He spelled it out. 'Apparently he does live near Staphorst. His address is a farmhouse just outside the town. I was just looking it up as you phoned. He's out of the office on appointments this morning. Chances are he'll be on his mobile though. I have the number here. I'll text it through with his address.'

'Good stuff, well done.'

'Why don't you go and check his address out first? Alison may be there. If there's nothing doing, you can try Miller on his mobile.'

'Fine, well done, Archie. Everything OK there?'

'Yes, all good thanks. One thing. The police sergeant lady came round again. She pointed out something we've not thought of, at least I hadn't. She said that the device on Paul's boat may well have been set off by remote control. She asked again if any of us had seen a stranger around. There must have been someone watching and set it off after Paul had picked up his parcel and returned to his boat.'

Sandy looked over at Pete, who raised his eyebrows.

'That means whoever it was knew bloody well they'd hurt him,' said Pete. 'Callous bastard. I wish I could get my hands on him.'

'There won't be a lot left if Judy gets there first. She was apoplectic.'

They were all quiet for a moment while they digested this latest information.

'OK, said Sandy, 'send that text over and we'll go from there. Thanks, Archie. Speak to you soon.' He cut the call.

A minute later the phone pinged again with Archie's text. Sandy reprogrammed the Sat Nav. Their target was four and a half kilometres away. They set off. The address was on the far side of town. On the drive in they saw lovely, picture-postcard houses lining the road. Each had beautifully thatched, gently sloping roofs - coiffured, as Sandy termed it, like a well-trimmed Beatles haircut. Each house was set with a gable end towards the road, as if the houses were all side on. Many were very large and stretched back away from the road. In fact, they appeared to have been added to as time had gone by. They were uniformly white, all with dark green window shutters and doors. The road on which they drove was cobbled and clean. The whole scene looked like the town had skipped a century.

When they arrived at Miller's farmhouse it was similar - white with green trim. They approached down a light-grey gravel drive bordered by post and rail fence and parked before the front door. The place looked deserted and there were no other cars in evidence. They got out and rang the door-bell which chimed inside. There was no reply. Pete stood back and peered up at the first floor.

'Nothing obvious,' he said. 'Looks like nobody's home.'

Apart from the odd car passing on the road a hundred yards away, there wasn't a sound.

'Peaceful spot, for sure,' commented Sandy. 'But you're right, it looks deserted. I'll see if I can get through to the brother.'

Pete went to investigate round the side of the house while Sandy made the call.

Five minutes later, Pete returned as Sandy ended his call.

'No one about round there,' said Pete. 'Looks like just a farmhouse. Doesn't seem to be a working farm. Not by them, anyway. Just a double garage and a shed. Did you get through?'

'Yes. He was very cagey. Wouldn't say much. Kept asking who I was and what I wanted. Asked me three times, like he was testing me, trying to catch me out. I told him we were in a fight with Alison's husband and that we had no intention of harming her in any way. I told him we would like her help, that we just wanted to talk to her. He wouldn't tell me where she was, not even if she was in Holland. I don't know whether I convinced him but in the end I asked him to pass my number on to his sister. I think he will. He'll talk to her, at least. But all we can do is wait and see if she calls.'

'We shouldn't wait here. There may be someone watching. It's nearly twelve. Let's go and find some lunch; it seems a long time since our ferry breakfast.'

They crunched back over the gravel and headed back towards town. They pulled in at a small, wood-built little restaurant set back from the road on its own. There were half a dozen cars in the car park by a small log-built structure that may have served as an outside bar in the summer. They entered and were shown to a table by a waitress wearing a black dress and stockings with a white apron. They ordered two cups of coffee and asked for a menu. Both were silent for a while, trying to make sense of the hieroglyphics on the menu. There were a few photographs but most of it was rather a haze.

'Snert,' said Sandy, pointing to a specials board. 'What on earth is that?'

'No idea. I think we need some help,' replied Pete, waving the waitress over.

She spoke good English and smiled as Pete asked what snert was.

'Basically it's pea and ham soup,' she said. 'It's slow-cooked and a very good winter dish. Warming and filling on a cool day like today. It comes with bread and butter. You'll like it, I'm sure.'

He raised his eyes to Sandy, who nodded.

'Yes,' he said, 'we'll have two of them, thank you.'

'Nothing ventured,' said Sandy as the lady went to fill their order.

They settled into a companionable silence that was eventually broken by

Pete. 'So, tell me about this Tim character.'

Sandy looked up. 'You don't want to hear about my fumblings.'

'Sure I do. Where's he from? What's he do?'

Sandy sighed. 'Well, he's from Kidderminster and he's an architect. We've exchanged a couple of emails and he seems intrigued by the fact I live on a boat. I emailed him my phone number and, well, that was him getting in touch.'

The waitress arrived with their coffees, accompanied by a couple of small dark brown biscuits wrapped in cellophane.

'That's exciting though, isn't it? Good news that he got in touch.'

'Good news he doesn't seem to think I'm a complete moron I suppose.'

Pete laughed.

'Don't be hard on yourself. You're a likeable chap. A better bet than many, I'll wager.'

'Hmm. It's nice of you to say so, but I've had so many false dawns I get a bit despondent sometimes. I know I'm a pain in the backside now and then, but at the end of the day I'm like anyone - I just want companionship. I'm fifty-eight for goodness' sake and. as Judy pointed out, in jest I know, I have a great future behind me.'

Pete smiled. 'She wouldn't hurt you on purpose. And it's not like you haven't got friends. But I know where you're coming from. As time marches on, it does feel like I may be destined to end up single too.'

'I know she was joking, but it still hits home a bit. As for you, if you want to make any progress you could start by getting a new hat.'

'There's nothing wrong with my hat! We've been through a lot together.'

'It looks like it. Yesterday morning was about the first time I'd seen you without it. I'm surprised it came off. Looked like it had been knitted into your very fabric.'

'Besides,' Pete went on, 'I'm not on the look-out really. Got myself badly burned once and don't want to go through that again.'

'You seem pally with our Judy.'

'I like her, but neither of us wants to get anything to get in the way of a friendship. Even if it is based on barbs and insults.'

It was Sandy's turn to chuckle. 'She's pretty forthright for sure.'

Sandy's phone rang.

'Eh up,' he said, looking at Pete and raising his eyebrows. 'Hello.'

After a one-sided conversation where Sandy said 'yes' and 'mm' a few times, he hung up. 'She says they'll meet us. Two-thirty by the memorial in the park in the centre of town. She sounded nervous.'

'I'm not surprised. It's a result anyway.'

The waitress arrived with their snert. Each was presented with a large bowl of bright green pea soup. There was a separate plate of dark brown sliced bread and a bowl of butter.

'By gum,' said Pete, 'that does look good.'

Sandy stirred the concoction with his spoon and blue-grey lumps of ham appeared.

'I hope you enjoy,' smiled the waitress.

'Blimey, what a plateful,' exclaimed Sandy. 'I'm sure we will.'

They did - it was fabulous.

Alison Hordley was wearing a long fawn coat, walking boots, a fur hat and sunglasses. She was accompanied by a man in jeans, black brogues, red shirt and black leather jacket. They approached warily, looking around as they came.

It was he who spoke.

'One of you is Sandy?'

'That's me.'

'And you are?'

'I'm Pete,' he said, 'Pete Crowther.' He held out his hand.

The man kept his hands in his jacket pockets.

'I am Simon Miller, Alison's brother. I assure you that this meeting is not my idea. Alison wanted to meet you. I advised her to stay away, but here we are.'

Miller towered over his sister by nearly twelve inches. He was about six foot five and had piercing green eyes. He had trim, dark hair, flecked with grey and didn't look like the kind of person to tangle with as he loomed over his sister protectively. He looked from one to the other, staring into their eyes. It was uncomfortable in the extreme.

Sandy coughed lightly. 'We understand your concern,' he said. 'I'd feel exactly the same if I was in your shoes. But, please be assured, we have absolutely no intention of harming or compromising Mrs Hordley. We would just like to speak with her, ask her a few questions. Then we'll go. We've come a long way and our return ferry leaves this evening.'

Sandy looked at Alison, who had remained mute behind her disguise.

'Will you help us?'

'What do you want?' she replied after a moment.

Sandy took a deep breath and looked away. The park was quiet. Two young children played on a see-saw in a nearby play area, watched over by a lady. Apart from that, the park was deserted.

'We, that is the residents of Watergrove, have had some trouble, at the root of which is your husband. There have been a few incidents which, quite honestly, have been more trivial and spiteful than anything else, and we've coped with them. However, last Monday, one of our number, a good friend, was seriously injured. He is in hospital with appalling burns. He may lose a leg. We strongly suspect that your husband is responsible. Of course, we can't be sure, but we're here to ask whether you know anything that may help us.'

All was quiet for a moment before Simon Miller spoke. 'What's this all about? Why would he do something so stupid?'

Pete explained about the boaters' efforts to thwart the house building and the various things Edward had tried to counter them. When he explained about the incendiary device on Paul's boat Miller frowned and looked down at Alison.

'The police are investigating,' continued Pete, 'and they told us that it's only by chance they're not conducting a murder investigation. That's how serious this is.'

She shook her head. 'How did you know where to find me?'

'Someone, I don't know who, contacted us anonymously. They saw an exchange of emails on your computer, between you and your brother. We didn't know you'd come here for certain; we just took a chance.'

Alison sighed and looked away.

'But, let me assure you,' continued Sandy, 'that neither the person who got in touch, nor we, have revealed this information to your husband or the police, nor do we intend to. Pete and I have come on our own initiative and I promise that we'll tell no-one where you are. Only a few boaters know we've come, and I assure you they'll say nothing.'

Alison looked at her brother and said simply, 'He'll find me. Sooner or later he'll find me.' Simon put his hand on his sister's shoulder. She turned to look at Sandy and Pete. 'He's done some pretty stupid things in his time, but if this stunt is indeed down to him...well, what can I say?' She shook her head. 'Of course,' she went on, 'I've heard rumours for years about his philandering and the way he treats people. To be honest, I've largely stayed out of his business. It may sound pretty stupid but, isolated out there in that big house, at least I was safe and secure. I was immune to it all, I suppose. But recently he's got worse, agitated, threatening even. Last week he had a go at me. Not physically, he's too cute for that. No, he accused ME of infidelity. Can you believe THAT? And after all he's got up to over the years. Anyway, at that point I'd had enough. That's when I decided to get out.'

She grimaced, then gave a weary smile. 'In all honesty it was liberating. Nerve-wracking, but liberating. Driving out of those gates. I felt quite....' she pursed her lips, 'empowered. Yes. that's the word, empowered. It's a long time since I've relied on myself, but to be doing something for me for a change felt good.' She looked down at the ground. 'I'm sorry about your friend,' she went on quietly. 'Truly. I hope he recovers.'

She walked a few paces towards the war memorial and gazed over the list of those who had given their lives. It was a long list for such a small town. She looked down on a small posy of dead flowers, then turned.

'I don't know anything specific about what happened to your friend, nor indeed the other things he's been up to. Edward always kept me at arms' length where business was concerned.' She paused, then said wistfully, 'He kept me at arms' length in most other areas too. What I can tell you is that he works with a company called Pegasus. I've seen some of them come and go at the house. Usually it was just the boss on his own; at least I always presumed he was the boss. He's a small wiry man, late forties or early fifties with short salt and pepper hair. If I'm any judge, he's ex-military. Fit, thin-looking man - reminded me of a rat. In fact, he and Edward didn't spoil a pair. I think he's called Martin. I always presumed that was his surname, but I can't be sure. Occasionally I'd see others with him. They'd arrive in a big four-wheel-drive car, always via the courtyard at the back. Big men the others - bruisers sums them up, often wearing leather jackets.' She paused.

'Anyhow he, Martin, was there last week. It may have been Wednesday, I can't be sure. Late, around ten, long after all the estate workers had gone home. He stayed for nearly an hour. I don't know if that's any help...but anyway, Pegasus is the name of the outfit.'

There was a pause before Sandy spoke. 'Thank you. That's a big help. It's certainly a darn sight more than we knew before. We'll pass it on to the police.' He paused and looked closely at her. 'Will you be alright?'

She smiled ruefully. 'Before you came, I dreaded anyone finding me. All the way over I imagined getting pulled over in the car or being challenged somewhere. I couldn't believe you came so soon, and when Simon said there was someone here to see me, I nearly had a fit. But now you're here, I'm glad. It's actually good to unload a bit.'

'Please don't worry. We'll not say where you are. We'll be careful. Is there a way we can keep in touch? There may be something else you think of, or we may have a question or two for you.'

'You have my cell number,' said Simon, speaking for the first time for a while. 'I'd rather you didn't call at all, but use that number if you must. Don't call my office; you've caused enough of a stir there already. Ali won't be staying at my house. Even you two knowing where I live is two too many. Just be careful what you say to anyone; I'd hate to have to come looking for you.' He emphasised the 'you' and stared at them each in turn.

He held his arm out and Alison went to stand next to him. She smiled sadly. 'Good luck.'

'You too,' replied Pete.

Simon laid his arm protectively round his sister's shoulder and they walked away.

During the drive back to the ferry, Pete phoned Archie to update him. He ended the call saying, 'Can you pass that on to the police? But don't tell them where you got the information; tell them it was an anonymous call. We promised we wouldn't compromise Alison. Besides, her brother is a big lad and I'd hate to see Sandy injured.'

Sandy looked over at Pete, who grinned, as he said, 'We'll see you tomorrow, Archie. Should be back around lunchtime. You too. Bye.'

On the return crossing, the Rampaging Goolies looked a bit worse for wear but discovered a second wind a couple of hours into the overnight trip. Buoyed by a couple of Bacardis they were soon tittering and squawking, and dashing back and forward to the fag deck. Abba had given way to a solo pianist whose repertoire included Nat King Cole and Elton John. At least it was a bit less fraught than the Swedish massacre of the outbound journey.

24

Gig in the Dog

J udy's threats had frightened the meteorological gods. Saturday evening was dry. The gig was due to start at eight but people began to arrive from five-thirty. Local advertising had started the beating of the jungle drums. This was a big deal for rural Shropshire. Rarely did the bright lights shine so bright out there in the sticks, so demand for tickets had been unprecedented. Apart from the allocation to sponsors from further afield, the vast majority of tickets had gone to local people. The pub itself was full by half past six. There were a few grumbles as guests were turned away from the pub and directed towards the marquee, but nothing serious. Eric's friends were imposing characters and were polite yet firm. Ale and wine flowed, and there was lots of excited chatter. A stage had been erected inside, framed right and left by two banks of speakers. Half a dozen guitars, microphones and a bank of keyboards sat silent before a gleaming drum kit. Behind the drums was a large screen. An arch had been erected across the front of the stage that was home to a bank of lights and two cameras. A spotlight focused on a single microphone front and centre. To the left of the stage a man sat behind a mixing desk, where LED lights flickered and danced. A temporary barrier defined a two-metre strip in front of the stage. This was the VIP area, occupied at this moment by two leather-jacketed security guards.

In the large car park, the marquee was full by seven-thirty. Two hundred and fifty people were crammed in, with more stood outside and able to see the large screen through the open side of the structure. The temporary bar at the back of the marquee was swamped. The screen showed a photograph of Rounded at a gig in the Hollywood Bowl. In front of the screen was a small stage housing a single stool and two microphones. A further two banks of speakers would relay the gig to the marquee, and the screen would show the gig live.

'Organised chaos!' exclaimed Judy. 'Wow, it's great to see the place buzzing.'

'I'm nervous,' replied Archie, 'and all I'm doing is watching. I know this is only a pub but just imagine the feeling before going on in front of twenty thousand people. Must be terrifying.' He turned to Judy. 'You got your speech ready?'

'Don't remind me. I'm bricking it!'

'Not you, surely? But remember, whatever you do, don't fall off the stage or trip over any cables.'

She rolled her eyes. 'Well, thanks a bunch. That really helps!' she said, thumping Archie playfully on the arm.

The boaters had stood in a group near the door as the guests poured in, welcoming and thanking them for their support and wishing them a good evening. A TV camera and sound engineer recorded the arrival of the concert-goers and an attractive, dark-haired lady interviewed excited guests. Shropshire radio was represented by a portly man in a brown leather jacket and jeans, who dictated into a hand-held voice recorder and recorded interviews.

At six forty-five both sets of reporters were invited inside to briefly interview Len and the rest of the band. At seven, the boaters had joined the VIPs in Eric's upstairs dining room for a champagne reception and hot buffet. On their way, they'd been introduced to the band who were getting ready in Eric's lounge. Each guest was given some signed memorabilia including T-shirts, caps and signed prints and photographs.

Diane Markham of Gardeners' Choice fame chatted with Pete and Roger. Judy had addressed everyone, thanking the sponsors for their support. She finished by saying, 'I'll be saying thank you more publicly before the gig, but this gathering is to show our gratitude for stumping up for us. From me, and all my fellow boaters, a sincere thank you.' She raised her glass.

At eight, Judy clambered onto the stage and engulfed a microphone.

'Right, shut up!' she boomed. 'Quiet! That includes you lot in the tent.' A distant cheer could be heard, along with some wolf whistles. She was wearing a metallic silver kaftan which glinted and dazzled under a single spotlight. Her purple training shoes went largely unnoticed, but not by Pete, who pointed and grinned.

'Get lost,' mouthed Judy. 'All right, calm down, calm down,' she went on. 'I realize it's not every day you're addressed by a goddess, but please try and control yourselves.' More cheers and whistling. Gradually calm descended. 'Firstly, thank you for coming. All of you. What a turn-out - fabulous.' She paused. 'Now some of you may be aware that we, that's us boaters, have had a problem. Some of you won't give a monkeys, but some people have. Some may question why we, as a 'privileged' bunch, need or deserve any support. Well, firstly, let me assure you that we are ordinary folk. I am privileged only by dint of the fact that I live with some lovely people. We are a normal, run-of-the-mill group. In fact, if you could see this lot slobbing around most of the time, the last thing you would call them is privileged.' She smiled down at her friends.

'We've just chosen to live a different sort of life, that's all. But what we have done is come together to fight for something we believe in. Our friendship has grown as a result of that – and if I am privileged, that is why. Some of you may think our little scrap unimportant, but it's not. Someone with power and apparent authority is trying to run roughshod over us - we the ordinary, simple people, like most of us, I think. Everyone can learn a lesson from what we've achieved so far. If there's something troubling you, don't ignore it or allow yourselves to be trampled on - fight it. We have proved we can all make a difference. Stick together and support each other, and anything is possible. She fell silent. As applause died away to nothing, you could have heard a pin drop. 'If you're in any doubt about how serious things got, look at this...'

A live feed from Paul's hospital room suddenly appeared on the screens. There was an audible gasp from the crowd. Paul was in bed within a clear isolation tent, surrounded by electronic equipment and drip stands. Two nurses, each wearing a white uniform, stood by his bed, one each side. There was utter silence. Paul smiled and waved. He gave a thumbs-up and silently mouthed 'thank you'.

'He can see us, just as we can see him,' continued Judy. 'Look up there.' she said, pointing to the arch. One of the cameras spun slowly through three hundred and sixty degrees. The image on the screen scanned the crowd, and people waved. Then the image switched to the mass of people in the marquee. They clapped, then cheered. Judy held her hands up. Gradually everyone settled.

'Yes, he's one of us. He's lost his home and very nearly his life. But he WILL get better; he WILL come home. And we'll be here waiting for him.' She wiped a tear away. The camera had returned to the stage. She looked up and above the renewed clamour mouthed, 'We love you.' She dug a tissue out of her robe and blew her nose 'Right. Enough of the sloppy stuff. He's had enough air-time.' She winked at the camera. 'OK. Nearly time for the main event.'

'Get 'em off!' someone yelled.

'Keep 'em on!' shouted another.

Judy laughed.

'I've taken a vote. 'On' wins.' Cue jeers and boos.

As everyone quietened down again, she went on to thank the sponsors individually. They were gathered in the area just below the stage and basked in their moment of fame. Judy spotted D.S. Crane and D.C. Williams by the door. She inclined her head towards them, a gesture returned by the lady detective.

'Now,' she boomed, 'one of you is in for the surprise of a lifetime. One of you is going to introduce the band.' She looked round the audience and there were some nervous faces. Some were wide-eyed, some looked down at the floor. 'YOU,' she pointed. 'Brad. Come up here!'

He looked dumbfounded and terrified. He shook his head and tried to shrink back but was pushed up on stage by Pete and Roger. Judy handed him the microphone. He stood shaking his head.

Eventually he muttered, 'Blimey, O dear Lord.'

'Come on man, get on with it,' someone yelled.

He looked down at Joy. 'This is you, isn't it? Your idea.' She beamed up at him. He shook his head again. 'OK, well. Hello. What can I say? I've been a fan of these guys for nigh on forty years. I spent my formative years listening to their music, but I never got to see them live. So, tonight for me, well, it's a dream come true. And, well, here they are...Rounded!'

A huge cheer erupted as the four musicians walked up on stage. They all shook Brad by the hand. Len, bringing up the rear, gave him a hug.

'What an intro,' he yelled, grabbing hold of the mike. He winked and gave Brad a thumbs-up. The lights in the pub were dimmed and stage was in darkness. The crowd fell silent. In the background, under a single spotlight, a snare drum beat out the sound of a train on a track - the intro to their hit, *Running On*. Another spot, and the base guitar joined in, thumping out the rhythm. A third spot and Bee's keyboard shrieked the whistle of an approaching train. As it passed by, the tone dipped and, with a blinding flash, Len's lead guitar played the chord that had been heard the world over – they were under way.

Song after song was cheered with increasing hysteria. The band played for an hour and a half before taking a break. After a thirty-minute interval Len appeared in the marquee. He took his seat to rapturous applause and played an acoustic set for forty minutes. He was accompanied by Bee who harmonised on vocals. Her solo rendition of *Never Alone* had the audience spellbound and brought some to tears. Written by Len and Jerry forty years ago, it paid homage to Ed, the friend who was there at the beginning, but who never got to play with the band. Len returned to the main stage for a final set. He asked one of the roadies, Jack, to bring his Fender Stratocaster up on stage. The band played *The World Over*. The track featured Len, who played a five-minute solo on the iconic Fender. The notes died away to a huge cheer. At the end of the song Len hushed the crowd. A photo appeared on the screens of the band playing in Sydney. Len was out front playing the same guitar.

Len spoke. 'We were asked to come and play here by my old mate, Pete.

We'd no real idea who we'd find or what to expect. What we did find was a pretty special bunch of people. They've made me welcome, all of us in fact. Thank you. I can't speak for the other guys, but I've enjoyed this evening as much as any I've ever played. This guitar,' he held it aloft, 'travelled the world with us, and there it is in Australia in 1989.' He pointed at the screen.

'As you heard, it still sounds pretty good, although my ageing fingers are not quite as supple as they were. It's been signed by the band, including Bee, and it holds some dear memories. But, it's time with me is at an end; it's time to pass it on. I've been lucky, very lucky, in my life. I'm in a position to be able to help someone who really needs a break. The initial idea was to auction the Fender off, but having spoken to Pete and his mates, we've had a change of mind. I want to help get Paul back on his feet, so the guitar is for him. I'm sure nobody would begrudge him that.' People clapped, then cheered. Half an hour later the gig neared its end. They finished with the title track from their first album, their best-known anthem, *The Time, The Place*.

Before the song started Len looked up at the camera. 'Paul mate, come home soon. This one's for you.' For those that didn't know the chorus beforehand, the words came up on the screen. By the end, to a person, the whole crowd joined in:

'Don't look back in time to seek
The when, the where, the how
Wherever you are, whatever you do,
The time, the place, is now.'

25

Arrest

The following afternoon, Pete drove Len to Birmingham where he presented Paul with his gift. Paul was in strict isolation to minimize the risk of infection. No physical contact was allowed, so Len suspended the Fender from the television bracket via its shoulder strap. Directly opposite the end of his bed, Paul would see it each time he woke from a drug-induced sleep.

'Thanks, that's awesome. Thanks a million,' said Paul, his voice muffled by the oxygen tent.

'You're more than welcome. I can think of no-one better to take it on.'

'I saw it, saw it all on my TV,' said Paul. 'Bloody brilliant. I kept asking the nurses to turn it up, but they wouldn't. There's some sickies in here apparently and we couldn't do with waking them up – or killing them off.'

Len laughed. 'Never mind - we recorded it. Those cameras were hooked up. I'll let you have a copy as soon as it's stitched together. You can blast away all you want when you get home.'

A dark cloud passed momentarily over Paul's face.

'They tell me I'm in for a long haul. Feels like months already, and it's not much more than a bloody week.'

'You'll get there.'

Paul nodded and smiled ruefully.

'I can't play it, you know,' he said, looking at the guitar.

'So what? Neither can I. I've been getting away with it for a lifetime. Besides, they tell me you've got an engineering degree. If you can master all that stuff, I'm sure you'll can manage a few chords. Tell you what, when you're fit again, come over and I'll show you some basics.'

'That would be good, thanks.' He smiled. 'Did you end up with any of Judy's underwear?'

'No,' he chuckled, 'she managed to restrain herself. That's one impressive gal though, eh?'

'She is that. Pete fancies her, you know.' He smiled and yawned.

Pete, who was keeping out of the way in an armchair in the corner, spluttered. 'Oi, keep me out of this.'

'Hey, Len,' said Paul. 'I really appreciate what you've done. We all do. Thanks.'

'You're welcome. No worries, as they say in Australia. It's been my pleasure. I genuinely mean that. Oh yes, I bought you a few bits and bobs too.' He turned to retrieve a bag he'd left on the table under the television. 'Nothing much, just a few things we've signed. Bit of a keepsake till you're up and about.' But when he turned back, Paul had fallen asleep.

At five-thirty the following afternoon, Sandy got a call from John Greenway.

'You heard?' said John. 'Hordley's been arrested.'

'You're joking!'

'No, Neil Grant's just phoned me. He said that the police arrived at about two in the afternoon and Hordley was driven away half an hour later.'

'What's he charged with, do you know?'

'No. But Neil said they came mob-handed. There are still two cars and a van in the yard. They look to be taking stuff away. He doesn't know what - computers and office files he presumes. Hordley was furious by all accounts, ranting and raving as they brought him out. Couldn't happen to a nicer bloke!'

'I'd love to have seen that. OK, thanks John. Keep us up to speed, will you?'

'Sure, bye for now.'

Sandy sent a text to Simon Miller.

"Please pass on to Alison. Just heard, EH arrested this PM. Details unknown. Will keep you informed. Sandy."

Later that evening Sandy, Pete and Judy were sharing a beer on the pontoon outside Judy's boat.

'Well, well, well,' said Pete. 'They've picked Hordley up. I thought they might look into what Alison told us, but I can't believe it happened so quickly.'

'He'll be out on bail before long. Mark my words,' said Sandy. 'Friends in high places.'

'Maybe, but he'd have to be made of stone if this hasn't dented his pride. There'll be a lot of people glad to see him taken down a peg or two.'

'That's for sure. But there's a couple of things bothering me,' said a pensive Judy. She looked over at Paul's boat deep in thought.

'And?' prompted Sandy.

'Well, firstly, who was close enough to set that device off and, less importantly, who was feeding him information?'

'Could be one and the same,' said Sandy. 'You're right, though, it's unsettling to think that someone we know was actually our nemesis.'

'I don't think it's the same person,' said Pete.

'Why not?' asked Sandy.

'The two things are poles apart, for one thing. It's one thing to pass on information, but setting off that device is in a different league altogether. There's something very warped in doing that, knowing you could actually kill someone. Either big money involved or a total lack of conscience, or both. No, my gut feeling is that whoever shopped us out to Edward is under pressure for some reason, and whoever set that thing off was hired to do a specific job – which, don't forget, would have included swapping or altering Paul's parcel.'

'Any ideas? asked Judy.

'Well, the obvious choice for the fire is that outfit that Alison mentioned. Someone would need plenty of technical know-how, and that seems to fit, despite what little we know about them. Having said that, it appears that at the end of the day, it all comes back to Hordley. He would have initiated it, and engaged whoever actually carried it out.' He paused. 'Then again, that is a huge step up for someone who is basically a farmer.'

'An angry and desperate bully,' said Sandy.

'Yes, but even so, it's drastic stuff, isn't it?'

'Maybe injuring Paul was a mistake,' said Judy. 'Perhaps they were just after the boat?'

'Perhaps you're right. We're just guessing.'

Len walked down the pontoon towards them, accompanied by Roger.

'Evening all,' he said. 'Anyone fancy a swift one in The Dog later? I'm moving on the day after tomorrow, at least for now, and it would be a fitting farewell.'

'Actually, we've already arranged a committee meeting for seven tomorrow. Come and join us if you want.'

'Oh blimey! OK then, as long as you let me pick up the tab.'

'We'll run it by Archie,' chuckled Pete.

26

A Sixteen-incher

That evening, Roger had once again invited selected guests to attend *An Evening With...* where he would recite his latest masterpiece. Having heard about these periodic soirées, Len had pleaded to attend.

'Your insanity is confirmed,' Pete had commented.

'I'm partial to malt whiskey.'

Also in attendance were Pete, Mike, Colin, Sal and Judy.

'Welcome everyone,' said Roger when everyone was settled on a seat.

As committee chair and the person considered responsible, by herself at least, for the prevention of the housing development, Judy awarded herself the only comfy chair, Roger's spinning, rocking recliner. The other guests, perched in varying unflattering poses, were consoled in part by a tot of one of Roger's malts.

'This time,' Roger continued, 'two for the price of one. The first is a ditty that came to me while idling about in The Dog, and the second a sort of personal reminiscence about my experience of French wine – a subject dear to my heart. So without further ado, let's away. The first one is called Duped.

'It's been a long winter. Boring, wet and cold. I'd been in a bit of a rut and I needed a challenge, something to perk me up. So I approached a bloke in a pub and started a conversation. Well, it wasn't so much a conversation as a monologue. I spoke at him. He was very polite, and didn't tell me to go away.

A SIXTEEN-INCHER

In fact, he was a good listener. He didn't say much, at least to start with - he didn't say much to end with either. In fact he never said a word at all. I rattled on about my miserable winter till I suddenly had a mind fizz. I'm not sure why, but I told him I was a writer. There wasn't much reaction. Probably because this chap was Ukrainian and didn't speak English, so I left him and tried someone else.

'So, you're a writer are you?' said the second person, a nice lady wearing pyjama trousers and a yellow raincoat. She was drinking a glass of white wine and reading a book. I judged that she would welcome some stimulating conversation.

I answered her confidently - 'I certainly am.'

'What sort of writing? What do you write about?'

'Anything.'

'Really?'

'Yep. I'll write you an article on anything you like. Go on, pick a subject.'

'Shoes.'

'Shoes?'

'Yep. Shoes.'

'Pick another subject.'

'What's wrong with shoes?'

'Well, nothing, but who the hell wants to read about shoes?'

'I do.'

'What size?'

'Eh?'

'What size shoes do you want me to write about?'

'Fives. That's my size.'

'Is it really?'

'Yes. In fact, I am very fond of shoes. I'm a fashion designer.'

'Are you?'

'No. Just like you're not a writer.'

'Bloody cheek. What makes you say that?'

'Deportment.'

'What about my deportment? What's wrong with it?'

'Well, it's just that there's nothing right with it. The vibes are wrong. I see a number of alternatives. One, you're a writer who has never sold anything, which means you're really bad; two, you're a writer who has sold something and dresses like someone in a dark alley in a historical drama for effect; or three, and I suspect this is the accurate one, you're not a writer at all and you've just come to sit down and pester me.'

'I like that dark alley bit. Might just use that.'

'In your article about shoes?'

'No, in the event I get commissioned to write an article about alleys.'

'What are the chances of that?'

'Slim, I grant you. You never know though. The last one I wrote was on hose pipes. I wasn't expecting that till it landed on my desk.'

'You have a desk?'

'Sure, every writer has a desk. It's a writing desk. At which I wrote my hose pipe article.'

'What was it about, this hose pipe article?'

'I don't really remember, but if I do recall there were references to coiled snakes and urination.'

'Oh, marvellous. How creative.'

'Thank you. It was a while ago, just when I was starting out - before I was awarded more worthy commissions.'

'Like articles on shoes, perhaps.'

'I haven't done that yet.'

'No, but after you've given birth to that masterpiece and released it into the wild to astonish the literary world, you could do one on a particular piece of clothing and call it an article article.'

'I like that. Might use that one, too.'

'Just in case you have to write an article on apparel, I suppose.'

There was a pause.

'I'm out of my depth here, aren't I?'

'Not necessarily. You're probably just a bit short of confidence, or ability - and a desk.'

'Thanks. That helps. You really know how to uplift a guy.'

'Well it's your own fault. If you'd come over and told me you want to be a writer and asked me to help, things may have turned out differently.'

'Oh. Will you help me to be a writer?'

'No.'

'Why not?'

'I don't know anything about it – like you.'

'You're smart though. I bet you could if you put your mind to it.'

'My book and my wine is as far as I want to put my mind right now.'

'That's not very friendly.'

'I never asked for your friendship. You just came over, sat yourself down and started lying.'

'I was being creative. It wasn't lying.'

'Course you were. Look, if you write a story it is being creative. When you make something up in that tortured mind of yours, you can get away with it when you write it down. Everyone knows it's not supposed to be true. When you tell me you are a writer and you're not, that's lying pure and simple.'

'Yes, but if I'd sat down and said I want to tell you a story about me being a writer you'd have told me to get lost. At least this way we've had a chat.'

'Mmm.'

'Anyhow, tell me about how you didn't get to become a fashion designer.'

'Get lost.'

'Seriously, I'm interested.'

'I have no intention of telling you anything about me. I'm a private person who came in here for a few quiet moments. Moments that you have turned into a shambles.'

'I knew you weren't a fashion designer the moment I set eyes on you.'

'Really.'

'Yes. It's those trousers.'

'They're Harrods.'

'King Harrod? He should have kept them.'

'I like that. I might use it.'

'Use it where? When you stop being a fashion designer, you mean, and pretend to be a writer – unlike me, who is a writer?'

It all got a bit surreal after that. A chap in a black cap came in and told my companion, Ms Rowling, that she must leave for her appointment. The last I saw of her was climbing into the back of a Rolls Royce. She'd left her book behind. Who on earth writes a book about a bloke called Potter? I ask you.'

'Oh,' said Colin.

'Splendid,' said Judy. 'Well done, Roger.'

Everyone applauded politely.

'I think you have a future, Roger,' said Len.

'But where? And doing what?' replied Pete.

'Thank you, Len. It's nice to have an unbiased intellectual with whom to share a tale.'

Colin, never one to get over-effusive, didn't disappoint. 'Where the hell did you drag that from? If your last story about the idiotic cyclist was the product of a diseased mind, this one really takes the biscuit.'

'Shut up, Colin. You're lucky to have been invited back after your outburst last time,' said Mike.

'Lucky, am I?'

'Don't listen to him, Roger love,' said Sal. 'I liked it.'

'Thank you, Sal.'

'OK, charge your glasses,' said Roger. 'Time for number two. But please be circumspect; I'm a struggling writer you know.'

'You can say that again,' said Colin.

A few minutes of glass tinkling and gurgling followed. Another seven inches was spirited away before the group settled down again.

'OK,' said Roger. 'This one's called *A Drop of Red* - some personal memories of my experiences of wine in France. It contains a little gentle humour, and you may even learn something. Right, here we go...'

I like wine. Not just any wine - cheap wine. Being English I have availed myself of inexpensive elixir whenever I have visited France. I always travelled in a commercial vehicle large enough to accommodate copious quantities of the stuff – I called it my van ordinaire. My wife and I are voyagers; in fact we lived on a boat in France for a spell. We travelled around for five years from hangover to headache, fuelled by wine's off-cuts, (or I did - my wife is teetotal). The supermarkets were loaded with budget wine, shelf upon shelf of the stuff. Each shop a slippery stepping-stone over the river to a knackered liver. Most of the cheap stuff is quite drinkable, but occasionally you wonder what went wrong - just every now and then you encounter a patio-cleaner, but mercifully they are few and far between. Yes, supermarkets are good, but I'd been told (by a chap who'd just fallen flat on his face outside the bank) that I could do even better – in a cave.

Adjacent the Canal du Centre in Burgundy (which is one of the world's wine hotspots) this cave was not the home of a troglodyte; no, this was a wine cellar, pronounced carve. Actually, it was a whitewashed barn attached to a peeling cottage; but, nevertheless, it was somewhere I reckoned I could pick up a bargain. I know I'm out of my depth when I see wine in real bottles with real corks. Most have sepia labels with Côte de 'some place recognizable', and a sketch of a châteaux. The very best vintages are displayed in a temperature-controlled cabinet with LED lighting and a strong lock to keep me out. The 'merely excellent' are arranged by highly paid interior designers, bedded on straw, in and around authentic wooden crates. Neither of the aforementioned has price labels.

I saw one chap (dressed in loafers and a straw hat) buy wine at 250 Euros a bottle. Five cases he bought (to save you the bother, that's 15,000 Euros) – and it would be for 'laying down' - and potentially revolting. This sort of wine can take years to mature, so he probably won't live long enough to taste the stuff. This means that either his undeserving descendants will get expensively pickled or he will sell it on for a handsome profit before he dies - to pay for replacement gargoyles on his country pile (and there are few things more aggravating than country piles). Wine is a commodity after all. People buy it untasted, unseen in fact, purely to make a profit. This is not for me - I'm after instant wine. The only 'laying down' I want to encounter is me after a couple of gallons.

Some of the expensive stuff is fizzy. The likes of Veuve Clicquot or Tattinger are Champagnes because they originate from the Champagne region and are made using the méthode champagneoise. Other fizzy wines, Crémant or Mousseux for example, which I'm told can be very tasty, are not allowed to call themselves champagne because they come from an 'inferior' region and are made using the méthode traditionelle. Fizzy wine is made the world over, but Champagne is Champagne and is sold as such, kudos and price tag attached.

In Russia bubbly is called Sovetskoye Shampanskoye, which doesn't have much of a ring to it - to non-Russian speakers anyway. In Germany the method of manufacture is klassische flaschengärung – which doesn't have much appeal either. If you requested either of those in Baltimore or Birmingham you'd probably be arrested. Genuine bubbly is destined for up-market weddings or corporate boxes at sporting events and the less expensive alternatives for the refectory tables of the middle classes where they wile away lazy afternoons under a shady trellis being bombarded by rat droppings. On my budget I am afforded the luxury of avoiding anything fizzy or locked in a cabinet, so I headed to the rear of the barn where the real stuff is on offer – the life-blood of the proletariat.

Natural light doesn't penetrate this far back so illumination is provided by a few low-wattage light bulbs powered by the owner's great-grandfather peddling a home-made generator out the back. When my eyes adjust, I see three gasoline pumps from which customers can fill their own containers. Priced variously at 1.80, 2.40 and 3.20 Euros per litre, they are certainly not overpriced. For those like me who hadn't thought to bring a container, there is another alternative - a selection of boxed wines.

Now, I'm partial to a drop of red and so with tingling taste buds I approach. The lady of the cave was almost overcome by my knowledge of supermarket boxed wine and agreed (with a 'bitter-lemon' expression) to allow me to sample each of the ten red boxes available. If she expected me to spit them out, she was mistaken. My philosophy is that it is important to ascertain the severity of crushing hangover one may end up with as part of the wine tippler's art.

I'm absolutely no expert (as the observant among you may have begun to notice) but all the boxes tasted exactly the same. I surmised that the contents had all leached straight from the hillside via a complicated arrangement of sewage pipes straight into a steel tank that had formerly contained hydrochloric acid. From there it had been pumped into vacuum-sealed bladders before being randomly encased in coloured boxes. Although not supposed to be fizzy, this stuff down the budget end of the dungeon had a lightly corrosive nature and gently effervesced, as if a mild nuclear reaction was underway. My wife had come with me and later said she was very proud that I decided not to buy anything at all. I pointed out that our medical insurance had lapsed.

My ignorance of all things wine knows little bounds. A couple of years ago we had cruised on our boat to a place in eastern France on the Canal des Vosges called Épinal. I was excited because Épinal is the Champagne capital of the world. I'd planned to mortgage the dog so I could afford a half bottle of genuine bubbly. Imagine, I thought to myself, sitting on my rear end in the sunshine sipping real Champagne, the evening sun refracting and dancing through the bubbles in my flute as I gaze out on the poor people. I would sample, just once, true contentment.

Then imagine my disappointment when I discovered that Épinal actually had nothing to do with fizzy wine. The Champagne capital is Épernay, about four hundred kilometres west, on another waterway in a different province. Mind you, I did get a decent suntan battling my way through a box of indeterminate red while contemplating my ignorance.

Wine comes in many different forms. Bottles (glass and plastic), bladders in boxes, bladders without boxes, barrels, even tankers and the joy of trying to identify a suitable anaesthetic is one of life's true pleasures. The great thing is that if you find a particularly nasty one, all you have to do is drink enough and you won't even remember it. The danger with inexpensive wine is that you forget everything else as well. But the cost of the budget offerings is compensation enough. It's amazing to wake up sometime the following afternoon to find you still have some paper money in your wallet.

On a visit to a purveyor of wine in Burgundy, I sampled six whites and six reds. It was an open invitation to an official wine-tasting. The tasting was accompanied by a variety of nibbles, including spicy vol-au-vents and rotting cheese – inducements indeed. The wines, to my finely-tuned palate, were basically unpleasant – and became considerably worse when I discovered the price. The town of Beaune, wine capital of Burgundy in the department of Cote d'Or, is only a short distance away. You would have thought that our hosts could have rustled up something that tasted half-decent. In fact, Beaune is known for its architecturally acclaimed hospice – no coincidence this, considering they produce Vin de Plutonium. I quickly realized that for the price of one bottle I could buy a veritable river of my usual stuff, sufficient to give a migratory herd of wildebeest pause for thought. It wasn't a case of quantity over quality; I genuinely didn't like it.

I make no apology for my alcoholic ignorance. I have tried many fancy vintages over the years. In fact, if I'd continued down that road I would have been bankrupt. This is the reason I now only purchase Châteaux Bog Standard. Through iron will and steely determination I have convinced myself that bottles with fancy labels should remain the preserve of the wine snob. No, remaining faithful to the stuff on which I have thrived would continue to see me enjoy thunderous hangovers and bouts of triple vision. I have had so many wonderful evenings of which I have no recall I must have been doing something right. As my friend said only last week after a particularly determined bout – 'that's another evening we won't remember in a hurry.'

'Voila!' he concluded.

'You're right, Roger,' said Colin. 'We did learn something. You know as little about wine as you do about anything else.'

'Ignore him, Roger love, it was very interesting,' said Judy. 'I didn't know you'd lived in France, nor that you had a wife!'

'Bit of literary licence with the last bit, but I did have a year or two travelling about on a barge. A good few years ago now. Fun though.'

'You realize that Jerry, our drummer, has a vineyard in France?' said Len. 'Do you mind if I send that on to him, he'll enjoy it.'

'Sure, by all means. I'll email it to you if you'll give me your address. We might be at differing ends of the wine appreciation spectrum though.'

'He hardly drinks; he gets his kicks by producing the stuff and seeing people enjoy it. Not sure I could be so disciplined, but there you go. Anyhow, good tales. Thank you.'

'You're welcome. And can I say, once again, thanks for all you've done for us. A taste of malt is the least we could offer.'

Len inclined his head and smiled.

There were a few minutes of chat and the odd rude comment before Roger's guests disentangled themselves from their various perches and headed off into the evening.

'Bye, everyone,' said Roger, as they made their way out. 'I'll see you tomorrow evening.'

A sixteen-incher – a relative success.

27

Unmasked

'Right, settle down,' said Judy. 'Welcome to the final meeting of Operation Vegetable. For the time being anyway. This may turn into an inquest about the shambolic goings-on in a quiet corner of Shropshire, but before we get to Roger's minutes I would like to welcome three honorary members. The fact that they are here at all has less do with their support of our cause than the fact that this meeting is being held in a pub. All three of them have been witnessed in a state of less than total sobriety on occasion, but the fact is they are here and that they have supported our cause is noteworthy.

Firstly, welcome Joy and thank you for your support. Through your sartorial elegance you raised our average appearance-level to a point or two above dreadful. You also stumped up cash for the cause, for which we are very grateful. Not a penny of it will be wasted, I can assure you. Please note, Archie, that you will NOT be getting any assistance with your bar bill. Your benevolence and willingness to sate our thirsts has been noted in dispatches and should be thanks enough.

'I'll be glad when this nightmare is over,' he muttered.

Judy smiled at him and winked.

'John, welcome to you too. You swapped sides. Fair to say I think that it was a brave move that benefited both parties.'

'Desperate more like. We did get him fired!' said Mike.

'Well, that's water under the bridge. But if I may offer one note of personal thanks. Your information was responsible, at least indirectly, for getting sloppy-drawers over there,' she pointed at Pete, 'out of our hair for twenty-four hours. Into another country no less, and for that we are eternally grateful. If we'd had a flag, we would have raised it.'

'Finally, Len. Without you, we wouldn't have had ringing ears and thundering hangovers last Sunday morning. Thanks for making such an effort for us. It's been a pleasure meeting you, and please pass on again our gratitude to the other band members. Although, it must be noted, they did bugger off as early as was polite on Sunday morning. A round of applause, please, for our honoured guests.'

Enthusiastic applause.

'Over to you, Roger.'

'Thank you, madam chairperson. Here are the minutes of...'

'Woman,' said Judy. 'Chairwoman. Democratically elected chairwoman.'

'I stand corrected. Not for the first time. Thank you, madam chairwoman. Here are the minutes of Operation Vegetable Three, held here at the Dog last Wednesday. Christ, was it only six days ago? Seems like a lifeti...'

'Oi, Mr. Minute Man,' boomed Judy. 'Your brief is to deliver the facts. Let's have less of the rejoinders. Leave interpretation of the facts to members with some common sense. Right, carry on.'

Roger sighed.

'Present at the meet.. no, I won't bother with that either,' he muttered. He hitched up his trousers and continued. 'The tone of the meeting was initially sombre as Pete relayed information about our friend Paul. However, we were offered some encouragement when we found out that, despite his condition, Paul's sense of humour was intact.' The meeting raised their glasses to him.

'Allegations that the man in the big house up the road may have been responsible for Paul's injuries caused our Matriarch to suffer the scale of eruption last seen with the destruction of the island of Krakatoa. Though we sympathized with her, many committee members were momentarily in fear of their lives as our local volcano erupted. Magma spewed, noxious gasses belched and unearthly rumblings were felt as far away as the ladies' lavatories.

When things had subsided…'

'Are you honestly surprised,' interrupted Judy, laughing, 'that I take the mickey out of you?'

With barely a pause, Roger continued, 'North Shropshire breathed a sigh of relief when the tumult finally subsided, and our matriarch went on to praise members efforts' in relation to the restoration of our allotments. The lumbering endeavours of those she termed 'the old dodderers' was a joy to behold, and the local pharmacy was deeply indebted to us for the sudden increase of sales of various restorative potions. The results of our labours are clear to see and, due to the influx of a group of youngsters, at least two generations below ours, I expect to see a forest of illicit substances spring up with the warming of the weather. The crew of one particular boat should be welcoming this with unbridled enthusiasm. Not everyone shares this fervour, however. Some believe the ingestion of various hallucinatory chemicals will coincide with an increase in music of dubious origin and questionable noteworthiness.

We discussed the gig, at length. Many members offered worthless, random titbits plucked from petrified grey matter in a vain attempt to say something worthwhile. BUT, I'm delighted to report that, DESPITE all our careful planning, the gig was a great success. This was due, in no little part, to the four people who actually knew what they were doing, namely Len and his three fellow band members. It's fair to say that without them the evening would have been much more peaceful. If anyone needed a lesson in how to plan and prepare for a sizeable function, our template is to be studiously ignored.

'You're straying from your brief again,' warned Judy.

'Finally, our chairper…woman thanked everyone for their meagre efforts and announced she had lost three pounds in weight, largely because her best friend is an appalling cook.'

He sat down to a cheer.

'Thank you, Roger. I think it fair to say that your minutes can be summed up in one word: unbelievable. The wit and imagination you have woven into your insightful tapestries do indeed make you stand out as the most accomplished writer on your boat. Well done indeed.'

'You're too kind.'

'Right, on a serious note, we have some news on our informer. Pete, over to you.'

Pete sighed and looked down at his notes.

'Well, I'm sorry to have to report, but it was Betty. She's the shop manager for those who don't know.'

'Well, the swine,' said Sal angrily.

'Hang on, hang on,' said Pete. 'Don't be too hasty. Wait till you hear what I have to tell you. OK, bearing in mind what John told us of Edward's late-night visitor, our suspicions were piqued when Archie saw Betty riding a motor scooter a couple of days ago. We decided not to say anything at the time, rather to go and have a quiet word with her instead. We went to the shop yesterday morning and challenged her. She didn't even bother denying it, merely broke down in tears. But, before you pass judgement, it turns out that she was being blackmailed. It transpires that her former husband, Steve Porter, used to work for Hordley Estates. About four years ago, he was responsible for the death of a fellow worker, indirectly at least. The allegation against him involved lack of maintenance on a potato harvester. Indeed, that he had been negligent. Whether the death was Steve's fault was open to question, but what was important was that he believed he was responsible. Hordley convinced him that the accident was solely his fault and threatened to release evidence to the authorities. He was told that this may have led to criminal charges. Although Steve continued to work for the Estate for a while, the pressure proved too great and he left about a month later.'

'All this put a huge strain on Betty and Steve's marriage, and they were divorced two years ago. Steve moved away but Betty stayed on, continuing to work in the shop. Not content with wrecking Steve's life, Edward also threatened Betty. He told her that he would implicate her in any cover-up up relating Steve's 'crime'. He said that one word from him would see her lose her job with the Waterway's Trust. He basically scared her half to death, and when this housing development kicked off, told her that if she didn't provide him with information she would not only find herself out of a job, but also facing possible charges. To protect his source, he created a sham when he sent his thugs to frighten Betty. She had been forewarned and knew what was going on, but had acted out her part in that particular charade out of fear.

Archie and I looked up the newspaper archives and there was indeed an accident where a man lost his life. Perhaps some of you remember?' he asked, looking round. There were one or two nods.

'It was in September, coming up four years go. The guy who died was a casual worker, a nineteen-year-old Romanian lad employed for the duration of the potato harvest. It appears that Edward wished to deflect any potential blame away from the Estate so set Steve up to take the fall, if necessary. As it turns out, the lad's death was investigated and ruled an accident, so no direct blame was apportioned. However, Steve wasn't aware of this ruling and Edward still threatened him with exposure - 'allow the truth to come out', was how Betty described it. Hordley told Steve that he would tell the authorities that 'new and important evidence' had come to light and, no matter what the initial ruling said, the matter could be re-opened at any time. The fact that it was all fabrication was irrelevant; Steve believed it, and it cost him dear. We spoke with Betty and we reckon the only reason why Hordley continued to hold this emotional tie over Steve was power - purely and simply the power of a big man over a minnow. That's how he gets his kicks, how he operates. It's a pretty sorry episode all told, and I hope that collectively we can forgive Betty.'

'The bastard,' muttered Roger. 'I really, really hope he gets his comeuppance.'

'Is there no end to this man's duplicity? asked Sal.

'I suspect that we haven't heard the end of it yet,' said Judy. She gave a shuddering sigh. 'Whatever, we've had one question answered and I for one am prepared to exonerate Betty. She's suffered enough by the sound of it.'

'She was really apologetic,' said Archie. 'But when she mentioned Paul, she was virtually inconsolable.'

'She might regret it now, but she did sell us out and she's likely to be targeted by the police as complicit in all that's gone on, whatever the circumstances.'

'Yes, Sandy,' said Pete. 'She's aware of that, despite that fact that we all know where the real blame lies. She did have an excuse, but how the police will view that I'm not sure.'

'Well, I hope they go easy on her,' said Terri. 'Poor lass.'

'She's one of us, by association at least,' said Cass, speaking for the first time. 'She doesn't deserve any more grief.'

'Despite the fact that she runs an appalling shop,' announced Archie, 'I will back her up.'

'The way you wind her up, I'd be surprised if she wasn't desperate to emigrate.'

'It's all in jest, Mike, she knows that.'

'OK, let's put that on the back-burner for now,' said Judy, 'and move forward. First, some good news. Paul is progressing well. He rang me this morning himself. They allowed him a phone in his oxygen tent, and he called to express his gratitude to everyone who has wished him well - which I duly pass on to you all. When I think back to ten days or so ago when he was injured it makes me shudder, but it looks as if he's beginning to turn a corner and he'll be alright, despite a long road ahead.'

She turned to Len.

'You're off tomorrow, I believe?'

'Yes, heading on off up towards Llangollen.'

'Well, I hope you enjoy the trip. Once again, can we thank you for all you've done? Not only your generosity, but the fact that you gave everyone a real lift when we needed it. Of course, we didn't know just how serious things were going to get when you agreed to come, but nevertheless it is sincerely appreciated and you've given us all some fond memories. Not sure how I managed to hang on to my underwear, but I'm glad I did.'

'He's glad you did too,' muttered Colin.

Everyone chuckled.

'It's a fond memory for me, too,' Len said, smiling. 'I wish you all well. I have a feeling that you're on top of things and it'll all turn out fine. You've turned into quite a force collectively.'

'Judy's quite a force collectively on her own,' said Pete.

'Oi, watch it scruffy-drawers,' she said, pointing. 'I'll have you know I've now lost eight pounds!' She ran her fingers through her hair and shook her head coquettishly.

'Ignore the ignorant oaf,' said Terri, 'You're just perfect.'

'You and I know that, love, and thank you for saying so. It's this lot you need to convince.'

John Greenway came through the door.

'Oh yes, I forgot. John!' she shouted. 'Come over here a minute.'

He stood stock-still.

'Don't look so nervous! Come and join us.'

He walked over to join the group.

'John has agreed,' she announced, 'to help out young Wayne and his family two days a week. His Dad took some persuading that there was no ulterior motive, but he finally agreed to let John give them a lift till young Wayne finishes his schooling and can return to the farm full-time. They can't afford to pay anything, so Joy said she would cover his wages for the time being. It'll be great experience for John and invaluable for the family. So, good for you John, and best of luck.'

'Here here,' the boaters chorused. There were nods of approval all round.

'Well, thanks, yes. I just hope I don't let them down.'

'No chance,' said Colin, in a rare show of benevolence. 'You'll be a life-saver. Good on you.'

John smiled sheepishly.

'Now bugger off and go and get yourself a drink,' said Judy. 'Here, have one on me,' she said handing over a ten-pound note.'

'Ta,' he said, smiling. He turned towards the bar but stopped and turned back. He looked round the group with a tear in his eye. 'Thanks to all of you. That's from my Mum and Dad too. We're starting a new life due to you guys. Sincerely, thank you.'

'Stop blubbing, man,' said Roger. 'Go and get yourself a pint before you set us all off.'

28

Just Desserts

Three months later.

A summer storm rumbled away eastwards, having battered Watergrove Marina for nearly half an hour. In the distance a dirty grey curtain hung below bubbling, angry clouds. Water dripped noisily from the boats in the storm's wake. As the sun broke through, wisps of vapour rose lazily from the boats and pontoons. The storm followed a week of stifling temperatures and brought the promise of more comfortable conditions. A narrowboat is not the best place to be in intense heat. Once hot, it's not easy to cool them down again as the steel and insulation trap the warmth. Air conditioning units are rare on boats - they are power-hungry and desk fans merely stir the air like a hot soup.

People were emerging having taken refuge from the thunder and lightning, safe within their Faraday's cages.

'Blimey, that was a humdinger,' said Roger, as Judy poked her head out of her front doors.

'Not half. Let's hope it heralds a relief from this heat. It's only people like you and me Roger, in peak physical condition, who can stand temperatures like that.'

'Indeed,' he replied with a chuckle. 'I bet Pete struggled down there in his cess pit.'

'Pffff. Doesn't bear thinking about. Haven't seen him for a day or two;

perhaps he's melted.'

Sandy walked down the pontoon to join them.

'That was a cracker, wasn't it?' he said.

'Yep, sure was,' replied Judy. 'You off to have another row with Betty?'

'No, I need some milk. If she's bothered to get any in.'

Sandy loped off towards the shop as Roger rolled up the canvas sides on his 'front porch', as he termed it. Many boats have a wood and canvas construction over the front well deck. They provide storage space for coal and wood during winter months. In the summer, the sides are rolled up to provide a pleasant place to sit while people enjoy the sunshine.

Since the furore about twelve weeks ago much had happened. Edward Hordley was charged with conspiracy to cause explosion likely to endanger life or property, and blackmail. He had been granted police bail, but his passport had been seized and he had to report to the police every Friday morning in Whitchurch. He had also been prohibited from contacting both his wife Alison and the inhabitants of Watergrove Marina. He had been seen very little in public since his arrest, and his trial was due to start within the month.

Gregory Martin, Chief Executive of Pegasus Security had been charged with causing an explosion likely to endanger life or property. He was tied to Edward Hordley following the examination of texts and emails between the two parties, seized in searches following Hordley's arrest. Surprisingly, Hordley had kept a record of their dealings. Sheer arrogance led him to believe he would never be implicated in any wrongdoing, but that was to prove his undoing. The search also uncovered documents relating to a number of employees of Hordley Estates, including fabricated evidence linking Steve Porter to the death of the Romanian estate worker used in the blackmail of both he and his wife, Betty.

Allegedly, a handler at the post sorting office was paid two thousand pounds to swap a package of medication for one containing Thermite, a mixture of aluminium and iron oxide. Though not large, within the confined space of a boat, the improvised incendiary device was highly destructive and potentially lethal. In an effort to court favour, Hordley told the police that the explosion was set off remotely by a drone operated by Martin. Hordley told the police that he never intended to cause personal injury and that the decision to use an explosive device was Martin's alone. Despite his protestations, he was to stand trial.

Three days before the trial was due to start, Edward Hordley was found by his secretary. Alerted by a gunshot blast, Mrs Featherstone rushed in and discovered her boss in his first-floor office, slumped on the floor by his desk. Behind his overturned chair, the curtains were blood-splattered and the man himself lay in a widening pool of blood. A shotgun was lying next to his body. Police found no note. In a twist, Hordley's secretary told the investigating officers that she believed she had heard a second noise a few seconds after the first - a sound not dissimilar to a gun-shot, but quieter, more muffled.

Speculation grew that the second noise was a door closing and that Edward Hordley had not been alone at the time of his death. As the main office door was visible from Mrs Featherstone's small office, the only viable option was the second door which led down to the dining room a floor below. But nobody unexpected had been seen arriving or leaving the house. Hordley's fingerprints had been found on the gun. That was to be expected, but nothing was found on the trigger, stock or empty cartridge case. This led the police to suspect foul play. Despite detailed forensic examination nothing was proved one way or the other. At the inquest into his death, suicide was ruled out and a verdict of death by person or persons unknown recorded.

The investigation is still officially ongoing, but nobody to date has been brought to account for the killing. Speculation focused on the person most at risk should Hordley be allowed his day in court, namely his accomplice, Martin. Despite the evidence of the texts and emails, nothing specific relating to the attack on Paul was discovered. The two men had met (on occasion with Main's colleagues) – that was not in question. Pegasus had carried out general surveillance and conducted searches for Mrs Hordley. They were also implicit in the staged threats to Betty Porter but, regarding the incendiary device and allegations of involvement with Hordley's death, nothing could be proven and charges were finally dropped.

'Well,' said Pete, sitting at the bar in The Dog one evening, 'it was a miserable end to a miserable man.'

'Not wishing to speak ill of the dead, but I for one will not mourn him,' said Archie. 'He was a cheat and a manipulator. How the hell he got away with it for so long is beyond me.'

'Money,' said Roger. 'Benjamin Franklin said, "Money never made a man happy yet, nor will it. The more a man has, the more he wants. Instead of filling a vacuum, it makes one." That about sums him up. Hordley lived in a giant vacuum. I bet he never had an actual friend in the world. Paid associates, yes, but a genuine friend? Huh! I doubt it.'

' A bit sad in a way. I wonder what will happen to the Estate?' sked Archie.

There were pursed lips and head-shaking.

Joy came in and joined the three boaters.

'Hi,' said Pete, 'how are you then?'

'Fine, thanks. Good evening, gents.' She was dressed casually yet elegant as always, in cream slacks and light grey cashmere sweater.

'Pinot please, Eric. Will you guys join me?'

'Don't mind if I do, thanks,' said Archie.

'You look all relaxed and casual. Not been working today?' asked Roger.

'Just having a couple of days to myself. Been mulling over an idea or two; thought I'd pop in and unwind a bit.'

'Same again, gents? asked Eric.

They drunk up and pushed their empty glasses towards Eric.

Joy was thoughtful for a moment. 'Can I run something by you?'

'Sure,' replied Archie. 'Don't expect any sensible answers though.'

She smiled.

'I had an interesting phone call a few days ago. Alison Hordley rang me and asked if I would consider going into partnership with her. She wants me to invest in Hordley Estates.'

The three men stared at her, wide-eyed.

'Don't look so surprised. I'm not as dumb as I look.' She laughed.

'Blimey!' said Pete. 'And?'

'Well, it transpires Alison now has inherited a rather large business, the running of which she admits she is clueless. She's asked me to go in with her.

I was as dumbfounded as you to start with but, the more I think about it, the more favourably I'm considering the idea.'

'Goodness me,' said Roger. He paused and went on, 'Well, my first question would have to be, how much do you know about farming?'

'I asked myself that too. The answer, frankly, is very little. But there are people who do. At the end of the day, a business is a business. I'll wager the Chairman, or woman, of Akzo Nobel doesn't know much about making paint. They'll employ people to do it. My theory is that there are workers there who can run things day to day - Neil Grant, the farm manager, for example. Strictly between us, I had a quiet word with him this afternoon. I thought the poor lad was going to have a seizure when I suggested the possibility of him taking on more responsibility. I've left it with him for now, but he's been there quite a while and knows how the farm operates. I see no reason why he can't step up. The workers know their jobs, they'll just need guidance. I'm sure they will be voids in my knowledge, but there are experts or consultants around who can guide us. It might cost a bob or two initially, but I have the feeling we'll get to grips with things. The other things swaying me is that the estate owns a lot of property. Some of it accommodates the workers, but a lot is rented out too – that's my game. I see no reason why we can't develop that side of the business.'

Archie scowled and pointed at Joy. 'If you try building on our vegetables, we'll set Judy on you!'

They all laughed.

'I wouldn't dare!'

She took a sip of wine and paused.

'The other thing that's gone through my mind relates to John Greenway. He wants a place of his own, and I wondered about the possibility of leasing him an acreage to run his own business. He's a bright guy who's shown a fair amount of initiative. By all accounts, he's doing really well over with Wayne and his family over there in Oswestry. Plus he's been learning the rudiments at college and has been looking at ways to strike out on his own. Perhaps this is an ideal opportunity for him. One or two others as well, maybe. There's plenty of land after all, and the idea of smaller, niche operations appeals to me. Rare breed animals, perhaps?'

They were all silent for a minute.

'Well, what do you think?'

'I think you're taking on a monster,' said Pete. 'Having said that, I really admire your guts for even considering it.'

'Don't think I'm not nervous, I am. It's a huge responsibility and, unlike some people I could mention, I realize I'm dealing with people's livelihoods here. Hordley Estates is a juggernaut, and my fear is I'll drive it into a ditch. Hopefully not, but I haven't got a crystal ball.' She paused. 'The other thing that's gone through my mind is what would happen if the estate was just sold off to an investment company or farming conglomerate. They certainly wouldn't consider local people. Conversely, I know that I'll be investing in a business, one that has to show a profit. If it doesn't, I'll be knocking on one of your doors looking for a couch to sleep on.'

'Don't worry, we could do with a live-in housekeeper,' said Archie, with a smile. He paused. 'Look, Joy. Don't take this the wrong way, you're a friend to all of us. No offence meant here, but you're the north side of sixty, at an age most people are considering winding down. Are you sure you want to get wrapped up in something this big, risky even?'

'No offence taken.' She smiled. 'Frankly, I'm not totally sure, no. But I'm pretty fit and I've got all my marbles, well, most of them anyway. Sure, I could spend the rest of my days pottering around, showing people round the odd house from time to time, but this excites me. I DO have an opportunity to make things better, to give people round here a better life, with real prospects. It can't be at the expense of going bust, but I believe that with good decisions and the right people around us, we can succeed. Financially it would be a separate venture to the estate and letting agency; I won't put that at risk - but the two could benefit from each other. It could be a pretty productive working partnership, I think.'

'You're making some pretty compelling arguments, I must say,' said Pete. 'Not that you really need it, but you have my support. And if you do go ahead, I'll wish you all the luck in the world.'

'That's a nice thing to say. Thank you, Pete. Keep it under your hats for now if you don't mind. Give me a few days to make my mind up; you'll be among the first to know either way. But thank you for listening.' She paused. 'You know, when Will died, I thought my whole world had collapsed. It did for a time, I guess. But it's with your help, and others who come here, that I managed to get back on my feet. I'll never forget that.'

29

Plans for the Plot

In charge of fundraising for Operation Vegetable were Archie and Paul, until his accident. In his absence Archie had met with Pete and Judy round her dining table to finalize the total raised.

'It really is quite remarkable,' said Sandy. 'The final total is just over ninety-thousand pounds.'

'It's unbelievable!' said Judy. 'I knew we'd done pretty well, but at the outset I never dreamed we'd manage a figure like that.'

'None of us did, I think; it just kept coming in. In fact, it still is! Eric still has a bucket on the bar where locals keep chucking loose change,' said Archie. 'There was an initial surge from local sponsors - nearly thirty thousand there. Then there was that anonymous donation of fifty-thousand pounds. Incredible. No note, just a cheque made out to Watergrove Residents Committee. You'll remember it was from a charitable foundation with offices in London. I had a look but couldn't find out anything about them. To be frank, I didn't try too hard after that initial internet search. Anonymous is what they want to be, I suppose. It would just be nice to be able to say thank you.' He smiled. 'There were further donations after the TV programme was aired, then gig tickets, raffle auction etc., etc. It all added up to ninety-one thousand four hundred pounds and change. I think people's generosity has been quite overwhelming.'

'I've drafted an announcement for the papers, and letters to all those who made significant donations. I know the main sponsors had plenty in return, thanks to Len and the band's generosity, but I still find the whole thing incredible. The spotlight fell on our little corner of the world for a while. Our fifteen minutes, if you will.'

'The problem we have,' said Pete, 'is what to do with the money. It was a war chest but, as we know, the legal fight fizzled out.'

'We owe you something for the guys with their digger,' said Archie. 'That came out of your pocket. But it still leaves a huge amount.' He paused. 'And there's another potential income stream from the recording of the concert...'

'Gig,' said Judy. 'Get with it, man. Concerts are for old buffoons in bow ties.'

'Or bassoons,' muttered Pete.

'Indeed... gig,' continued Archie, ignoring Pete. 'It's up to Len and the band naturally, but...well, it's something perhaps we'll have to consider in the future.'

'I have one idea,' said Judy. 'The whole thing was focused around our allotments. Part of that is now given over to the youngsters, thanks to Diane and her team. Let's get that equipped properly for them, a place where kids can come and learn skills that could offer them a genuine future, rather than merely a place to grow illicit substances for Pete.' She winked at him. 'We can stock that shed of theirs with some decent equipment; give them somewhere to be proud of. Let's make them welcome and feel part of our community.'

'Sounds good,' said Archie.

Pete raised his eyebrows. 'We might even have enough left over to buy our leader some new trainers. She's likely worn out her last pair charging around administering her chairpersonly duties.'

Ignoring her friend, she continued, 'Archie, could you include a note in your letters to the sponsors explaining our intentions? I'm sure they won't object, but it's polite to keep them appraised, don't you think?'

'Quite right. Yes, I'll do that.'

'I'm sure we can help out with the new barn and the narrowboat restoration too,' said Pete.

'True. And on that topic, it appears that romance is blossoming at

Watergrove,' said Judy with a smile. 'Sandy appears to have found a soul-mate.'

'Friendship rather than romance if you ask Sandy, but yes it's good to see him blooming. Seems a decent guy does Tim,' said Archie.

'Very convenient that he's lucked in with an architect just as he's taken on the Dutch Barn project,' joked Pete.

'You are cynical,' chuckled Archie. 'He's pretty well thought of is Tim. I Googled him a couple of days ago. He's won some prestigious awards and done some mighty impressive work, at least to my amateur eyes. I doubt a rural barn will stretch his talents.'

Indeed, Sandy was thriving as plans for the barn took shape. He'd used his talents as a meticulous planner (with Tim's help) to design a building that could be used initially for excavation of the site then subsequent building of the wooden narrowboat. Thereafter there was the option to change the use to a livestock shelter. It was to be classed as an agricultural building, therefore not subject to prohibitive planning legislation. The frame would be constructed from green oak, be open-sided and topped with a barrel-vaulted, galvanised roof. At forty yards by twenty-five it was large, around nine thousand square feet, and the estimated build cost was to be around twenty-five thousand pounds.

Sandy discovered early on that a wide range of largely lost skills would be required to build the boat. He came across the Nurser family, who were wooden boat-builders from the start of the twentieth century. William Nurser and his four sons built boats up till the early 1940s when the yard passed to the Barlows. One of the sons, Charles, made notebooks of various builds that are still housed in museums such as the British Waterways Museum at Stoke Bruerne and the National Waterways Archive at Ellesmere Port. Many of the notes were hieroglyphics to Sandy, but he was contacting people who were keeping traditional skills alive.

Joy had spoken to Alison Hordley and both ladies had backed the scheme wholeheartedly. They'd both agreed that Hordley Estates needed some positive PR after years of ill-feeling and suspicion. Benevolence in any shape or form was a notion never historically associated with the Hordley name –

it was time to change people's perceptions.

Watergrove was looking it's best on a lovely summer afternoon in late July. Drinking a cup of coffee, Judy stood on the pontoon near her boat and looked over the scene. The marina was busy during peak holiday season, many boaters taking advantage of a settled spell of weather. Boat owners painted, cleaned and polished. Water hoses snaked along the pontoons as tanks were filled. Isolated chatter and laughter could be heard and the sun shone. She knew the cosy feeling of being part of a community. She could hardly believe that the angst and worry of the previous few months had dissipated. She smiled to herself, proud of her friends, happy to feel part of it all.

Some private boats had left for extended cruises, but many took shorter trips, a week or so up to Llangollen and back. Hire boats called in regularly to water up and buy supplies from the shop. Many would stay the night before heading off early the following morning to ensure they made the most of their limited time on their boats. She smiled, recalling Archie's ill-fated cruise earlier in the year. Someone had called it 'the chicken run,' and the name had stuck. A story for Archie's memoirs, and recounted round a crackling fire in The Dog.

Yes, there had been some excitement, but this was better.

30

The Time, The Place

Two weeks later an ambulance pulled up close to the shop in the marina car park. Despite the crew insisting that he used a wheelchair, Paul clambered down the rear step with the aid of a pair of crutches. He'd been told that the ground-floor apartment to the rear of the shop had been made ready for him. All the boaters had gathered to welcome him home. They cheered and clapped as their friend slowly hobbled towards them. Despite his obvious discomfort he had a huge smile on his face. He received hugs and handshakes and a chorus of 'welcome homes', and more than one person shed a tear.

'Welcome back, love,' said Judy, enveloping him in a huge hug. 'You, my lad, are a sight for sore eyes. You don't know how much we have all looked forward to this day.'

'You're not the only one, I can assure you,' he said, smiling. His hair was cut short and, although he looked rather pale, his eyes were bright. 'Thanks, everyone. Getting back here has been a real goal for me for the past few months. It gave me something to aim for, and when I had down days I thought of you lot. Well, most of you anyway,' he added, laughing. 'Seriously though, it's brilliant. I can't thank you enough.'

He looked round and took a huge breath, smelling the surroundings.

'Boy, does that feel good.'

'Right,' said Pete, 'let's get you settled in.'

Paul turned and took a couple of faltering steps towards the shop.

'Where the hell do you think you're going?'

'Over here, where do you think?'

'You might want to reconsider.'

'Eh?'

'That's your new home,' said Pete, pointing to a gleaming blue narrowboat moored next to the bank on the residents' pontoon.

Paul look dumbfounded.

'What?' He stared at Pete.

'Yep, it's yours.'

Paul turned to look at the boat again. 'What?' he said again. 'You're joking.'

'Nope. It's a gift. From a friend of yours.'

He turned back to Pete again.

Judy said, 'It's from someone who developed a soft spot for you when he saw your courage and determination. Someone who would like to teach you to play the guitar.'

Paul stared at the boat for a moment then broke down and sobbed. Months of fear and frustration poured out as he leaned forward on his crutches. Judy and Cass went to support him and hugged him. He said through his tears, barely audibly, 'I don't believe this.'

'Well, believe it,' said Cass through her own sniffs. 'It's yours.'

Finally, he calmed down and hobbled over to the boat. He stood and stared for a good two minutes, then clambered onto the rear deck and looked around him. He smiled and slowly shook his head as the boaters gathered round.

'Blimey,' he said, 'I still don't believe it.'

'Go on then, have a look inside,' said Archie.

Carefully, Paul climbed down the steps into the rear cabin, the bedroom. A red quilt covered the double bed, and the room was illuminated by ceiling-mounted spotlights. Beyond he could see the bathroom. He made his way slowly forward, past the three-quarter bath with gleaming taps and shower attachment. Nobody else followed, allowing him to soak it up on his own. As he shuffled into the kitchen the boat rocked gently, squeaking against its bank-side fenders. More spotlights illuminated solid oak worktops, duck-egg blue cupboards and a stainless-steel sink. He looked out of the window and waved to his friends. They waved back as Paul leant on the worktop and bowed his head in disbelief.

Out on the quay, Judy took Pete by the hand. 'You, my friend, should be proud as punch. You have initiated one of the kindest, most generous acts I have ever had the privilege to witness. Well done you.' She leaned over and kissed him on the cheek.

Paul turned to the right. In the adjacent lounge were two high-backed black leather chairs, each with a foot-stool. They faced a new television on one side of the cabin and a multi-fuel stove on the other. The double doors at the bow opened onto the well deck. One chair swivelled round.

'Welcome home, my friend.'

Len sat with Paul's Stratocaster in his lap. The two men stared at each other, one with a huge grin on his face, the other with tears streaming down his cheeks. Via Bluetooth, the guitar was linked to the boat's multi-speaker music system. A familiar chord rang out. and Len sang quietly....

Don't look back in time to seek

The when, the where, the how

Wherever you are, whatever you do,

The time, the place, is now.

More from Jo May

Jo's websites

Jomay.uk features Jo's other books and a series of articles and you'll find all sorts of eclectic things at abargeatlarge.co.uk, including:

- A photographic record of his and his wife's boating days
- A collection of stories and articles
- A health warning! (The fat bloke gets into difficulty)
- Links to his other books

(Jo would love to hear from you - there are contact forms on each site.)

Jo's books

Biographical travels on three different boats in the UK and Europe:

- A Barge at Large
- A Barge at Large II
- A Narrowboat at Large

Fiction:

- Flawed Liaisons
- Operation Vegetable

Printed in Great Britain
by Amazon